The Foaming Deep

A Yorkshire Murder Mystery

DCI Tom Raven Crime Thrillers
Book 8

M S MORRIS

Published by Landmark Media, a division of
Landmark Internet Ltd.

M S Morris® and Tom Raven® are registered
trademarks of Landmark Internet Ltd.

msmorrisbooks.com

ISBN-13: 978-1-914537-40-0

CHAPTER 1

The path across the cliffs was muddy in places and slippery after the recent rain. The moon remained stubbornly hidden behind thick clouds, making the darkness complete. Anna reached into her jeans for her phone to light the way, but her pocket was empty. Shit, she must have left it behind in Robin Hood's Bay.

Never mind. The phone was only a cheap model and could easily be replaced. Besides, she couldn't go back to look for it now, even if she could remember where she had last used it. It was too late. And too risky. She would have to find her way in the blackness.

With the absence of vision, her hearing became more acute. The night was full of sounds. The crash of waves on the rocks below, the hoot of an owl inland.

Her own ragged breathing.

She reached out her right hand and felt a stab of pain as her fingers closed around the long thorny stem of a bramble. 'Ow!' She released it with a cry and took a moment to regain her footing. To her left was a barbed wire fence, and beyond that the flat clifftop before the plunge down to the sea.

She needed to calm down or she would be over the edge of the cliffs before she knew it. She had walked this path a hundred times and had often thought she could do it blindfolded. Well, now was the test of that claim.

She set off again more slowly, one step at a time, her battered old trainers landing in puddles she couldn't see. Cold water oozed through the cracked soles, soaking into her socks but she ignored the sensation, concentrating on her balance. If she just kept going she would arrive at the youth hostel at Boggle Hole soon enough. And tomorrow she would be back on the coach to London. She'd got what she had come for. Now it was time to leave the past behind and focus on the future.

No going back. Ever. She had burned all her bridges.

She came to a wooden gate and scrambled over it, not bothering to hunt for the iron latch in the dark. It couldn't be much further now. Then suddenly the darkness grew even thicker and she knew she had reached the spot where overgrown branches formed a natural tunnel over the path. Another couple of minutes and she'd be back in the safety of the youth hostel. She longed to take off her muddy footwear and climb into her bunk bed.

She had just emerged from the tunnel when she heard a fresh sound behind her. She paused. Had she imagined it? No, there it was again. The squelch and suck of feet in the mud. Was someone following her? She turned and was immediately blinded by the piercing white light of a phone.

She raised a hand to shield her eyes. 'Who's there?' She did her best to sound brave, but her voice betrayed her, quivering and uncertain.

The follower advanced without speaking.

Anna turned and ran.

CHAPTER 2

DCI Tom Raven glanced surreptitiously at his watch. How early could he leave without appearing rude? The black tie dinner in the Palm Court Ballroom of the Grand Hotel was an annual police fundraiser for local charities, an opportunity for the Scarborough force to pat themselves on the back and hand out awards for bravery, outstanding service to the community, and say farewell to those retiring into the sunset. Raven wasn't up for any award and he didn't ever expect to be. That wasn't why he did the job. And he was a long way off retirement, having exhausted all his life savings renovating his house. Besides, what would he possibly do with his time if he wasn't spending it being a police detective?

He had been to police dinners before and was already counting down the minutes until he could return home to his daughter, Hannah, and his dog, Quincey. Previous experience had taught him that the speeches would be interminable, the atmosphere stifling, and the company tedious. There was nothing worse when you were sober than being in the company of drinkers.

At least he didn't mind dressing up in formal attire. Unlike many of his fellow diners, tugging at their bow ties, clearly uncomfortable in dinner jackets, Raven had always liked to look his best. He might not be an adventurous dresser, but he felt most at home in a smart suit.

He glanced around the ballroom, decorated with ornate ceiling mouldings and sparkling chandeliers. The décor was intended to evoke the opulence of the hotel's Victorian past. But for Raven, the sight transported him back to the nineteen-eighties, when he had first peered at the grand setting around the legs of his mother, who had worked as a chambermaid at the hotel and had sometimes brought him here after work.

The formal seating plan positioned him on a circular table of eight between Detective Superintendent Gillian Ellis's businessman husband, Gordon, and Police Superintendent Brandon Holt, who had also come alone. Everyone else on the table had brought their partners.

'I see they've put us single chaps together,' said Holt, introducing himself at the start of the evening and giving Raven's hand a vigorous shake. 'What will you have, red or white?'

'I'll stick with water, thanks.'

Holt eyed Raven as if unsure whether he was joking. 'Is this your first time at one of these evenings? They can drag on a bit without a little lubrication.'

'Yes, it's my first year here in Scarborough,' said Raven, taking a sip of mineral water and seeking to deflect curiosity about his reluctance to drink anything stronger.

'I thought so.' Holt poured himself a generous measure of red from the bottle on the table and lifted his glass to Raven's. 'Well, I don't know how I'd make it through the evening without a few drinks to take the edge off. Cheers!'

'Cheers.'

Superintendent Holt – 'Call me, Brandon. No need for formalities here. Half the force will be legless by the end of the evening. Let's hope the villains don't know that.' – was a few years older than Raven with thick grey hair, a well-developed paunch that betrayed a long history of fine wine and dining, and the confidence that came from occupying a respected, senior position. Or was it that confidence that had won him the job in the first place? It was the kind of conundrum that Raven had never fathomed – one of the many reasons he would never reach the dizzying heights of superintendent himself.

Holt was effectively Gillian Ellis's opposite number and headed up the uniformed officers at Scarborough Police Station. From what Raven had seen, he spent most of his time behind a desk, shuffling paper, shaking hands and making occasional TV appearances while wearing his most serious face. His serious expression was not much in evidence this evening, however. Holt seemed to be in his element, regaling the table with entertaining and witty anecdotes and generally revelling in the company. That was another reason Raven knew he would never get promoted beyond the rank of detective chief inspector.

Social skills, or lack thereof.

He listened as Holt recounted a tale, which may or may not have been true, about a regular offender who had been acquitted from his latest misdemeanour only to be promptly re-arrested on his way home from court for driving without insurance. Of more interest to Raven was the dinner guest seated to his left. Gordon Ellis was his boss's husband, and Raven wondered what kind of man might choose to spend his life with her. Gillian was a forbidding woman, with austere tastes in art, music and reading material, and Raven was intrigued to discover more about her husband.

Gordon didn't present quite the conventional appearance Raven had anticipated. His hair was a little too long and wavy, his face browned and adorned with a well-trimmed silver beard. Amid a sea of identically attired men, Gordon was the only one wearing a burgundy bow tie. He carried an air of mystery but appeared keen to enlighten Raven about his past. 'I had a misspent youth,' he said with a sidelong glance at his wife and a hand gesture that hinted at all kinds of nefarious activities.

'Similar to me, then,' said Raven, who had spent his teenage years bunking off lessons and hanging out at seafront amusement arcades in the company of various undesirables, eventually dropping out of school at sixteen after scraping through his final exams.

'Yes,' continued Gordon. 'After an Art History degree, I moved to Paris and sampled the starving artist scene for a while. Do you know the Marais district?'

'Not really,' said Raven. His first trip abroad had been to the Bosnian conflict courtesy of the British Army. Gordon's misspent youth didn't sound so similar to Raven's after all.

'It was a crazy year,' mused Gordon, 'but living in a garret, drinking absinthe and smoking spliffs loses its appeal after a while, so I returned to Scarborough and knuckled down to some hard work.'

Gordon's hard work had evidently paid off, judging from the enormous period house that he and Gillian now owned at the smart end of town. But Raven was still no nearer to understanding how Gordon had gone from impoverished artist to millionaire businessman.

'My business is in international trade,' he explained vaguely, leaving Raven not much the wiser. 'But as I grow older I'm becoming more interested in how I can give back to the community. Let me tell you what I'm up to these days.'

While Brandon Holt entertained Gillian with some hilarious story involving a night out with a judge and a magistrate, Gordon engaged Raven in an earnest discussion of the charitable activities of the local Rotary Club, in a thinly disguised attempt at recruitment. Raven listened politely, but found it easy to resist Gordon's efforts to get him involved, pleading long and unpredictable working hours as his excuse.

'Pushes you hard, does she?' asked Gordon, with a nod toward his wife who was by now debating the merits of literary prizes with the wife of a senior officer from Traffic.

Raven offered him a smile that he hoped was enigmatic. He had no wish for his feelings towards his boss to be reported back to her.

'Yes,' said Gordon, seeing through the ruse immediately. 'That makes two of us.'

As the evening wore on, more bottles of wine were emptied – enough to keep a small vineyard in business. Police dinners were not famous for abstinence. Voices became louder, laughter more raucous, body language more flamboyant. Raven found himself withdrawing further into his protective cocoon.

The Traffic operations manager sitting opposite was growing increasingly boisterous. When the cheese arrived and the wine gave way to port, he raised an arm and levelled a finger at Raven's glass of water. 'You don't have to worry about being over the limit tonight. No one's brought a breathalyser with them!'

Raven said nothing, but Brandon Holt came to his defence. 'Put a sock in it, Crawford,' he drawled good-naturedly. 'At least he won't be puking in the gutter later! Not like that time you had to be bundled into a taxi.'

The rebuke had the desired effect and Crawford fell silent, turning his attention to his stilton instead.

'Thanks,' whispered Raven, grateful for the intervention. He studied his watch once more. The superintendent had been right about the event dragging on. The food wasn't yet finished. And the awards and speeches were still to come.

Raven turned to glance at the nearby table where the more junior detectives from his team were seated together. Detective Sergeant Becca Shawcross and Detective Constables Tony Bairstow and Jess Barraclough seemed to be having a better time than him, judging by their hoots of laughter. Raven was pleased to see Becca enjoying herself. She had recently split up from her defence lawyer boyfriend but seemed to have picked herself back up again. She and Jess were laughing at a joke and even Tony seemed to have let his hair down a little, sitting between two young female officers and chatting amiably. Raven wished he was sitting on their table too, instead of being placed with the bigwigs. Even Detective Inspector Derek Dinsdale appeared to be happily seated on a table of middle-ranking officers.

Once the plates were cleared away it was time for the awards to be doled out and the acceptance speeches made. Raven sipped his coffee and dutifully laughed at the jokes and clapped in all the right places. He felt he deserved an award himself, for enduring it. Not much longer now, and then he could make his escape.

The final award of the evening was presented to Superintendent Brandon Holt for an annual reduction in drug-related offences in the Scarborough neighbourhood.

'Oh, God,' muttered Holt to Raven as he scrambled to his feet, 'I haven't even thought about what to say.' Nevertheless, he took his place on the podium with a practised display of modesty and accepted his award graciously from the Chief Constable. He gave his acceptance speech fluently and without hesitation, carefully acknowledging the contribution of his "hardworking colleagues who truly deserve all the credit." He was clapped enthusiastically as he returned to his seat.

'I think I pulled it off,' he whispered to Raven with a wink.

And then the dancing started. Raven didn't even have to check his watch to know that the time had come to slip away. He shook hands with Gordon Ellis and Brandon Holt, said a few words to Gillian, and escaped at last into the cool night air.

The evenings were growing chillier as autumn took hold, and Raven welcomed the change. Summer was gone, and with it the crowds and the easy living. Raven preferred life to be a little harder. It seemed more real that way. He turned up the collar of his black coat and took the flight of McBean Steps that led down to the Foreshore between the side of the hotel and the central tramway.

He recalled riding the funicular cliff railway with his

mum, so many summers ago, and pushed away the familiar rush of nostalgia and melancholy that threatened to overpower him at such times. The trams weren't running this late at night, but after sitting at a table for hours, Raven welcomed the fresh air and the exercise. The hundred and fifty-three steps were manageable, even with his bad leg, as long as he took them slowly and steadily.

Heavy cloud covered the moon, and treacherous pockets of shadow concealed the steep stairs. Raven descended with one hand pressed to the stone wall of the hotel, gripped by a terrifying sensation of descending into a bottomless pit. In the distance the sea made an oil-black slick against the infinite void of the heavens, and it seemed that if he lost his footing he might fall forever. Only the light from a single boat blinking on the horizon broke the illusion.

At the foot of the steps, he hurried past the closed amusement arcades that had claimed so many hours of his school days. More memories here, some good, some bad, but all of them painful to him now. How he envied Gordon Ellis, who considered his year spent in Paris pursuing a career as an artist a wasted opportunity. Raven had squandered his education and hadn't even managed to make it out of Scarborough until he had fled his hometown into the embrace of the army. He knew nothing of Paris's bohemian districts, but was willing to bet that Gordon Ellis had not been shelled or come under enemy fire during his time there.

He continued past the deserted West Pier and turned into Quay Street. His house, a three-storey Georgian terrace, stood in darkness. It was gone midnight and Hannah was sensibly in bed. He let himself into the house as quietly as he could. Quincey, his Black Labrador, padded into the hallway to acknowledge his arrival and then returned to his sleeping basket in the front room.

Raven climbed the stairs, got undressed, tumbled into bed and fell into a dreamless sleep.

It was barely light outside when the phone rang. Raven

emerged from deep sleep, leaving behind vague memories of a dream in which a Hercules transport plane descended towards a Parisian garret, Gillian Ellis in the cockpit, and answered the phone on autopilot. He was jolted wide awake when he heard what the duty sergeant had to say. The body of a young woman at Boggle Hole.

'I'll be there as soon as I can.'

It was only after he hung up that he wondered if Boggle Hole was a real place or if this was a wind-up.

CHAPTER 3

When Raven picked up Becca from outside her North Bay apartment, she was wearing dark glasses and didn't seem particularly chirpy. He had last seen her taking to the dance floor at around midnight on Saturday. Now it was six thirty on Sunday morning. Probably not long enough to have made a full recovery after a night of drinking and dancing.

'Late night?' he asked, doing his best not to smile. 'Your face looks a little green.'

She lowered her glasses and gave him a withering look. Or was it more of a withered look? Her eyes were bloodshot and sunken in shadow. 'Just drive slowly for once, will you? No need to take the corners like a Formula One driver.' She shielded her eyes with the sunglasses again and cradled her forehead in her hand, bringing conversation to an end for the moment.

At that hour on a Sunday morning they had a clear run north out of Scarborough on the Whitby road. It seemed a pity to take the journey at a sedate pace. Yet Raven complied with her request, sticking carefully to the speed limit and slowing down around bends. He didn't want her throwing up over the leather seats of his beloved BMW.

As they made their way across the rolling moors, all carpeted in purple heather, Raven's mind returned to the subject that kept coming back to haunt him. At the end of his last big case, a visiting detective superintendent from Northallerton, DSU Lesley Stubbs, had left him with a tantalising piece of information. Many years ago, as a uniformed rookie officer in Scarborough, she had taken statements from the public regarding a fatal hit-and-run incident. An eagle-eyed witness had given her the registration number of a vehicle seen driving away at high speed. But when Lesley wrote up her report, word came down from on high to drop it. Lesley had given Raven the registration number as a parting gift, putting two and two together and realising that this was likely to be the vehicle that had killed Raven's mother. He had been sixteen at the time and her death had shaped his entire life.

On the spur of the moment, Raven had asked Becca if she would help him follow up the lead. It would just be the two of them, working alone, off the record. A case that had been closed for more than thirty years, with nothing more to go on than an unverified witness statement, recalled from memory after the passing of the decades following a chance encounter between Raven and Lesley Stubbs. What was the likelihood that such an investigation would bear fruit? Yet Becca had readily agreed to help.

But that was six weeks ago and they hadn't made a start. Raven knew it was up to him to get the ball rolling, so what was holding him back? Was he frightened of what he might find? Or more afraid he would find nothing? That the trail would lead nowhere, merely compounding the agony of never knowing who was responsible for killing his mother.

He had never made peace with the idea that the driver was out there somewhere, walking free and unpunished. But he had found a way of living with that knowledge, burying the thought beneath layers of subterfuge. The army psychiatrist he had seen after being shot by a Bosnian

Serb soldier had sensed the presence of some deeply submerged trauma. 'Is there something else you'd like to tell me, Tom?' he'd probed. 'What made you choose to join the army?' But Raven had kept his lips sealed. His leg injury had healed by being left alone, not by cutting it open to bleed afresh. He was not about to slice open the wound in his mind.

Either way, there was no time to do anything about it now. The body of this young woman would be his focus for the foreseeable future.

He turned off the main road a short while after the turning for Ravenscar. His car had once broken down on this isolated stretch of highway, but today the M6 purred like a leopard. Raven was keen to unleash its power, but a sideways glance at Becca's huddled form was enough to dissuade him from pushing down any harder on the accelerator. A sign pointed to Boggle Hole and the youth hostel. Three miles to go. This road was narrow, with passing places in case of oncoming cars. Farmland stretched out to either side, sheep grazing in long grass, dry stone walls hugging the contours of the land, five-bar gates enclosing each field. The hedgerows were as purple as the moors. Clouds drifted overhead, the light shifting from muted grey to bright sunlight and back.

Becca groaned as the car neared the coast, the road becoming steeper and narrowing to little more than a track.

'I'm driving slowly,' said Raven, following the twists and turns of the bumpy path, the sea growing steadily larger before him.

'Mm,' moaned Becca. 'Not slowly enough.'

A little further and the road was cordoned off with police tape. A local bobby directed them into a small, tarmacked car park at the side of the road. Signs indicated that the last quarter of a mile to the youth hostel was inaccessible to traffic in any case. Raven pulled to a halt and got out. A stiff wind ruffled his hair and the air held a chill that hinted at colder weather to come. Becca slid out too, stretching and yawning and drawing her jacket around her.

'Come on,' he said. 'The fresh air will do you good.'

'Not as much good as a few more hours in bed.' But she removed her dark glasses and folded them away, following him reluctantly.

They ducked under the police tape and set off along a lane bordered with high hedges. The path sloped downhill and Raven felt the familiar ache in his leg as his muscles worked to steady him. He was still an old wreck, when it came to it. Becca, on the other hand, might have been nursing a hangover, but was perking up noticeably now they were out of the car and breathing in the bracing sea air.

'There's the youth hostel,' she said, as the hedges on their left fell away to reveal an old mill nestling at the bottom of a green valley. The view from the path revealed a collection of dark stone buildings clustered around a courtyard. They occupied a picturesque spot tucked away at the back of the cove.

'It's a bit inaccessible,' said Raven. 'Is this the only way to reach it?'

'Yes, a slipway leads down to the beach but you can only reach the hostel on foot. There's this path or the path across the clifftops. If the tide is out, you can walk along the beach from Robin Hood's Bay.'

They continued down the path, arriving in a small cove bordered by high cliffs. The beach was sandy but dotted with rocks and rockpools that made the going difficult, at least for Raven. He stumbled across the seaweed-strewn rocks, dragging his injured leg like a lead weight, doing his best not to lose his footing. Becca appeared more at ease, striding confidently over the terrain towards the focus of activity at the mouth of the bay.

The CSI team was already busy at work, the team leader, Holly Chang, directing operations, her bossy voice reaching across the sands. She came to meet them as they approached. 'Good morning. Glad to see you've both made it after last night. I opted to stay home with the kids instead.'

'Very wise,' said Raven. 'You've obviously been to one of those dinners before.'

'One or two. The usual carnage, was it?'

'A free bar, and then dancing,' said Raven. 'I'll bet there were a few casualties. But you'll have to ask Becca about that. I left early, if you can call midnight early.'

Becca gave him a scowl and put her dark glasses back on. 'Where's the body?'

'Come this way.'

Holly led them around the corner of the cliff to the opening of a large cave. The cave mouth cut a dark and gaping hole in the almost vertical cliff face, seeming to swallow all light. Fallen rocks and scree littered the sand and Raven glanced upwards, fearing further rock falls.

The body of a young woman was propped against the entrance in a posed, seated position. Her head hung forward over her chest and her limp, blonde hair, matted with blood, covered her face like a veil. Her hands lay lifeless at her side, palms up, fingers curling inwards. A curious sea crab was crawling toward the fingers of her right hand. Holly plucked it up and deposited it in a nearby rockpool.

'We're going to have to work quickly,' she explained, 'because the tide will be back in a few hours and then this area will be completely submerged.' She indicated the presence of the advancing sea, still some distance away from the cave entrance. In the morning light, the water drew a steel blue stripe against the shoreline. Mirrors of shallow pools caught the sky between patches of sand and rock. A flock of seagulls took to the air, cackling loudly.

'Any ID on her?' asked Raven.

'Nothing. No bank cards, no driving licence and no money or phone. Fully clothed, and no obvious signs of a sexual assault. She has a nasty head wound, but she didn't necessarily die in this spot.'

'Why do you say that?'

'As you can see, there isn't much blood here, apart from

on her hair and skin, but there's a lot more blood near the bottom of the steps that lead to the path to Robin Hood's Bay.' Holly lifted her white-gloved hand, pointing to a spot at the head of the bay.

'Show us.'

She took them a roundabout way across the beach to the bottom of the steps, avoiding the markers that the CSI team had placed in the sand. 'This is where she appears to have sustained her injuries. A single set of footprints leads from here to the cave entrance where her body was discovered, but they're not hers. It looks as if someone carried her body to the cave. After that the footprints go straight to the youth hostel.'

'Can we see the footprints?' asked Becca.

'Sure.' Holly led them to the nearest marker, where a large and clearly defined trail of prints had been preserved in the sand. 'Men's size eleven trainers, suggesting someone tall. Jamie has taken photos and sent them over to forensics. They ought to be able to pin down the brand easily enough.'

Raven took in at a glance the route left in the sand. From the bottom of the steps to the mouth of the cave and then back up the beach to the entrance of the youth hostel. The outgoing prints were deep, as if the person who had made them had been carrying a great weight. The returning prints were lighter. No attempt had been made to conceal the tracks.

At the bottom of the steps, Raven and Becca stooped to examine the blood. It was just as Holly had said: a significant amount. It had soaked into the sand and splashed across rocks, staining them copper in the weak sunlight.

'Any sign of a weapon?' asked Raven.

Holly shook her head. 'None.'

'Who found her?'

'That chap over there.' She indicated an elderly man dressed in waterproofs and Wellington boots sitting at one of the picnic tables outside the hostel. He was talking to a uniformed policeman who Raven recognised as Sergeant Mike Fields from Whitby. The two of them had worked together to solve a spate of murders at the Whitby Goth Weekend earlier that year. Raven and Becca went over to say hello.

'DCI Raven,' said Fields. 'And DS Shawcross. How's it going?'

'Not so bad.' Raven was a fan of Fields's down-to-earth manner and appreciated his local knowledge, but the two men had not parted on the best of terms, with Raven suspecting Fields of leaking details of the previous investigation to the press. The allegation had never been proven however, and Raven decided to give the man a second chance.

'This is Mr Foster,' said Fields, introducing the man in Wellingtons. 'He found the body at six this morning.'

'Pleased to meet you,' said Foster. 'Inspector Raven, was it?' He was a thin and wiry man with a nut-brown face and silver hair. A pair of metal-framed glasses perched on the end of his nose. On closer inspection, he was perhaps a few years younger than Raven had thought, but his weathered complexion made him seem older.

'What were you doing down here so early?' asked Raven.

'Fossil hunting.' Foster was carrying a rucksack and a thermos flask. He had clearly come prepared to spend the day here. 'Boggle Hole is one of the best sites in the country to find ammonites, particularly the *Asteroceras obtusum* species. The Redcar mudstone formation is exposed right here on the foreshore. It's a combination of mudstones, siltstones, sandstones and limestones. It's one of the finest Lower Jurassic locations in Europe.'

Foster's arms were in motion as he spoke, pointing out the various rock formations that spanned the bay, from the foot of the cliffs all the way down to the approaching sea. The nerdiness of the amateur enthusiast.

Raven made a mental note to add fossil hunters to his

list of helpful members of the public. A list that already included dogwalkers, delivery drivers and nosy neighbours.

'Are you local?' he asked.

'I live in Whitby, but I like to come here whenever the conditions are good.'

'And when might that be?'

'Mostly during the winter months when the fossiliferous zones are exposed, but the tide has to be right too, of course. That's why I was here so early today. High tide was at midnight last night. Low tide was at six this morning.'

'Six o'clock.' Raven turned his attention to the cave opening at the foot of the cliffs about halfway down the beach where a temporary screen had been erected to shield the victim's body. 'So at midnight all of this cove would have been underwater?'

'That's correct.'

'From what time would the cave entrance have been dry?'

'About two o'clock this morning,' said Foster. 'So the body must have been placed by the cave sometime between two and six.'

'Placed?' said Raven sharply.

Foster looked alarmed. 'I mean, you can clearly see the footprints in the sand leading to the body. Someone must have carried her there.' His eyes turned to the youth hostel. 'Before going into the youth hostel.'

Raven nodded. It was obvious from the size of the footprints that it wasn't Foster who had carried the body down the beach. But the man was observant, you could say that for him. If he hadn't been out fossil hunting at such an unearthly hour, the body might not have been discovered until later, giving the CSI team less opportunity to scour the scene of the crime for evidence before the rising tide erased it.

'You found more than you bargained for, Mr Foster,' said Becca.

'Well, yes. I did, rather. When I first saw her, I thought she was just sitting there. But then I realised she wasn't moving. But I didn't touch her. She was clearly already dead. I had this silly idea... no, you don't want to hear what I thought.'

'Go on,' said Raven.

'It's just that in times gone by, local people used to believe that hobgoblins lived in these caves. That's why the bay is called Boggle Hole. Boggle is another name for goblin. My first thought when I realised she was dead was that the goblins had killed her.' He took off his metal-framed glasses and rubbed his eyes. 'Sorry, but it's been quite a morning.'

'We'll need a signed statement from you,' said Raven. 'And then you can go home. Perhaps Sergeant Fields could take a written statement?'

'Leave it with me,' said Fields. 'I'll make sure it's all sorted and sent to you as quickly as possible.'

Raven turned to Becca. 'As for us, I think our next stop is the youth hostel.'

CHAPTER 4

The smell of fried bacon and scrambled eggs assaulted Becca's senses as soon as she entered the youth hostel. The thought of breakfast was unimaginable after consuming so much alcohol the previous night and she fought down a wave of nausea.

She was grateful to Raven for taking the drive to Boggle Hole at such an uncharacteristically steady pace. But as a teetotaller, what must he be thinking of her? She didn't consider herself to be a heavy drinker, but she'd been feeling down since splitting up with her boyfriend, Daniel. Her housemate, Ellie, wasn't a good influence on her, with her easy drinking habits. And watching Ellie slobbering all over Becca's brother, Liam, every time he came to the flat was becoming a strain. The truth was, Becca was lonely and had decided to have a good time and let her hair down. And now she was paying the consequences.

But none of that explained precisely why she was so bothered by what Raven thought of her.

The manager of the hostel emerged from the kitchen and came to meet them. He was late thirties or early forties, tall and broad with a thick ginger beard and shoulder-length hair tied back in a ponytail.

'Kevin Brighouse.' He wore a navy and white striped apron over his shirt and jeans and wiped his hands on a tea towel before shaking Raven and Becca firmly by the hand. 'I'm the manager and general dogsbody around here. Sorry I'm in such a state' – he indicated his grease-smeared apron – 'but the kitchen lad hasn't turned up for work and people are waiting for their breakfasts. And that's on top of everything else.' He lowered his voice to a whisper. 'The body, I mean. Your man, Sergeant Fields, was saying that no one is allowed to leave the youth hostel until further notice. Now everyone's asking me how long they'll have to stay. What should I tell them? Some people have trains to catch, and so on.'

'I'm sorry about that,' said Raven. 'But we'll need to speak to everyone staying here. Do you live on site yourself?'

'Aye, as do most of the staff when they've got an early or late shift.'

'What about this lad who hasn't turned up for work?' asked Becca. 'Does he live here too?'

'Rory. Yeah, he does.'

'When did you last see him?'

'Yesterday morning. It was his day off.'

'Has he failed to show up for work before?' asked Becca.

'No,' said Kevin. 'He's normally completely reliable.'

'I'll ask Sergeant Fields to track him down,' said Raven. 'In the meantime, we'll need to interview all the guests and staff. I realise you're busy, but perhaps you can spare us some of your time now.'

It was clear from Raven's tone of voice that this wasn't a question and Kevin reluctantly indicated the way to his office. 'Aye then, it looks like folk will just have to wait a while longer for their bacon and eggs. Come this way.'

Raven gave an order to a passing constable to begin a search for Rory the kitchen lad, and he and Becca followed Kevin into a small room at the end of the corridor. She took a seat opposite the manager's desk while Raven lurked to one side, standing. He leaned his back against the wall, his black coat wrapped around him like a second skin even though the office was hot and stuffy. Becca loosened her jacket, feeling a fresh round of turbulence in her stomach.

'This body on the beach,' said Kevin. 'Is it a woman?'

'Why do you ask?' Becca asked.

'Well, there's a lass here, one of the guests, who's been getting a bit hysterical. She says she travelled up from London with a friend yesterday morning, but her friend didn't return to the hostel last night.'

'Where is this lass now?' asked Becca.

'In the dining room.'

'We'll speak to her next,' said Raven. 'But first, did you notice anything unusual last night or early this morning? Any problems with guests? Any arguments? Any noise?'

'Nothing,' said Kevin. 'I slept like a log. First sign of trouble was when Rory didn't show up to cook breakfast. And then the police came knocking on the door... since then I haven't had time to think.'

'I hear what you're saying,' said Raven. 'We'll take a written statement from you later, but if you can introduce us to this girl from London, we'll let you get back to your duties.'

'Thanks. I appreciate that.'

Kevin took them into a light and airy room with tables down both sides. A young woman who couldn't have been more than twenty was sitting at a corner table, a steaming mug of coffee in front of her. Her jet-black hair was scraped off her face in a tight ponytail and her nose and ears were pierced in multiple places. She looked jittery and jumped up as Raven and Becca approached.

'Are you the police?' She spoke in a strong South London accent. ''Bout fackin' time you lot showed up, innit?'

'Well,' said Raven in a calm voice, 'we're here now.' He nodded to Becca, and she understood this to mean that she should take the lead in this interview. Great, just what she needed. More aggravation. Perhaps Raven thought she would find it easier than him to form some kind of bond with this fidgety young woman. The girl was more tightly wound than a watch spring.

'I'll leave you to it, then,' said Kevin and disappeared back into the kitchen, seeming only too happy to leave them in the company of his guest.

'Well, wot you got to say?' asked the girl.

Raven looked at Becca expectantly but said nothing. Great.

'Let's sit down,' said Becca, pulling up a chair. 'What's your name?'

'Lexi.' The girl nibbled at a piece of loose skin by her fingertip. Her nails were bitten to the quick.

'Lexi what?'

'Lexi Greene. What's yours?' Her tone was insolent.

'I'm DS Becca Shawcross and this is DCI Tom Raven. We're from Scarborough CID.'

Lexi glanced suspiciously at Raven who had taken a chair a little back from the table. Becca read distrust, even dislike, in her eyes. Raven certainly wasn't making any effort to be pleasant. Then again, when did he?

It was up to Becca to play the good cop.

'So, Lexi, the manager told us that you're worried about your friend.'

'It was 'er idea to come 'ere. Not mine. And now she's gone missing. We should never 'ave come.'

'What's her name?'

'Anna. Anna Capstick.'

'Could you describe Anna for me, please, Lexi?'

'Thin, white, long blonde hair. 'Ang on, I've got a photo somewhere.'

She scrolled through her phone at lightning speed then angled it so that Becca could see the screen. She held on tightly, not letting the phone out of her hands, and not allowing Raven to see.

Becca leaned in closer to look. The photo on the screen showed Lexi and another girl pulling faces at the camera on a night out. It was definitely the woman on the beach. Becca gave Raven a brief nod of confirmation. 'You're from London, is that right, Lexi?' she asked.

'Yeah, sarf London. Peckham.'

'And is Anna also from London?'

'Nah, she's from Robin Hood's Bay, innit?'

Robin Hood's Bay was the settlement closest to Boggle Hole. A small fishing village nestled in the gap between two cliffs, it was popular with tourists and quickly became crowded during high season. Its narrow, twisting streets and stone cottages harkened back to centuries past.

'So was Anna returning to visit friends or family?'

Lexi looked away. 'Summink like that.'

Becca sighed. So much for forming a bond. She was going to have to work harder to get Lexi to open up. 'Why don't you start at the beginning,' she suggested, 'and tell us how you know Anna and why you both came up to Yorkshire.'

Lexi nibbled at her fingernails, shooting a mistrustful look in Raven's direction, before pulling her chair closer to Becca. 'We're mates. We flat share in London an' work at a coffee shop near Tower Bridge.'

'When did you arrive in Boggle Hole?'

'Yesterday morning. We took the overnight coach from Golders Green 'cause it was the cheapest way to get 'ere. It didn't leave till gone midnight. I tried to sleep on the coach but it was too fackin' uncomfortable. Then we got the bus from Scarborough.'

'So what time did you arrive at the youth hostel?'

''Bout midday.'

'And how long were you planning to stay here?'

Lexi looked at Becca as if she had taken leave of her senses. 'Jus' the one night. Why would anyone 'ang around 'ere any longer? I should be off now. I've gotta go to work tomorrow.'

'It's a long way to come for one night,' said Becca.

'Yeah, that's wot I said, but Anna wanted to see 'er mum. She lives in Robin Hood's Bay, innit.'

Raven leaned closer, casting a dark shadow across the table. 'If Anna has family in Robin Hood's Bay, why are you staying at the youth hostel in Boggle Hole?'

Lexi drew away from him defensively. 'You callin' me a liar?'

Raven shook his head and leaned back in his chair, nodding again for Becca to resume.

'We have to ask these questions,' Becca explained to Lexi. 'So that we can build up a complete picture.'

'Yeah, I guess.' Lexi gave Raven the evil eye once more before turning her attention to Becca. If Raven's intention had been to cement the fragile bond between the two women, then his plan had worked. 'Anna 'adn't seen 'er family for, like, a year. She didn't get on with 'er dad. I fink she was afraid of 'im.'

'Was he abusive towards her?'

'Dunno.'

'Talk me through what you did yesterday after arriving here.'

'We dumped our gear in our room. Then we walked over to Robin Hood's Bay.'

'Which route did you take?'

'The path over the cliff. But when we got there, Anna said she 'ad stuff to do on 'er own and I was like, well wot d'you expect me to do all day in this place? And she said, well 'ave a look around, it's quite pretty innit, and I fought, yeah but there's nuffink to do.'

Becca could imagine how a young woman who had spent her entire life in the urban environment of South London might not appreciate the charms of a quaint Yorkshire village like Robin Hood's Bay. 'Did you see where Anna went?'

'Yeah. She went into an 'ouse opposite the pub overlooking the square.'

'Her mum's house?'

'Dunno.'

'Did you meet up again?'

'Nah.'

'What did you do all day, then?'

Lexi shrugged her thin shoulders. ''Ung out. Got a coffee. Got an ice cream. Got bored. Came back 'ere and went to bed. There was nuffink to do and I was knackered 'cause I 'adn't slept on the bus. When I woke up, Anna wasn't there. I fought mebbe she'd stayed wiv 'er mum after all, but then I 'eard there was this body on the beach and I jus' knew it was 'er. Is it 'er?' Lexi had come close to tears.

'We'll need to formally ID the body,' said Becca, 'but it looks as if it might well be your friend. I'm sorry.'

'Oh, God, that's fackin' shite.' Lexi's eyes were brimming with tears. 'I wish we'd never come to this shithole!' A tear slid down her face and Becca reached for her trusty pack of tissues. Even witnesses who tried to play it tough like Lexi were prone to burst into tears when they heard bad news, and Becca often felt that giving people the worst possible news was her main occupation. Lexi took a tissue and blew her nose loudly.

'Is there anything else you can tell us?' probed Becca. 'Anything Anna said or did? Did she mention anyone else she planned to visit in Robin Hood's Bay or speak to anyone here in the hostel?'

Lexi's mouth fell open as if she'd just realised something important. 'God, yeah, there was this geezer 'ere in the hostel when we arrived. He and Anna said hello, but I didn't like the look of 'im.'

'Why not?'

Lexi pulled a face. 'I know yer not supposed to say stuff like this, but he wasn't all there if you know what I mean.' She tapped the side of her head. 'He was simple, like.'

'But Anna spoke to him?'

'Yeah. They knew each other from school or summink.'

'Could you describe him?'

'Tall, lanky. Like, really tall. Needed a wash, if you ask me. He was the same age as us. Like I said, I fink Anna knew him from school.'

'Do you know what he was called?'

'Anna called 'im Rory. Don't know 'is surname.'

Becca glanced at Raven. It seemed almost certain that this was the kitchen lad who hadn't appeared for work this morning. Raven gave a curt nod to show that he'd understood.

'We'll just take a look at the room you and Anna were sharing,' said Becca.

'Wot for?' Lexi was immediately back on the defensive. 'Wot you looking for?'

'It's just routine,' Becca reassured her, 'when someone has died in unexplained circumstances.'

'Yeah, well okay. But can I go now? I've got to get back to London today, innit. I gotta work tomorrow.'

'No,' said Raven, his deep voice cutting across Lexi's thin inflection. 'You'll need to stay in Boggle Hole until we say you can leave. We'll sort things out with your employer if necessary.'

Lexi shot him a look of pure loathing.

'Can you show us to your room?' said Raven, rising to his feet.

'Don't 'ave much fackin' choice, do I?' said Lexi sullenly.

Becca and Raven followed her out of the dining room and along a corridor to a small dormitory room containing two bunk beds. ''Ere,' said Lexi. She watched from the doorway as they worked their way through the small room. The search revealed nothing unusual. Anna's overnight bag contained a change of clothing and an assortment of cheap toiletries and makeup brands.

'Are you 'appy now?' asked Lexi.

They were interrupted by the arrival of Sergeant Mike Fields. 'Raven, there's no trace of this kitchen lad, Rory Gamble, anywhere in the hostel. But we've been searching his room. You need to come and see this.'

'Oh God,' said Lexi. 'What 'ave you found? I knew it was 'im.'

Raven gave her an angry stare. 'You stay here, Lexi,' he told her. 'Fields?'

Raven and Becca followed the Whitby sergeant up to a small room at the top of the hostel. It was the same size as the girls' room but contained only a single bed. A uniformed constable stood guard in the doorway.

'Show them,' said Fields.

The constable stepped back inside the room and showed them an item of clothing that had been thrown into the far corner of the room. A yellow T-shirt crumpled like a rag. It was smeared from top to bottom with dark stains of dried blood.

CHAPTER 5

It was possible to walk along the Cleveland Way from Boggle Hole to Robin Hood's Bay, but the footpath was off limits, as the CSI team was scouring the area around the steps where Anna had sustained her injuries. Besides, a steep walk along a rough track held little appeal to Raven when his car was available to him. So after issuing an alert for Rory Gamble, he and Becca retraced their route from Boggle Hole to the car park and drove the inland route via the village of Fylingthorpe.

A steep road descended into the lower half of Robin Hood's Bay and Raven took the last part of the journey in low gear, one foot pumping the brake. He'd had enough of steep hills for one day already.

The road twisted and turned, narrowing as it approached the heart of the village close to the shore. Tiny cottages and old houses built from solid Yorkshire stone crowded in on both sides. They passed a pub, a toy shop, a craft shop, a dinosaur and fossil museum, a fish and chip shop, and a place selling ice-cream, buckets, spades, and fishing nets. The tight bends were only barely wide enough for the M6 to squeeze around, but the village was quaint and charming and Raven could see why it was popular with visitors.

At the foot of the hill the road widened into a cobbled square. On the side overlooking the sea was a public house that doubled as a hotel. On the opposite side of the square stood the house that Lexi had identified from Google Street View imagery as belonging to Anna's parents. A slipway led down from the square to the beach, and in front of it a collection of rowing boats and small fishing boats were dry-docked on the cobbles.

There was nowhere to park, but Raven ignored the double yellow lines that surrounded the square and parked the BMW next to the boats. He opened the car door and felt the cool sea breeze on his face. The tide was still some way out, but the gentle hiss and roar of the waves washing the shore made a calming background murmur.

The tranquillity was broken by a shout. 'Oi, mate, what ya' doing? You can't park there!' A man working on one of the boats was staring at Raven, an ugly scowl on his face.

'This says I can.' Raven flashed his warrant card. 'Police. We're here to speak to the parents of Anna Capstick. Do you know them?'

The man's scowl deepened into a brooding frown, dark enough to turn milk sour. 'I'm Davy Capstick. Wha's this about our Anna?'

'You're her father?' The man looked to be about the right age – Raven guessed mid-forties.

'Yeah, what of it?' Anna's father might have been strong and muscular in his youth, but his body was now running to fat. His thick forearms were heavily tattooed with symbols of the sea – an anchor, a mermaid, ropes and knots. He had been tinkering with the outboard motor on a boat when Raven arrived and wiped his oily hands on a dirty rag.

'I think we'd better go inside,' said Raven.

Davy tossed the rag into the boat and set off up a flight of steps to the tall, narrow house across the square. The door was unlocked and he threw it open, banging it against the wall. 'Kate, where are yer?' he hollered up the stairs. 'Cops are 'ere! Summat 'bout our Anna.'

Raven and Becca followed him inside. The house felt ancient, reminiscent of Raven's own house back in Scarborough before he had sunk a small fortune into its refurbishment. The Capsticks' house was firmly in an unrenovated state, creaking floorboards and flaking plaster on bare brick walls, warped timbers in ill-fitting doors and a pervasive smell of damp making it feel like the cabin of an old fishing boat, scarcely seaworthy.

Davy was standing at the foot of a dark, twisting staircase that led upstairs. 'If Anna's done owt daft, I'll knock 'er bleeding 'ead off,' he muttered.

Footsteps echoed overhead, followed by the creaking of floorboards, and a woman appeared at the top of the stairs. 'What's 'appened?' She sounded scared.

'How the 'ell do I know? Now get down 'ere, woman, so we can find out and I can get back to the boat!'

It was plain to see why Anna had chosen to stay at the youth hostel in Boggle Hole rather than with her parents in this house. Lexi had said that Anna was scared of her dad and it was already clear that Davy Capstick was a domineering and aggressive bully.

His wife, on the other hand, made a very different impression. She descended the stairs timidly, her birdlike gaze darting between Raven, Becca and Davy.

'Mrs Capstick?' prompted Raven.

'Yes?' She was a small and thin woman with straight brown hair, perhaps a year or so younger than her husband, although it was difficult to tell as her face was creased with worry. She pulled her sleeves down over her arms, but not before Raven had seen the dark, purple bruises.

'Perhaps we could go through and sit down?' Raven said kindly.

Davy didn't wait for his wife, but marched straight through to the small front room that overlooked the square, ducking his head as he walked through the doorway. Raven and Becca followed him in, Raven also ducking low beneath the heavy oak lintel. The room was sparsely furnished with an old sofa, a battered wooden dining table and chairs, and a rusty iron anchor propped on the hearth next to an open fireplace.

Kate joined them but didn't go to her husband who was standing in front of the window. Instead, she moved further into the room, retreating into a darkened corner and taking a seat at the dining table.

'I'm afraid we have some bad news about Anna,' said Raven. There was no easy way to soften the blow. 'A body matching her description was found this morning on the beach at Boggle Hole.'

Kate blinked but didn't take her eyes off Raven. 'Our Anna? Dead?'

'Fookin' 'ell,' said Davy. He drew a pack of cigarettes from his trouser pocket but his hands were shaking so much that he dropped them. 'How'd that 'appen?'

'We haven't yet established the cause of death, but we're treating it as suspicious,' said Raven. He stooped down to pick up the fallen cigarettes and handed them back to Davy. A Polish brand, he noted.

Kate's eyes were wide with shock, but she hadn't yet begun to cry. Only a trembling of her lower lip suggested that tears were on their way. 'Anna were here yesterday,' she said, as if in denial of the news. 'She were right as rain, weren't she, Davy?'

Davy Capstick fumbled a cigarette into his mouth and lit it with a match that he tossed into the fireplace. He took a drag and blew smoke towards the low sloping ceiling. 'She were always gonna come to a bad end, that one.'

'Why do you say that?' asked Raven.

Davy looked as if he wished he'd kept his mouth shut. 'Anna were always rebellious, wouldn't listen to a word she were told. She left home nigh on a year ago, doing God knows what down south. We 'aven't seen 'er or 'eard nowt from 'er in all that time, and then she shows up yesterday out of the blue like she's the bleeding Queen of Sheba or summat.'

It was quite a speech and Davy turned away at the end of it to gaze out of the window, taking another long drag of his cigarette and making no effort to comfort his wife.

He seemed to have said all he was going to say on the subject, but Raven wasn't done, not by a long way. 'Why did she come back?'

Davy glanced up, a sharp look of resentment in his eyes. He really did know how to scowl. 'God knows. You'll 'ave to ask 'er.' He pointed his cigarette at Kate who flinched as if she'd been struck.

Kate seemed to shrink into her seat, putting as much distance between herself and her husband as she could without actually leaving the room. 'She just turned up,' she said in an apologetic voice. 'I had no idea she was coming. Honestly I didn't.'

Raven motioned to Becca to continue the interview. Kate looked fragile enough to break if she weren't handled very gently.

Becca understood his meaning and took a seat next to Kate at the dining table. 'Perhaps you could tell us what time Anna arrived here, Mrs Capstick?'

Kate shrugged. 'About one o'clock, I suppose.'

'And how long did she stay?'

'About an hour.'

'Did she say why she'd come?'

Kate's eyes flitted around the room, looking anywhere except at Davy. 'Just to tell me how she were getting on in London. She'd got a job. She were doing fine.'

'What else did she say?'

'Not much. She'd made a friend, I forget her name. The friend came with her on the coach, but she didn't come to the house.'

'You didn't meet her?'

'No. Why would I?'

Why, indeed? It seemed that Anna had gone out of her way to keep her two lives apart. She'd told Lexi little about her home life, and her parents next to nothing about what she was doing in London. Didn't people keep in touch on their phones nowadays? Why would Anna make such a long journey just to tell her mum she'd got a job?

'Was there nothing else that Anna told you, Mrs Capstick?' pressed Becca. 'You told me that she spent an hour with you.'

Kate lifted a hand to her mouth as if physically trying to avoid speaking. She stared at the empty fireplace, her eyes watery.

'Mrs Capstick?'

Kate's eyes returned to Becca. 'Anna asked how we were doing. I said all right. I asked her if she were going to come back to the Bay, but she said no, she were only stopping for the day. She had to get back t'work.'

Raven sighed in frustration. Coaxing information out of Kate was like trying to pull a limpet from a rock. They would have to speak to her on her own later without her husband's menacing presence.

'Can either of you think of any reason why someone would want to harm Anna?' Raven asked. 'Did she mention any problems she was having in London? Money, drugs, boyfriends? Anything?'

Both Kate and Davy shook their heads. 'Are ya' done yet?' enquired Davy, 'only I've got work to do.'

Raven squared up to him, his temper barely contained. What kind of father reacted to news of his daughter's death in such an offhand manner? Only one who didn't give a damn what had happened to her. 'No, Mr Capstick, we haven't finished yet. I'd like to know where you were at the time of Anna's visit yesterday.'

'Me? I were out.'

'Out where?'

'Fixing the boat. Someone's got to pull their weight around 'ere.'

'The boat is just across the square,' said Raven. 'Didn't you see Anna arrive or leave?'

'Nah. She must have sneaked in and out. Didn't want to see me, no doubt.'

'And why might that be, Mr Capstick?'

Davy blinked, perhaps realising that he'd said the wrong thing. 'We didn't always get on, me and Anna. Like I said before, she wouldn't listen to a word she were told. It were best when she moved out. Better still if she'd never come back.' He folded his arms as if that settled the matter.

'Has your family always lived in Robin Hood's Bay?' asked Becca.

Her non-combative approach seemed far more to Davy's liking. 'Oh, aye, this 'ouse belongs to Kate's dad. The family's been 'ere for generations. But it weren't good enough for Anna,' he added darkly. 'She always 'ad grander ideas.'

'Such as?' asked Raven.

'Make her fortune down south.'

Raven wasn't sure that working in a coffee shop and sharing a flat in Peckham counted as making a fortune, but at least Anna had succeeded in getting away from home and standing on her own two feet. 'What is it exactly that you do for a living?' he asked Davy.

'Fishing mainly. In the past, leastways. These days, we have to work a bit harder to make ends meet. Bit o' fishing, bit o' tourism, bit o' this and that.'

'We?'

'Me and Sid, Kate's dad.'

'And where is Sid now? Is he around?'

'Gone to Whitby for the day. We need a new part for the boat.'

The town of Whitby was just five miles away by road, but perhaps if you had no car and depended on public transport, it was a whole day's trip. They would have to come back some other time if they wanted to meet Kate's father.

Raven sighed again. The meeting with Anna's parents hadn't gone exactly the way he'd expected. But he was determined to leave with something more than a depressing picture of a coarse brute and his downtrodden wife. 'Can you explain to me exactly why Anna decided to leave Robin Hood's Bay in the first place? You told us that she left a year ago and didn't keep in touch. Did something happen to trigger her departure?' He addressed the question to Kate, hoping to draw her out.

Kate shrugged. 'Anna just wanted to get away.'

'Nah,' interrupted Davy. 'It was 'cause of that boyfriend of 'ers.'

Raven's ears pricked up. 'Boyfriend?' A boyfriend, or an ex-boyfriend was definitely worthy of following up.

'Connor Hepworth.'

'And where can we find this Connor?'

Davy chuckled. 'Right there.' He pointed out of the window to the pub and hotel across the square, which was called the Waterfront. 'His parents run that place.'

'What about friends?' asked Becca. 'Did Anna have any close friends in the village?'

'There's Fern Adams,' said Kate. 'She and Anna were at school together. You'll find her in the craft shop.'

'What about a lad called Rory Gamble?' asked Raven, keeping his voice in neutral tones. 'He works at the youth hostel. Was he a friend of Anna's?'

Kate looked up sharply. 'Rory? Why are you asking about him?'

Raven ignored her question. 'Do you know him?'

'Everyone in the Bay knows Rory,' said Kate. 'His dad's a local builder. His mum died when he was little. He's a bit... simple, if that's the right word.'

'You didn't answer my question,' Raven pointed out. 'Were Rory and Anna friends?'

But it was Davy who butted in to answer. 'Our Anna were never friends with that boy,' he said, his voice raised, his face dark with renewed anger. 'Did he kill her?'

'Why would you ask that, Mr Capstick?' said Raven.

'Because he's not right in the head. Never has been.'

Raven was about to ask more, but he was interrupted by an incoming phone call. It was Sergeant Mike Fields. He stepped into the hallway to answer it. 'Raven speaking.'

'Raven, we've just had a call from the vicar at Robin

Hood's Bay.'

Raven's brow crinkled with puzzlement. 'The vicar?'

'Yes. He says that Rory Gamble is in the church with him. They're having a friendly chat, apparently.'

'A friendly chat,' repeated Raven. 'Make sure that the vicar keeps him in the church. I'll be there in a few minutes.'

CHAPTER 6

'What did you make of those two?' asked Raven as he executed a seven-point turn in the tiny, cobbled square in front of the house and began the slow crawl back up the hill through Robin Hood's Bay.

'You noticed the bruises on Kate's arm?' said Becca.

'Of course.'

The bright sunlight hurt Becca's eyes but having spent a short while in the company of Kate and Davy Capstick, her hangover had slipped a long way down her list of concerns. 'I feel nervous about leaving her alone with that man.'

'We'll check with social services if there's any history of domestic abuse,' said Raven, 'and whether Davy Capstick has a police record.'

His response went only halfway to reassuring Becca. They were already dealing with one violent death. If another woman lost her life at the hands of the same man, she would never forgive herself. 'That man is a brute,' she told Raven. 'He didn't care a jot that Anna was dead. Is that because the news was no surprise to him?'

'We can't jump to conclusions,' said Raven. 'But it's clear that Anna went out of her way to avoid him yesterday, and that there was a deep rift between father and daughter.'

'That's one way of putting it,' said Becca. 'Kate was terrified of him. Did you see the way she shrank from him?'

'I know. We need to speak to Kate again, alone, and find out more about Anna's visit. Anna must have had a real reason for coming back. Not just to say hi.'

'I agree.'

The BMW whined its way up the steep road and entered the newer part of the town at the top of the hill. The gradients here were shallower, the roads broader. It was still pretty though, with neat gardens in front of well-kept houses. Yet Becca had been a police officer long enough to know that even the prettiest façade could hide ugly secrets.

The church was an imposing stone building with a tall tower and a red-tiled roof. Parking spaces, once again, were conspicuous by their absence. Raven left the car on the roadside in front of the porch and they entered through the open door.

The church was large for such a small village, with pillars and a domed apse over the altar. The vicar was waiting for them just inside. 'Good that you could get here so quickly,' he said. He was a youngish man, energetic and keen, dressed in a black cassock with a white clerical collar looping his neck. 'Reverend Mark Taylor.' He shook their hands and looked at his watch. 'You'll have to be quick. The service is about to start at eleven.'

Becca didn't even need to look at Raven's face to know that this wouldn't have gone down well with her boss.

'This is a police inquiry and we're investigating a suspicious death,' Raven informed the vicar in a tone that left no room for dispute. 'We'll take as long as necessary. Now, where is Rory Gamble?'

Reverend Taylor was caught off guard by Raven's blunt response. 'Um, yes, of course. I didn't mean to suggest it wasn't important. Rory's in the vestry.'

'You left him there on his own?' said Raven, making no effort to disguise his disbelief.

'Don't worry,' said the vicar. 'He won't have gone anywhere. The only way in and out of the vestry is a door inside the church.' He set off at a brisk pace down one of the side aisles, Raven close at his heels, his right leg moving stiffly as it always did when he was agitated or in a hurry.

Becca followed some distance behind. She could almost feel the waves of fury coming off Raven and didn't want to get caught in the backwash.

At the end of the aisle, the vicar pushed open a heavy wooden door and ushered them into a room filled with church paraphernalia – hymn books and Bibles stacked on a bookcase, candles and holders on a shelf, and vestments hanging on a rack. A young man sat hunched on a wooden chair, his elbows propped on his knees, hands clasped in front of him. His right leg twitched up and down in agitation and he lurched to his feet as the vicar entered.

'It's all right, Rory,' said Reverend Taylor in a soothing voice. 'This man and lady have come to ask you a few questions. Just answer them truthfully, and everything will be fine.'

Rory Gamble was exceptionally tall, his arms and legs too long for the cramped space of the vestry. He looked strong too, and filled with a wild, nervous energy that he could barely contain. He danced from one foot to another, unable to remain still for longer than a second. His eyes were downcast, fixed on a point somewhere on the vestry floor.

'I found Rory sitting by the church door this morning when I came to open up,' the vicar explained. 'He was very upset and when I asked him what the matter was he told me that he'd–'

Raven interrupted him. 'If you don't mind, Reverend, I'd like to hear what Rory has to say for himself.'

'Of course.' Reverend Taylor dropped his voice. 'But you have to understand that Rory is a vulnerable adult, so if you don't mind, I'll stay here with him.'

Raven nodded his assent. He pulled up a spare chair and sat down in front of the hulking young man. 'Hello, Rory. I'm Detective Chief Inspector Tom Raven. Why don't you sit down?'

Becca marvelled how Raven could switch his demeanour from undisguised anger with the vicar to calm patience with Rory. His voice was gentle and soothing, and the young lad ceased his movement, lifting his eyes to meet Raven's. He studied him through long, straggly hair. 'Am I in trouble?'

'No,' Raven assured him, 'we just need to ask you about something.'

'Are you the police?' There was a childlike naivety to his question.

'That's right,' said Raven. 'We're from Scarborough.'

Rory seemed to accept this explanation. He lowered himself to his chair, which was hardly big enough to contain him. He turned his head to look at Becca. 'What about her?'

'I'm from the police too,' said Becca. 'My name is Detective Sergeant Becca Shawcross, but you can call me Becca, if you like.' The lad was visibly calming down, his features becoming bland and trusting.

'Now, Rory,' said Raven, 'the vicar here says you've got something to tell us.'

Rory looked up at Reverend Taylor for approval before speaking. He really was like a child in a man's body.

'Go on, son,' said the vicar. 'Don't be afraid. Tell this man what you told me.'

Rory turned to Raven again but was unable to hold his gaze for long. He bowed his head once more, fidgeting with his big hands.

'You work at the youth hostel,' prompted Raven. 'Is that right?'

Rory nodded. 'At Boggle Hole.'

'What do you do there?'

'I work in the kitchen. I help Kevin with the meals.

Sometimes I cook the breakfasts on my own.'

'You must have to start work very early in the morning. Do you live at the hostel?'

'Yes. My dad lives here in the village, but his house isn't big enough for the both of us, not now I'm all grown up. Anyway, I like it better at the youth hostel.'

'Were you at the hostel last night, Rory?'

Another tentative nod.

'Did something happen last night? Something you want to tell us about?'

'No.' Rory shook his head but dropped his gaze to the floor once more.

'I see,' said Raven. 'What time did you get up this morning?'

'Five o'clock. I always get up at five when it's a breakfast day. I set my alarm so I won't sleep in. Once, I overslept and Kevin was cross with me, so I won't do that again.'

'Five o'clock is a very early start,' agreed Raven. 'Tell me what you did after you got up.'

'I had a wash and got dressed. There isn't time for a shower when I'm on breakfast duty. And then I went downstairs.'

'What did you do downstairs?'

Rory hesitated. 'I should have gone straight to the kitchen and started work.' He came to a halt once more.

'But what did you do instead, Rory?' said Raven patiently.

'I went outside.'

'Down to the beach?'

Rory nodded. 'I walked to the steps and I found... I found...' He hid his face in his hands and let out a low moan. He started rocking from side to side.

Reverend Taylor laid a hand on his shoulder. 'It's all right, Rory, these people are here to help. There's no need to be afraid.'

Rory dropped his hands and ceased his rocking almost as quickly as it had begun. He looked up at Raven, his gaze steady now. 'I found her at the bottom of the steps. She was just lying there. I knew that something bad had happened.'

It was the spot where the CSI team had found the blood.

'Who did you find?' asked Raven.

'It was Anna.'

'Was Anna your friend?'

'Yes.'

'So what did you do?' asked Raven.

'I asked her if there was something wrong, but she didn't answer. She wasn't moving either, but I didn't think she was sleeping.'

'Why didn't you think that, Rory?'

'Because of the blood.'

'So what did you do next?'

A look of agitation passed across Rory's face. It was with some difficulty that he said, 'I took her to the cave. I carried her across the sand so that she wouldn't get wet, and then I sat her up against the rocks.'

'I see,' said Raven. 'And why did you do that?'

'So the goblins would make her better.'

'The goblins?' Becca recalled what the fossil hunter, Mr Foster, had said about hobgoblins living in the cave. Foster's irrational fear had been that the goblins had killed Anna. 'Why would the goblins make Anna better, Rory?'

But it was the Reverend Mark Taylor who answered her question. 'It's a local legend. Boggle Hole was believed, like many other places on the moors, to be home to goblins, or boggles. It was thought that they had the power to help local people, or to play mischief on them, according to their whim. Mothers used to take their sick children to the cave at Boggle Hole in the hope that the goblins would make them better. Of course, it's all just superstition.'

'I know that,' said Rory. 'I know the goblins aren't real. But I didn't know what else to do.'

Raven nodded. 'I see. So you left Anna at the cave,

Rory. But then you ran away. Why did you do that?'

Rory shrugged. 'I was scared I'd done the wrong thing. I didn't hurt her. But I thought I'd get into trouble.'

'Rory came here looking for sanctuary,' added the vicar.

'Well, Rory,' said Raven, 'you're not in trouble. You should have phoned the police or told someone when you found Anna's body instead of moving it. But I'm not going to arrest you for that.'

'You aren't?'

'No. But I do have another question for you. Did you take Anna's mobile phone from her?'

'No,' said Rory, smarting at the suggestion. 'That's stealing, that is. I would never steal from anyone.'

'Okay, Rory.' It seemed that Raven was willing to accept the lad's story at face value. 'Just one more question. Do you know of a reason why anyone would want to hurt Anna?'

Rory shook his head sadly. 'Anna was nice. She was kind to me.'

'All right.' Raven stood up and addressed himself to the vicar. 'Rory will need to come into the station later and make a full statement. Would you be able to bring him in?'

'Of course, after the service.' In the main body of the church an organ started playing. 'Just one other thing.' Reverend Taylor drew Raven and Becca aside, a fresh look of concern on his face. 'How has Anna's mother taken the news? I assume you've informed her.'

'Yes,' said Raven. 'How well do you know the family?'

'Quite well. Kate, especially. Her husband doesn't come to church, and nor did Anna, but Kate attends services from time to time.'

'She was upset on hearing the news of her daughter's death, as you can imagine,' said Raven. He paused for a beat. 'But I can't say the same about Anna's father.'

'Ah yes,' said the vicar. 'Davy.' The name hung heavy in the air, and he seemed reluctant to say anything more.

'We noticed bruising on Kate's arm,' prompted Becca.

'Do you know how that might have happened?'

The vicar seemed to be wrestling with his conscience. 'It's not for me to break confidences, but let's say that the Capsticks are not the happiest family in the parish, and that I have concerns about Kate's welfare.'

'You're saying that Davy abuses his wife?' said Becca.

'I'm not saying that at all,' said the vicar hurriedly. 'At least, I have no proof of that.'

'In your opinion,' said Raven, 'Could Davy have killed Anna?'

The vicar squirmed in discomfort. 'I couldn't possibly speculate, one way or the other.' He checked his watch. 'And now, you really must excuse me. The Sunday morning service is due to begin.'

Raven let him go and then he and Becca slipped out of the church, the stares of the gathered congregation following them as they left.

CHAPTER 7

Goblins. Discovering a dead body was a nasty shock for anyone, and if even Mr Foster, the fossil hunter, had been struck by the crazy notion that hobgoblins had killed Anna, then Raven could understand how a simple lad like Rory might have persuaded himself that carrying her body to the cave so that the goblins might help her had seemed like a realistic option. Rory's belief in the legend of the goblins clearly didn't go very deep, and his primary reaction when asked to account for his actions was embarrassment. That explained why he had done a runner after moving Anna's body, instead of reporting it to the manager of the youth hostel, Kevin Brighouse.

A consistent timeline was beginning to take shape in Raven's mind. Anna's death from an – as yet – unknown injury at the foot of the steps leading down from the path to Robin Hood's Bay. Rory's discovery of the body sometime after five o'clock and his moving of it to the cave entrance, leaving footprints in the sand and blood on his shirt. Foster's arrival at the cove at six o'clock, and his subsequent phone call to the police.

'Thoughts?' he asked Becca when they were back in the

car.

'I think you're probably right to trust Rory's version of events. He didn't seem capable of constructing an elaborate lie, and his story is consistent with the known facts. But we can't rule him out. He's very strong. Even if he didn't mean to harm Anna, something might have happened between them, leading to him killing her accidentally.'

'It's possible,' agreed Raven. 'So who should we speak to next?' He had already formed his own idea on the matter but wanted to give Becca the chance to arrive at the same conclusion.

'Let's find this ex-boyfriend of Anna's.'

'Good call.'

Frustratingly, that meant manoeuvring the car back down the hill into the heart of the old village. By now the place was crawling with daytrippers and Raven navigated the road even more slowly than before. The summer season was finished, yet stalwart tourists prepared for all weathers in showerproof coats were filling the narrow streets, browsing in shop windows and generally getting in the way.

Raven parked on the cobbled square as before, ignoring indignant looks from passers-by. The chill of earlier had gone as the sun began to warm the day, and Raven unbuttoned his coat. Davy was back working on the boat again. He downed his tools as Raven and Becca got out of the car and followed them with his dark eyes as they made their way across the square to the pub opposite.

It was hard for Raven to ignore the obvious similarities between Davy Capstick and his own father. Alan Raven had been a fisherman too, scratching a living from the sea, and spending most of it on alcohol. He had often taken his fist to Raven's mother, leaving her bruised and beaten, and she had suffered his blows in silence, never complaining. She had done it to protect him, Raven realised looking back. Yet if he could have taken those blows in place of her, he would have done.

The Waterfront was a large pub, more like a hotel, with rooms available for guests on the two upper floors, and a good-sized bar and restaurant on the ground floor. It sat right on the edge of the town, one side facing the sea, built directly above the retaining wall of the waterfront. On a spring tide with stormy weather, waves would lash that wall, spraying white foam across the upstairs windows of the hotel. The sea was returning up the beach now, the advancing waves almost lapping against the stone wall, and Raven hoped that Holly and her team had managed to find and record all the available evidence before it was lost to the rising tide.

He held the door open for Becca, wrinkling his nose at that familiar smell of stale malt he associated with pubs. The scent brought painful memories, of slaps and bangs and his mother's tears, but here it was tempered by a mixture of wood polish and the aroma of cooking as the staff prepared to open the restaurant for Sunday lunch.

A few early drinkers were already seated at the bar. Old and middle-aged men, for the most part. They looked up as Raven and Becca entered, curious at the newcomers. No doubt news had got around of something afoot at Boggle Hole. People liked to gossip and speculate, particularly on a Sunday morning when there was not much else to do, especially in a place as small as Robin Hood's Bay. The window of the pub enjoyed a good view across the bay, and you could almost see the spot by the cave where Anna's body had been discovered. Dogwalkers and tourists would have been turned back by police guarding the cordon as they tried to cross the beach or walk the Cleveland Way that morning.

'Have you booked a table for lunch?' The man behind the bar was early middle-aged, robustly built but with a gentle smile. He looked the kind of man who would deal effectively with troublemakers and then return to chatting amiably about the football with the regulars. Not that there was likely a lot of trouble in an establishment such as this.

'Are you the landlord?' Raven asked him.

'That's right. Joe Hepworth's the name. Are you the police? I hear there's been a body found at Boggle Hole.'

All eyes in the bar turned to Raven.

'Yes,' said Raven. It would be silly to deny it. He walked to the end of the bar, out of earshot of the drinkers. 'We'd like to speak to your son, Connor Hepworth.'

'Connor?' The landlord's smile disappeared. 'May I ask why?'

The kitchen door opened and a woman emerged. Her face was round with rosy cheeks and she wore a navy apron over a casual top and skirt. She was of a similar age to the landlord and came to join him behind the bar. 'What's happened, Joe?' She laid a hand on his arm. 'Is it about Boggle Hole?'

'Yes it is,' said Raven. 'We're from Scarbrough CID.'

The woman gave Raven an appraising look. 'I'm Joe's wife, Sarah. Is it true what they say? That it's Anna Capstick who's dead?'

'We haven't yet made a formal identification of the body.'

Sarah nodded, drawing her own conclusion from Raven's statement. 'Poor kid. She grew up across the square from here. I suppose you know that. You'd better tell me what you want.'

'We just want to ask your son, Connor, a few questions.'

Sarah's eyes narrowed. 'What has it to do with him?'

'We understand that he was Anna's ex-boyfriend.'

Her voice grew cold. 'What if he was? That relationship was long over. Anna dashed off to London some twelve months ago. Connor hasn't seen her since.'

'We'd like to speak to him anyway, if you don't mind.'

'What for? You can't think he had anything to do with her death.'

Good grief, the woman was dogged in her persistence, even by Yorkshire standards. 'We don't think anything at the moment, Mrs Hepworth,' said Raven patiently. 'But we do want to speak to as many people who knew Anna as we can. We're trying to build up a picture of her life and piece together her movements yesterday in Robin Hood's Bay.'

Sarah still seemed unconvinced, but her husband rested a hand on her shoulder. 'Sarah,' he said softly, 'Connor's got nothing to hide and we want to help the police find whoever harmed Anna. We don't want a murderer loose in our village, do we?'

Sarah remained tight-lipped but nodded her reluctant consent.

'Connor's down the cellar,' Joe said to Raven. 'If you wait here, I'll go and fetch him.'

★

Connor Hepworth took more after his father than his mother, Raven was relieved to find. A young lad, about the same age as Anna or possibly even younger, with a slim build and a good-natured face. His father had fetched him from the cellar, and he was dressed casually in jeans and a T-shirt proclaiming the name of some band Raven had never heard of.

'Is this about Anna?' he asked, his lips tight. 'It's not really her, is it?'

'Let's sit down, shall we?' said Raven, gesturing to a table in front of the window, well away from the bar. He had no desire for Joe or Sarah to listen in to his conversation.

Becca sat down with the window behind her, and Connor took a seat looking out across the bay. His eyes were as grey as the sea and darted anxiously from Raven to Becca. 'There's been talk all morning of a body on the beach. Someone said the police had called at Anna's house. Please tell me it's not her.'

Raven looked to Becca. She was always so much better at this sort of thing than him. 'I'm sorry to break the bad news to you,' she said. 'But our belief at this stage is that it is Anna's body.'

The lad's grey eyes filled with tears. 'What happened to her?'

'That's what we're here to find out,' said Raven gently. 'What can you tell us about her? The two of you were a couple, is that right?'

Connor pulled out a hankie and blew his nose. 'Yeah, but we broke up just before she left the Bay.'

'How long were you together?'

'About six months, I suppose, although we'd been good mates for much longer than that. We were in the same year at school and obviously we lived almost next door to each other so we saw each other a lot. I can't remember a time when Anna and I weren't friends.'

'Why did the relationship come to an end?'

Connor's eyes were still wet and his hands were trembling. He held onto the table, as if afraid of falling. 'She broke it off. I didn't want it to end. If it had been up to me, we'd still be together.'

'So why did she bring things to an end, if you don't mind me asking?'

He shrugged. 'She just said she didn't want to spend her whole life in Robin Hood's Bay, that there wasn't enough to keep her here. I asked if that included me and she said yes. That really hurt.' He shivered at the memory. 'I even offered to go with her, but she refused. She said she needed a fresh start. Then she left and she wouldn't even reply to my messages. I didn't see her for a whole year.'

'Until yesterday.'

Connor nodded.

'Did you know she was coming back?'

'No. She just showed up here in the pub on Saturday afternoon. I couldn't speak to her straightaway because we were finishing off the lunch shift and it gets right busy on a weekend. She said she was starving but she had no money to pay for food. I gave her a tenner to go and get fish and chips and then I joined her on the beach after I finished work.'

'What time was that?'

'About half two.'

Raven nodded. The time fitted what Kate had said about Anna leaving the Capstick's house at two.

'What did you talk about?'

Connor shrugged. 'We had a lot to catch up on after a whole year. I told her what I'd been doing and asked what she was up to.'

'What did she tell you?'

'Not that much, really. It didn't sound like her life in London was all that. I mean, she'd found a job and was living with a friend called Lexi, but apart from that, not much. It didn't sound like a lot, for a year. I asked her if she was happy, and she said she was, but...'

'But?'

Connor shook his head. 'I dunno. I couldn't help thinking there was something she wasn't telling me. Something she wanted to say but couldn't find the right words. She kept asking me if I was okay, but she was the one who looked out of sorts.'

'Out of sorts in what way?'

'Just like there was something weighing heavily on her mind. I asked her outright if she had thought about stopping in the Bay, but she said she could never live here again. She had just come for the weekend and then she'd be off. I got the impression that... that this was her final visit and she planned never to come back again.' His gaze drifted to the horizon and his eyes began to cloud with tears once more.

'Connor,' said Becca, 'did Anna explain to you why she'd returned to Robin Hood's Bay?'

'No. She just kind of avoided the topic. But I felt there was something she'd come back to do. I don't think she was here just to see me.'

'What do you think it might have been?'

'I really haven't a clue. I thought I knew her better than anyone, but since that day when she broke up with me, she's been a mystery.' He lapsed into a dejected silence and Raven gave him a moment to compose himself before asking his next question.

'So, Connor, you told us that you met Anna at two thirty on the beach. How long did you spend with her?'

'About an hour, I guess.'

'And did you see her again?'

Connor shook his head. 'No. That was the last time.'

'Did she say where she was going next?'

'No.'

'I have to ask you one last question, Connor,' said Raven. 'Did you and Anna ever argue?'

The lad raised his chin defiantly to Raven, his grey eyes clear again. 'You mean, did we fight?' He gave a vigorous shake of his head as if the idea disgusted him. 'I never hit Anna, and I would never have done anything to hurt her. I loved her. Can't you see that?'

Raven thought he could, if love was something tangible that you could see or hold. If love was real and not simply a fable we told ourselves, then Connor gave the distinct impression of never having stopped loving his former girlfriend for the whole year she'd been gone.

'Okay,' he said, rising to his feet. 'But don't go anywhere for the time being. We might need to talk to you again.'

'Where would I go?' said Connor, his face ashen.

CHAPTER 8

'Well, we've certainly no shortage of suspects,' said Becca as they walked back to the car.

'No,' agreed Raven. 'Now we just need some clear pointers from CSI and the pathologist to steer us in the right direction, and we'll have this case wrapped up in a day or two.'

Becca smiled. They both knew that police work was never so simple. There was nothing at present to implicate any of the people they had interviewed. Until the postmortem had been carried out, they couldn't even be certain that Anna had been murdered. At the moment her death was unexplained.

One thing was sure. There wasn't much more they could do in Robin Hood's Bay that day.

'Do you fancy some fish and chips?' asked Becca. It may not have been in the best of taste to feel peckish after hearing about Anna's last lunch – possibly her last meal ever – but Becca had started work early that morning after a very late night and she was feeling ravenous.

'I thought you had a hangover,' said Raven.

'Fish and chips is a well-known cure for that,' said

Becca with a grin.

'Is it really?'

'Definitely.'

'All right then.'

Becca's nose led them to a tiny chip shop up a narrow alleyway off the square, and before long they were enjoying some of the finest fish and chips she'd tasted in a long time. She didn't know whether the cod had been landed at Robin Hood's Bay or Whitby or had been brought in from further afield, but wherever it had come from it felt good to be eating while gazing out across the North Sea. The beach was entirely covered now, the waves washing the shore, the tide already turned and heading back out. The cove at Boggle Hole would be washed clean of Anna's blood, all traces gone.

Raven scrunched up his empty bag. 'You going to finish yours?'

'You still hungry?' Her stomach had offered no great resistance to the food, other than a mild gurgling protest, but it was probably best to quit while she was ahead. 'Go on,' she said, passing the remaining chips to him. He devoured them as if he had never seen food before.

They returned to the car and set off, the BMW climbing the hill with ease. Raven accelerated to his normal speed as they left the village behind.

Becca wondered if this was a good moment to broach the subject that had been on her mind ever since Raven had asked her to help him investigate his mother's death. At the time, she'd sensed he was eager to get started, but weeks had passed and he hadn't done a thing about it.

She didn't want to pressurise him, but was he still serious about looking into the hit-and-run? Had he changed his mind about wanting her help? Knowing Raven, it was possible he'd already started his investigation without her.

In the end she decided there was no point speculating. She would just ask him outright while she had him behind the wheel.

'You know that thing we talked about?'

'What thing?' He kept his eyes glued to the road and didn't look at her.

'You know. Looking into your mother's death.'

For a moment he said nothing and Becca wondered if she had spoken out of turn. It was obviously a deeply personal matter. And yet, he had trusted her enough to confide in her.

'What about it?' he asked at last.

'Do you still want to do it?'

Raven signalled and turned onto the A171 before answering. 'Yes, but...' He trailed off.

'But what?'

Now he did turn to look at her. 'I've been scared of what I might find.'

Becca nodded. It was brave of him to admit that much. 'More scared than being in battle?' They had rarely spoken about his time in the army. And yet she knew his story well enough. Posted to Bosnia with the Duke of Wellington's Regiment, shot in the leg and discharged after being awarded the Conspicuous Gallantry Cross in acknowledgement of his bravery.

Raven's face betrayed no emotion. 'In battle, you don't have time to be scared. Everything happens too quickly.'

'So what are you afraid of now?'

He gave her a flat stare and she wondered if she'd gone too far. She knew he liked her to talk back to him, but maybe this was too close to the bone.

But after a second or two he broke into a smile. 'You're right,' he said. 'If there's one thing I learned from my army days it's that fear is the true enemy. And the only way to defeat it is to face it.'

'So we'll do it?'

'We'll do it.'

'There'll be time when we get back to Scarborough, if you'd like to make a start today.' It was still only mid-afternoon.

'You're a hard taskmaster, Becca Shawcross.'

Becca smiled to herself. If she'd known that all he needed was a little encouragement, she'd have spoken up sooner.

★

Becca's prompting had been the push Raven had needed to finally overcome his fear. Now that he'd agreed to do it, he was eager to get on. Desperate, even. How many years had he carried this misery around with him? For most of his life, it seemed. From the age of sixteen, at any rate. A quick search on the police computer and he would know.

Know what, precisely?

Something, at least. Whether it would supply the closure he so desperately craved remained to be seen.

He and Becca climbed the stairs to CID and went into his office. The station was quiet on a Sunday, the top floor practically deserted. Anyone who didn't have to be in today was at home recovering from the dinner the night before. Raven took a seat at his desk and fired up his computer.

Becca stood behind him. 'You've got the registration number of the car?'

'Naturally.' He opened his wallet and unfolded the slip of paper that DSU Lesley Stubbs had given him. He had carried it around all these weeks, keeping it safe for when the time came.

That time was now.

He typed the vehicle registration into the police database while Becca watched over his shoulder. His heart was beating unusually hard.

Just a few seconds now, and he would know.

He checked the number he had entered, seven characters that held the answer to the question that had haunted him for so long, then hit the return key. The system took moments to process the request, although it felt like an age. And then the result appeared on the screen. Raven stopped breathing.

A match had been found in the database to the car the witness had seen speeding away from the scene of the crime. A Mark III Vauxhall Cavalier 2.0i. A five-door saloon. Grey.

The registered owner was North Yorkshire Police.

CHAPTER 9

'And you've got dry rot in these joists too, mate. Look.'

Liam Shawcross watched with dismay as Barry Hardcastle, his builder, knelt down and broke off a fragment of darkly discoloured wood. It crumbled into a fine powder as he rubbed it between his big thumb and forefinger.

'That's a fungal infestation,' explained Barry. 'Nasty stuff, isn't it, Reggie?'

Barry's young assistant, Reg, nodded sagely, giving a small shudder of horror as he observed the demonstration.

Barry blew the dust away and wiped his hand on his trousers. Now that the floorboards were up, the timber joists of the Victorian building resembled cracked and flaking driftwood washed up in a storm.

'Gets into the wood and eats it up from the inside,' continued Barry. 'These days we call it brown rot, because even dry rot needs a certain level of moisture to get started. And that brings us to the root cause here. The leaky roof.'

The dry rot was just one more problem to add to the long list of headaches that this house had thrown up. Barry raised one finger to indicate the enormous roof that spanned the loft space they were standing in. It was covered with slates, supported by an elaborate network of joists, rafters and purlins. The timber was sagging, the slates cracked or missing, leaving the building fabric open to the wind and rain in several places. Barry had already established that the whole thing needed to be replaced.

Liam had budgeted for repairs when he'd bought the house. He'd thought he had it covered. Old buildings like this grand Victorian villa always needed a lot of work, but Liam had never known anything like it. His plans to transform the property into six luxury apartments were turning to dust as quickly as its timber fabric.

The ground beneath the house had subsided, making the foundations unstable and in need of underpinning, the wiring had been written off as dangerous, the water supply and drainage pipes were all corroded, and he had even discovered asbestos contamination requiring the services of a specialist waste disposal firm to remove. The money Liam was sinking into the project was enough to repair a small street.

'So how much is all this going to cost?' he asked Barry.

Barry seemed to find the question amusing. He gave Reg a good nudge in the ribs and chuckled to himself. 'How much, he asks. What do you think of that, Reg? He ought to know better by now.'

Liam clenched his jaw as the builder paused before launching into a long-winded explanation. 'It all depends, you see. First we'll have to assess the full extent of the damage. It might not be as bad as we first thought. Then again, it could turn out to be a whole lot worse. If that's the case, we're looking at chemical treatments, which can get costly very quickly. But it's more likely we'll have to rip the whole lot out and start over. Then you run into structural issues. We don't want the whole place falling in on us, do we?'

'No,' said Liam through gritted teeth, although at this very moment the prospect of the building collapsing on top of the builder and burying him and his infuriatingly uncommunicative apprentice in a mound of rubble was surprisingly appealing.

'All in all, it could cost quite a bit, mate,' concluded Barry. 'But you still haven't paid me for the work we've done already.'

Liam had been hoping Barry wouldn't bring up that particular issue. 'Yeah, mate, don't worry about it. I just need a few days to sort things out with the bank. You know what they're like.' He gave Barry one of his winning smiles, although he hardly felt like smiling.

Oh God, where was he going to find the money? He was already mortgaged to the hilt. He had sold his own flat and moved in with his girlfriend, Ellie, in order to finance this project. The bastards at the bank had lent him enough to buy the house but had balked when he asked for more to complete the growing list of renovations.

When he'd first come across this place, he'd thought it would be the one to take him to the next level in the holiday letting game. The house was a beauty, and perfectly located for the high-end rental market, which was where the big bucks were these days. Liam had crunched the numbers and had hardly been able to believe his good fortune when he learned he'd made the winning bid at auction.

Yet now the project seemed more likely to ruin him.

The last repair bill had been paid with money borrowed from a loan shark. He couldn't believe he'd had to stoop to such desperate measures. He couldn't tell Ellie what he'd done, and he certainly couldn't confide in his sister. Becca was always quick to judge, and if she knew he'd got involved with an illegal money lender, she'd be on him, even though he was the victim here.

Five hundred percent interest.

Liam felt ashamed just admitting to himself that he'd been so stupid. Yet what choice did he have? It was just to tide him over for a short period while he got the house converted and sold off the apartments. There was still a profit to be made if he could see the job through to completion.

But now this latest bad news had come along like a kick in the teeth when he was already on his knees. Dry rot in the attic. Life couldn't get any worse. He'd have to think of something pronto or his entire business would collapse into this sinkhole.

'Leave it with me,' he told Barry. 'I'll get you the cash, don't worry. I just need you to get things moving as quick as you can.'

*

'Go fetch, Quincey!' Hannah Raven hurled the tennis ball as far as she could and watched it spin away down the beach, bouncing and kicking up sand as it landed. The Black Labrador bolted after it, never tiring of the same game, however many times they played it. There was nothing like a dog for lifting your spirits when you were feeling down.

And it was good to have a friend too. So far, Ellie Earnshaw was the only good friend Hannah had succeeded in making since coming to Scarborough that summer. She had hung out a bit with Ellie's boyfriend, Liam, and his sister, Becca, who happened to be her dad's sergeant, but Ellie was the one Hannah saw most often.

When she had messaged Ellie that morning and suggested they meet up for a walk with the dog on the North Bay, Ellie had responded positively.

Great idea. Liam's still with his builder and I could use some fresh air. See you soon.

Thirty minutes later the two friends were strolling across the sand while Quincey ran back and forth, the ball between his jaws.

'So are you a full-time dog-minder now?' asked Ellie.

Hannah laughed. 'Not exactly. Quincey still goes to Vicky's some days, but I'm happy to take care of him the rest of the time, especially with Dad working such long hours.' Vicky Hardcastle, who was married to the builder who had renovated the house in Quay Street, ran a professional dog minding service, and Quincey was one of her favourites. 'So how are things with you?'

Ellie always liked to wear bright colours. Today she was dressed in a patterned top and ripped turquoise jeans. Her hair was dyed in all the colours of the rainbow.

'Everything's going great actually. When Liam suggested we should try living together I wasn't sure it was a good idea, but now that he's moved in, it's wonderful. I know it was a wrench for him selling his flat, but it proves just how committed he is to our relationship.'

'I'm pleased for you,' said Hannah. 'Have you taught him to pick up his smelly socks yet?'

Ellie laughed. 'I'm working on it. Men aren't as easy to train as dogs.'

Quincey bounded back up the beach and dropped the increasingly soggy and matted tennis ball at Hannah's feet. She bent down to pick it up and threw it into the air again. Quincey dashed away.

'What about you?' asked Ellie. 'Have you had any more thoughts about what you're going to do next?'

Hannah sighed. It was the subject that weighed on her mind most heavily. She had awoken that very morning at some unearthly hour, staring into the blackness, wondering how she was going to fill the rest of her life. It was okay living with her dad for the moment, spending her days in Quincey's company, but it wasn't what she'd expected after leaving university. After completing her Law degree, she'd come to Scarborough in high hopes of pursuing a career in law. But her internship with a firm of defence lawyers had ended badly and now she had no idea what she wanted to do. 'Mum thinks I should go back to London,' she told Ellie. 'She says that coming to Scarborough was a mistake and that I should get a job with a firm in the capital.'

'But you're not so sure?' said Ellie.

'I just don't know. I like London, but I'm not sure I

could face renting a room in a shared house in Clapham and commuting on the Tube every day.'

'Couldn't you live with your mum?'

'Are you kidding?' Hannah loved her mum, but Lisa wasn't an easy person to live with. She could be uptight, and since divorcing her dad, she had gone from one relationship to another. Hannah couldn't be around her at the moment. 'Besides,' she told Ellie, 'I'd miss all this.' She turned to face the sea, her arms stretched wide, the wind blowing her hair. 'You can't breathe air like this in London.'

'Good point,' said Ellie. 'Listen, I know this isn't a long-term career move, but if you want to earn a bit of cash while you sort yourself out, Dad needs a new waitress. He pays a decent rate.'

'At the bistro?' Ellie's dad, Keith, ran a small restaurant in the centre of town. Hannah had been there a few times with Ellie and had grown to like him. He was a kind man, and generous to a fault, always insisting on letting Hannah eat for free. 'That would be brilliant,' she said. She was running short of cash and didn't like scrounging off her dad.

'Great,' said Ellie. 'I'll give him a call.'

*

Superintendent Brandon Holt reversed his Mercedes into the driveway of the house on Wheatcroft Avenue and killed the engine. His visits to the home of retired Chief Superintendent William Seagrim wouldn't go on for much longer, surely. The old man was dying and might shuffle off his mortal coil any day. Although, Holt reflected as he walked to the front entrance, he had been thinking the same thought for years, and still Seagrim clung on relentlessly to life, refusing to let go.

Holt knocked briskly on the door of the detached mock-Tudor house and waited. The door was opened by the private nurse who had been hired to attend to the sick man. Seagrim was adamant that he wasn't going into a nursing home or hospital. He could easily afford the luxury of round-the-clock care, and what else was he going to spend his money on, anyway?

'How is he today?' asked Holt, stepping into the hallway.

'He's awake and comfortable,' said Nurse Bradshaw. She was always formal and maintained a professional distance with him. She had never told him her first name. He had never asked.

'I won't stay long.' Holt found these visits increasingly depressing and continued them mainly out of a lingering sense of duty. There was a bond between him and his former boss, one he found he couldn't easily break. The old man had a hold on him just as strong as his grip on life. Seagrim was a determined old bugger, you could say that for him.

Nurse Bradshaw nodded curtly and led Holt to the old man's room. The former dining room of the house had been converted into a sick room complete with hospital bed. Holt stood on the threshold and glanced wearily into the room, his eyes taking in the once warm and inviting space where family and friends had gathered for meals, and which was now dominated by the business of dying.

The old dining table had been removed to make way for the enormous metal-framed bed and all its apparatus. A sideboard that had once held plates and silverware was now stacked with medicine bottles, packets of pills, tubes and devices whose function Holt could only guess at. A pair of dining chairs remained, now placed on either side of the bed for the benefit of visitors, although who, other than Holt himself, would want to visit this grumpy old man who clung to life primarily, it seemed to Holt, to torment the living?

The room's single occupant lay ensconced in the bed, crisp white sheets tucked in at the corners. Seagrim's breathing was laboured, a heavy wheezing like the groaning of a ship caught in a heavy swell.

'You've got a visitor,' said Nurse Bradshaw, bustling into the room. She plumped up Seagrim's pillows and checked his catheter before allowing Holt to enter the room.

Holt went in warily, his nose wrinkling at the antiseptic smell that concealed layers of even less pleasant odours. His gaze lingered on the large window which gave a good view over the rear garden. Yellow leaves from a tall silver birch were scattered across the lawn. The last roses had died and needed deadheading.

Time brings all things to an end.

Holt had no intention of spending his final days like this. All that money Seagrim had accumulated for himself and what good did it do him? None. Holt intended to retire within the next two years and make the most of his future, preferably somewhere a good deal warmer than North Yorkshire.

Eventually Nurse Bradshaw finished her fussing and left the room with her usual admonishment. 'Don't tire my patient out, Superintendent.'

He always felt like replying, 'What does it matter? He's got nothing to live for. All this money and he's reduced to this!' But he kept his thoughts to himself and waited until she closed the door behind her before he approached the bed.

He took a chair and sat down. He wasn't going to insult Seagrim by asking how he was. Any fool could see the man was no livelier than a scarecrow. In any case, Seagrim wasn't one to wallow in self-pity. He would want to hear what was happening in the world outside these four walls, in the land of the living.

'It was the annual awards dinner last night.'

'Oh, aye? You win anything this time?'

'Oh yes, in recognition of my contribution to a reduction in drug-related offences in the Scarborough neighbourhood.'

Seagrim's upper body began to shudder, a gurgling, rattling sound emanating from his chest as a wave of coughing convulsed him. The coughs came in short staccato bursts, trailing off into a wheezing rasp. The old man was laughing.

'I thought that might amuse you,' said Holt.

'You jammy bugger,' said Seagrim once his mirth had died down. 'If only they knew the truth.'

'I had to make a speech, of course,' said Holt. 'The usual crap about how I couldn't have done it without my team. You know the drill.'

Seagrim chuckled but once again it turned into a hacking cough. Holt waited for it to subside before continuing.

'I sat next to this miserable bastard called Raven. He didn't touch a drop of alcohol all night. Those evenings aren't as much fun as they used to be.'

'We had some good times, didn't we?' croaked Seagrim, his eyes clouding over.

Now that the old man was lost in memories of the past, Holt braced himself to say what he'd really come here to tell him. 'Something's come up at Robin Hood's Bay. Police are crawling all over the place.'

'What sort of thing?' Seagrim's attention was suddenly back in the present. His bony fingers closed around Holt's wrist. His grip was surprisingly strong.

'Nothing you need to worry about. Some lass staying at the youth hostel in Boggle Hole was found dead on the beach. It's nothing I can't handle.'

Seagrim's grip tightened on his arm like a vice. He leaned forwards, the straggly muscles in his neck craning. 'Make sure you do.'

CHAPTER 10

Raven rose early on Monday morning after a broken night's sleep. The revelation that the car that killed his mother had been owned by the police had been a shock and had raised more questions than it answered. If he was hoping for closure, he had instead achieved the exact opposite, opening up a Pandora's box of questions.

Perhaps he should have suspected something like this. He already knew there had been a cover-up. But the truth was darker and murkier than he'd anticipated, and the number of questions swirling around his head and keeping him from sleep was multiplying. Who had been driving the car? Who had known about the hit-and-run? And who had ordered the inquiry to be dropped?

Becca had urged him to take the matter to Detective Superintendent Gillian Ellis, but Raven wanted to find out as much as they could on their own first. This was too important to him. He needed to know who he could trust.

Quincey was already up when Raven went downstairs, and he gave the dog's head a good rub. But he wasn't fooled by the animal's attention. 'You just want food, don't you?' he said, scratching Quincey's nose. But it was too early for breakfast, and Hannah would see to the dog's needs when she awoke later. He left a note for her on the kitchen table and went into the station, hoping to get some work done and settle his mind before the rest of the team got in.

But Gillian was there early too and intercepted him as soon as he arrived. 'Tom. I'm glad I bumped into you. Come into my office.'

He wondered if she'd arranged to ambush him in this way, but how could she have known he would be in so early? Perhaps she had something on her mind too, and like him, had been unable to sleep.

She took up position behind her desk, sitting upright, her big hands clasped in front of her. Raven stood waiting. She had this knack of making him feel small, even when he'd done nothing wrong. At least, he didn't think he'd done anything wrong.

'I hear that Gordon's been telling you tales about his younger days.'

Raven frowned in puzzlement. 'Yes, ma'am.' Had Gillian summoned him to her office just to talk about her husband?

She pursed her lips. Was that embarrassment he detected in her eyes? Was she afraid of what Gordon might have told him after a few drinks? 'Just bear in mind that my husband likes to tell entertaining stories at these kinds of dinners. Let's say that he often embellishes the past.'

Raven nodded. 'I see, ma'am. You wouldn't want me imagining that these days he was anything other than a respectable businessman.'

She tipped her head in confirmation.

'And you wouldn't want me to think any less of you either, ma'am.'

'I'm glad you understand, Tom.' She shuffled a sheaf of papers on her desk. 'Now, to other matters. I hear that you are investigating an unexplained death.'

'That's right. A woman's body was found near Robin Hood's Bay on Sunday morning. Sergeant Shawcross and

I interviewed a number of witnesses and persons of interest yesterday.' Raven would give her more details if she asked for them, otherwise he'd keep his answers brief. He really did need to catch up on his emails.

Gillian raised an inquisitive eyebrow. 'Persons of interest? Is there any reason for thinking that this is more than just a tragic accident?'

'I don't understand, ma'am. What do you mean?'

She let out a short, exasperated sigh as if the meaning of her question should have been obvious. 'What I mean is that the body of a young woman was found at the foot of some steps after she'd been out on a Saturday night. Isn't the most obvious explanation that she slipped and fell on her way back to the youth hostel in the dark?'

'That's one possible explanation, ma'am. But I don't want to pre-empt the inquiry.'

'Of course not, Tom. I'm not suggesting that. But why do you think there might be more to it?'

Raven didn't know quite why she was pursuing this line of questioning. It was his duty to investigate unexplained deaths to establish the cause. But he found himself becoming defensive of the inquiry. 'There are factors that suggest it may not have been an accident. I feel there's more to it.'

'You *feel* there's more to it?' Gillian's scorn was evident in her voice. 'Do you have concrete grounds for suspecting foul play?'

Raven tightened his jaw. He really could do without having to justify his job this early on a Monday morning. 'There are a number of factors that need following up. The woman's body was moved, her phone is missing, there are signs that her father may have been abusing her, there's an ex-boyfriend on the scene, and the post-mortem hasn't been carried out yet. I think there's plenty of work still to be done.'

Gillian took a moment before coming to a decision. 'Very well, Tom. We'll see what the post-mortem tells us. But for now, I'd like you to proceed on a low-key basis. I don't have the resources to turn this into a larger investigation.'

'Very good, ma'am.'

He returned to his desk knowing he had only limited time to prove that Anna's death wasn't simply an accident.

*

Gillian had told him not to turn the investigation into a larger one, but Raven knew he couldn't make much headway with just himself and Becca working on it. So once everyone was in, he summoned DC Tony Bairstow and DC Jess Barraclough to a meeting. Gillian could hardly rebuke him for enlisting the help of two junior detectives. That hardly constituted a major inquiry. Besides, with four of them working on the investigation, he could hopefully get things wrapped up before she even noticed.

He began the meeting by bringing Tony and Jess up to speed with what he and Becca had found out the previous day in Boggle Hole and Robin Hood's Bay.

'Anna Capstick was nineteen years old and grew up in Robin Hood's Bay. She left the village a year ago to make a new life for herself in London. On Saturday morning she reappeared, having taken the overnight coach with a friend and booked into the youth hostel at nearby Boggle Hole.' Raven paused in his delivery to see if anyone would laugh or ask about the name of the cove, but it seemed that he was the only one who found it peculiar. He pressed ahead with his summary.

'On Sunday morning her body was discovered at the entrance to a cave in Boggle Hole by a fossil hunter. Blood found at the scene strongly suggests that she died at the foot of the steps leading down from the Cleveland Way that connects the cove to Robin Hood's Bay, but her body was moved to one of the nearby caves on the beach. A young man with learning difficulties called Rory Gamble confessed to moving the body because of a local superstition that goblins in the cave have the power to make people better.'

Again Raven stopped, aware of how absurd this sounded. Thank God he hadn't mentioned goblins to Gillian Ellis or she'd have told him to get a grip.

'I know that area well,' said Jess, her blonde ponytail bobbing as she spoke. 'I've walked the Cleveland Way many times.' Jess was the team's resident long-distance walker. Always keen and full of energy, she had grown up in the heart of the North York Moors at Rosedale Abbey and thought nothing of long slogs up steep moorland trails. She had even completed the Lyke Wake Walk, a punishing forty-mile trek across the moors to the finishing post at Ravenscar just south of Boggle Hole. 'The youth hostel is quite isolated. If you're on foot from Robin Hood's Bay, you'd have to walk along the beach or take the Cleveland Way over the clifftop.'

'According to the fossil hunter who found the body,' said Raven, 'the beach would have been under water until around two in the morning.'

Jess pulled a face. 'I wouldn't like to walk that path in the dark. Even with a phone or torch to light the way, you could easily trip and fall. Those steps leading down to the cove are treacherous.'

Raven nodded. A fall in the dark was the most likely explanation, just as Gillian had said. But Raven wasn't in the habit of making assumptions. He preferred facts. 'We can't rule out a simple accident, but I think we need to dig deeper. There are too many unanswered questions. What happened to Anna's phone? It hasn't yet been found. Why did she leave home a year ago and why did she suddenly return without telling anyone she was coming? Her parents and her grandfather live in Robin Hood's Bay but Anna chose to stay at the youth hostel rather than with them. Why? Her travelling companion, Lexi Greene, told us that Anna was afraid of her father and I have to say that Davy Capstick didn't endear himself to me or Becca when we visited the family home yesterday. Kate, Anna's mother, has bruises on her arm. Is Davy responsible for them? Anna's ex-boyfriend, Connor Hepworth, whose family runs the pub and hotel in the village, says Anna finished their relationship without an explanation. He must feel hurt as a result. And then there are questions for forensics and the pathologist to answer. Where exactly did Anna die and what was the cause of death?' He turned to Becca. 'Have we had the report from the CSI team yet?'

'Holly sent it this morning,' said Becca, holding up a print-out. 'Anna's phone still hasn't been recovered. But they did find a receipt in her pocket from a craft shop in Robin Hood's Bay. The receipt was dated Saturday and was for the purchase of a necklace, but Anna wasn't wearing a necklace and no jewellery was found among her possessions at the youth hostel.'

'Has the post-mortem been booked in?'

'Felicity says she'll do it this morning.'

'Good.' Raven liked it when things moved quickly. 'Tony, can I ask you to trace Anna's phone calls and put out an appeal on social media for anyone who saw her in Robin Hood's Bay on Saturday? We need to trace her steps, find out where she went and who she talked to. All we know at the moment is that she went to see her mum between one and two pm and then met Connor on the beach for fish and chips at about two thirty. According to him, they spent an hour together. He says he bought lunch for her because she was skint. Look into her bank account and speak to her employer. According to Lexi, she worked at a coffee shop near Tower Bridge. And while you're at it, see if Kate Capstick has ever reported any instances of domestic violence or if Davy Capstick has any kind of record. Got all that?'

'I'll get to work right away, sir.' Tony was the kind of detective who would never complain about being given a long list of tasks. He was a bit of a plodder at first sight, and still a DC in his mid-thirties, yet Raven had come to value him greatly over the past twelve months.

'Jess, I'd like you to visit the craft shop where Anna

bought the necklace.'

'Sure,' said Jess, brightening visibly at the prospect of a day out.

'And Becca,' said Raven, 'let's see if we can speak to Kate Capstick again. On her own this time, without the presence of her husband.'

CHAPTER 11

The day was overcast, threatening rain, and the sea was a resolute grey just like the sky. Few day-trippers had ventured out on such a dreary weekday in September, and Raven was glad to see the Bay less crowded. There was still no place to park, though, so he left the M6 on the double yellow lines on the cobbled square just as before. Let someone complain. He would soon put them in their place.

'Davy's not around today,' said Becca, casting an eye over the boats by the slipway. 'Perhaps he's at home.'

'If he is, I'll ask him to leave,' said Raven, crossing the square to the house where the Capsticks lived. He knocked on the door of the house and waited.

The door creaked open to reveal the heavily lined features of an old man. 'Aye? What d'you want?' The man's face was brown from working outdoors, and gnarled like a tree. He leaned against the doorpost, looking almost as ancient as the timber frame of the house itself.

'It's Mr...?' enquired Raven.

'Sutcliffe,' said the man sullenly.

'Sid Sutcliffe? You must be Kate Capstick's father. We

were hoping to speak to her.'

'Well, she ain't 'ere.' On closer inspection Sid wasn't quite as ancient as he first appeared. Maybe about seventy. But he hadn't aged well, his stiff joints betraying years of wear and tear, the deep wrinkles in his skin like ripples in the sand.

'Did she say where she was going and when she'd be back?'

'Nah, she didn't.'

Sid seemed as unwilling to impart information as his daughter had been the day before, but Raven was determined not to waste his journey. 'In that case, maybe we could speak to you instead, Mr Sutcliffe?'

The man regarded them through hooded eyes before nodding his assent. 'Everyone calls me Sid. And you must be the police, I reckon.'

'That's right.'

The old man didn't ask to see any proof of that, but yanked the door wide open before shuffling back inside to let them enter.

They followed him into the room where they'd spoken to Kate and Davy the previous day. Sid took a seat at the dining table where parts of an old transistor radio were scattered. He appeared to have taken it apart for repair.

'You're good with your hands, Mr Sutcliffe?'

'Sid, I said you could call me. And yes, if you've got no other way to make a living, you'd best be good with your hands. My father taught me to mend things not chuck 'em out.' He gestured to the dining chairs. 'Why don't you haul up some seats?'

Raven pulled out two of the chairs. Now he studied them more closely he saw that they were mismatched, perhaps reclaimed from various sources over the years. Sid clearly took his make-do-and-mend philosophy seriously.

Raven waited for Becca to take a chair first and then sat down himself. 'You're Kate's father, Anna's grandfather, is that right Mr Sutcliffe? Sorry, I mean Sid.'

'That's right.' He returned his attention to his work and

didn't look up as he spoke.

'Have you always lived in Robin Hood's Bay?'

'Aye. I come from a long line o' fishermen.'

'My own father was a fisherman,' said Raven.

Sid looked up, his interest caught like a cod on a line. 'It's a hard life and gets harder with every passing winter. But the sea's in my blood, I can't keep away. These days there's no profit in fishing, so I take people out on trips during the summer months. Folk will pay good money to catch summat they can cook 'emselves. Some of 'em don't even want to fish, they come hoping to see a porpoise.' He sounded dismissive, as if he secretly despised the tourists who paid good money to go out in his boat.

'What do you do during the winter?' asked Raven.

Sid shrugged. 'Bit o' this and that. Fixing boats and so on. We can still go out in good weather, me and Davy that is.'

'Is there enough work to support the two of you?' asked Becca.

Sid looked at her. 'We get by. I took Davy on as an apprentice and taught him all I know. He's not a bad bloke really.' It was an admission of sorts that his son-in-law didn't necessarily make the best business partner.

'Did you take Davy on before or after he married Kate?' asked Becca.

'Before. That was how they got to know each other. I were right pleased when our Kate decided to marry him.'

Raven knew where Becca was going with this line of questioning and let her continue.

'And are you still pleased with her choice?' she asked.

'Of course I am. I don't understand what you mean.' Sid's attention returned to the dismantled radio on the table.

'What I mean,' said Becca, 'is that when we spoke to Kate yesterday, she seemed frightened in Davy's presence.'

'Frightened?' Sid shook his head. 'You must have read 'er wrong.'

'We noticed bruising on her arm. Does Davy mistreat

her?'

'No,' said Sid firmly, jumping to his son-in-law's defence. 'Davy's not like that. He may not be the sort o' man to show his feelings, but that don't mean he don't care.'

'He didn't seem to care much about his daughter's death.'

'Ah,' said Sid, his eyes clouding over. 'Anna were a lovely lass. We're all cut up about her something rotten, Kate most of all as you'd expect from a mother. But we 'ave to carry on, don't we? We 'ave to pay the bills.' He wiped his eyes with an old handkerchief that, like everything in the house, had seen better days.

Raven gave him a moment to collect himself before asking the next question. 'Did you see Anna on Saturday?'

'Not for more than a minute or two. I were working on the boat that day. I saw 'er come into the house to talk to Kate and then afterwards she went over to the pub. I said "'ow do?" and she told me she were getting on all right down south. Later I saw her walking on the beach with Connor, but I don't know what she did after that.'

'You didn't see her again?'

'No.'

'Anna and Connor were together for a while,' said Raven.

'Aye,' said Sid cautiously. 'Stepping out, they were, for a good few months. But then they split up and Anna decided to leave home.'

'Did she tell you why?'

Sid gave a hollow laugh. 'No chance. Anna always kept her cards close to her chest. But if you want my advice, you should go and ask Joe Hepworth what he knows.'

'Connor's dad? We've already spoken to him.'

'Aye. Comes across as a good bloke, don't he? But you mark my words: there's summat he's not saying.'

★

Jess loved the drive across the moors at any time of year, but when the heather was in bloom the journey was the best in all the world. The purple flowers were past their peak now and the sky was dull and cloudy, but she still preferred to be out here than back at the station in Scarborough.

She had walked the moors earlier that year all the way from Osmotherley to Ravenscar. It had been a gruelling test of her endurance, but after the blisters had healed and the aching in her legs had faded, she found her appetite for walking undiminished. In fact, she was already considering her next challenge. The Yorkshire Three Peaks was a possibility, or even the Coast to Coast Walk that passed through the Lake District, Yorkshire Dales and North York Moors national parks, beginning at St Bees in Cumbria and ending at Robin Hood's Bay. But she would have to do her research, and then make a firm plan.

Her battered old Land Rover clattered into Robin Hood's Bay and she decided to leave it in the car park at the top of the hill rather than drive it further down. The road was narrow and steep, and there was hardly anywhere to park near the village square. You'd be daft to try.

Besides, she felt like stretching her legs after the drive, and the walk down to the sea would do her good. The days were turning cooler and wetter after the scorcher of a summer they'd enjoyed but Jess didn't mind that one bit. All you needed was the right clothing, and you could get out at any time of year.

Her long legs carried her smoothly down the hill and before long she found the craft shop she was looking for on a particularly steep bit of the main road. She pushed the door open and stepped inside. A bell jangled overhead. The small shop was a treasure trove, selling everything from pottery to pictures to jewellery to teddy bears. Everything was mixed in with everything else in a great jumble and Jess thought how her mum would love it here, hunting around for knick-knacks. Perhaps she would bring her here for a day out sometime.

A young woman with braided hair was arranging postcards of the local area showing seascapes and delightful old cottages into a rotating stand. She wore a chunky multi-coloured jumper that looked handknitted. Seashell bracelets like the ones on display rattled on her wrist, together with matching earrings and necklace.

She smiled at Jess. 'Can I help you? Are you looking for anything in particular? I recommend the jewellery. It's all handmade locally.'

'I'm afraid I'm not here to buy anything,' said Jess. 'I'm from Scarborough Police.'

The woman's eyes opened wider. 'Are you here about Anna?'

'Yes,' said Jess. 'Did you know her?'

'We were at school together.'

This was better than Jess could have hoped for. An old schoolfriend – if indeed the pair had been friends – might shed some valuable light on Anna's personal life. From what Raven had said at the morning's briefing, Anna's family seemed a bit dysfunctional, to say the least. 'And your name is?'

'Fern Adams.'

'Is this your shop, Fern?' The woman was about the same age as Jess and seemed young to own her own shop, but she had a proprietary air about her, more than if she simply worked casually behind the counter.

'It's my mum's shop. We work together. I make all the jewellery.' Fern twirled her wrist, showing off the bracelets that had been made by knotting polished stones and shells together with thin cord.

Jess leaned in to admire Fern's handiwork. It gave her just the opening she needed. 'We found a receipt that shows Anna bought a necklace from here on Saturday.'

'Yeah, she came in,' said Fern. 'Just turned up out of the blue. I hadn't seen or heard from her for a year.'

'Were you close before she moved to London?'

Fern shrugged. 'I wouldn't say we were best friends. But you can't grow up in a place the size of Robin Hood's

Bay and not know people. Everyone knows the Capsticks. Sid and Davy are always out on their boat or making repairs on the boats down by the seafront.'

Jess acknowledged the truth of what Fern was saying. Having grown up herself in the tiny village of Rosedale Abbey in the heart of the moors, she understood how it worked. Everyone knew everyone else's business, or made it their business to find out.

What was strange was that no one in Robin Hood's Bay seemed to know what had happened to Anna.

'What kind of necklace did Anna buy?' asked Jess.

'One like this.' Fern moved across to the jewellery display and held up a simple clam shell threaded onto cord with a couple of beads for decoration. It didn't look like an expensive item.

'What time did she come into the shop?'

Fern thought for a moment. 'About half four. We shut at five.'

Jess jotted the times down in her notebook, pleased to have filled in another blank in Anna's timeline. 'How did she pay for the necklace?'

'Cash. In fact...' Fern hesitated.

'Go on.'

'Well, I got the impression it was all the money she had. It was her last five pound note.'

'And she spent it on a necklace?' Jess glanced again at the shell dangling from the cord. She wouldn't have paid five pounds for that necklace, especially if it was the only money she had left in her pocket.

'That was Anna all over,' said Fern. 'Money was like water to her. If she had it, she spent it.'

'I see,' said Jess. The way Fern was talking about Anna hinted at a certain disdain for the dead woman. Fern had admitted they weren't great friends, which was surprising for two girls of the same age who had grown up in such a tiny village. Had there been a falling out?

'So what did you and Anna talk about?'

Fern replaced the necklace on the display stand,

perhaps disappointed she hadn't been able to tempt Jess into parting with her money. 'Oh, you know, I asked her how she was getting on in London. She told me she was working in a coffee shop. I asked what it was like living in a big city.'

'And what did she say?'

Fern shrugged. 'Can't remember exactly, but it didn't sound all that amazing.'

'Why? What did she tell you?'

'I don't remember. To be honest, I wasn't really paying much attention. Big cities aren't my vibe. They're too impersonal, you know? There are so many people around, it feels quite lonely. Do you know what I mean?'

Jess did. She was a country girl herself. But she sensed that Fern was holding something back. 'Did Anna tell you about her plans for the rest of the day? Did she say where she was heading next?'

'No.'

'Did you notice if she had her mobile phone with her?'

'Yeah, she was looking at it when she came in. It was one of those cheap smartphones you can buy for almost nowt.'

'And did she definitely take the necklace with her when she left the shop?'

'Well, she bought it, didn't she?' A stroppy edge had crept into Fern's voice, a defensive note that seemed quite unnecessary in response to such an innocuous question.

Jess sensed she was getting closer to some truth that Fern was doing her best to conceal. 'That wasn't my question, Fern. Did Anna take the necklace with her?'

Fern maintained a look of defiance, but after a few seconds it crumbled and she lowered her chin. 'No,' she admitted. 'She left it behind on the counter. We had a kind of argument and she stormed out. She was like that, Anna. Hot-headed, you know?'

Jess nodded, satisfied. 'What did you argue about?'

'I asked her why she'd come back, and she told me she'd just seen Connor on the beach. They used to be an item.'

'I heard about that,' said Jess, beginning to sense the reason for Fern's anger.

'But that was, like, well over a year ago. Anna had her chance. If she wanted to be with Connor she shouldn't have dumped him and run off to London, should she?'

'Are you and Connor together now then?' asked Jess.

'Yeah, we've been seeing each other for a while. I didn't want Anna coming back and poking her nose in, trying to steal him back.'

'Do you think that was her intention?'

'Dunno. She didn't say. Anna never said nowt if it didn't suit her.' Fern's face had become sulky. Perhaps Anna had been volatile like Fern said, but Fern was temperamental too, her mood as changeable as the sea.

The door opened and the bell tinkled as a middle-aged woman entered the shop. She hovered on the threshold, seeming to register the charged atmosphere inside. After a beat she took her leave, withdrawing diplomatically back onto the street.

'Did you see Connor afterwards?' asked Jess. 'Did you ask him about Anna?'

'Yeah. He said there was nowt going on between them.'

'Did you believe him?'

Fern nodded. 'That bitch broke his heart when she left him. It was mean of her to come back after all this time. Why couldn't she just stay away for ever? I don't mean I'm glad she's dead. I just wish she'd stayed in London.'

Jess folded away her notebook, satisfied that Fern had now told the truth about her encounter with Anna. The interview hadn't moved the investigation much further forward but it had pinned down Anna's movements up to five o'clock on Saturday afternoon and explained the mystery of the missing necklace. 'Is there anything else you can tell me that might help our inquiries?'

Fern hesitated. 'Well, there is one thing. I spoke to Connor on the phone after Anna left the shop, but I didn't see him again until eleven, because he was working. As I was crossing the square where the boats are dry-docked I saw Anna outside the pub with Connor's dad.'

'Joe Hepworth?'

'That's right.'

Jess reopened her notebook and wrote down the name, along with the words *with Anna outside the pub at 11pm.* 'And Joe and Anna were talking?'

'Not exactly,' said Fern, her ears flushing pink with embarrassment. 'They were embracing.'

CHAPTER 12

'A classic cut and shave, please,' said Liam, taking his seat in the chair at the Turkish barber's. Just because his building project was going down the pan, there was no reason for him to let his appearance slide. Liam prided himself on looking smart and sharply styled at all times. It created a good impression. Particularly if he had to beg the bank manager for an extension on his loan. Or go cap-in-hand to that obnoxious loan shark again.

The barber whisked a cape around Liam's neck and set to work with clippers and scissors. The buzz and snip of his tools were strangely hypnotic and Liam began to unwind after his fraught discussion with Barry.

'Quiet in here today,' he remarked. 'Is it just you?' Normally Yusuf worked alongside his cousin.

'Kerem is visiting family in Ankara.'

'Ah, that's nice.' Liam really ought to pop round and see his own mum and dad soon. Now that he had moved in with Ellie, he didn't see them so often. But the guest house in North Marine Drive was only a short walk from the flat so he didn't have the excuse that they were four hours' flight away. 'Does he usually go there for his holiday?'

'Is not a holiday,' said Yusuf brusquely. 'His father drop dead. Heart attack. Is very sudden.' The clippers buzzed close to Liam's ear.

'Oh, I'm sorry.' No wonder the barber was being uncharacteristically curt.

'Turn head this way,' said Yusuf, taking hold of Liam's chin and twisting it to the left. The blade of a razor slid across the back of his neck, scything hairs as it went.

Liam decided the best thing was to shut up.

When the haircut was finished, Yusuf wrapped a hot towel around his face. Liam closed his eyes, enjoying the sensation of being cocooned in a warm dark place. He could happily stay here in the comfort of the barber's chair, forgetting all about his money worries. But the solace of the towel only lasted for a minute or two. Soon Yusuf removed it and plastered Liam's face and neck in white shaving foam. He flicked open his straight razor with a practised movement.

But the promised shave didn't happen.

'Excuse me, one minute.' Yusuf laid the razor down in front of the mirror. 'Back soon,' he whispered and disappeared into a room at the rear of the shop.

Liam stared at his reflection in the mirror, his thoughts drifting into unpleasant but familiar territory. 'Idiot,' he mouthed at the guy in the mirror. How had he got himself into this situation with the renovation? He'd been in the property business ever since leaving school and regarded himself as a pro. He knew the problems old houses could throw up, and he'd allowed himself plenty of contingency. And yet this latest project had gone wrong in almost every conceivable way. Bad luck didn't even begin to sum it up.

He wondered where Yusuf had vanished to. There were no other customers in the shop and he was starting to get bored.

The back door opened, but the man who stepped through it wasn't Yusuf. Liam had never seen him before.

He watched him warily in the mirror as he approached the chair. The new arrival had a buzz cut, bulging muscles and wore dark glasses even though the day was overcast and he was indoors. He looked like a bouncer from a nightclub. Or maybe a professional wrestler. A bald man followed him in, attired in a sharp suit and Liam gave a gasp of horrified recognition.

Donovan Cross, the loan shark he had gone to for cash.

Never mind Kerem's father – Liam's heart almost came to a halt too.

He grabbed at the armrests of the chair and struggled to get to his feet. But the bruiser with the shades was already behind him. Two giant hands like gammon steaks grasped Liam's shoulders, forcing him back into the chair.

'Liam Shawcross,' drawled Donovan Cross as he sidled up at a leisurely pace. 'You weren't planning to rush off, were you?'

'Of course not,' said Liam, doing his best to fix a smile to his face.

'What a pleasant surprise meeting you here,' said Donovan, although Liam wasn't fooled for one moment. This was no surprise but a set-up. Somehow, Donovan had known he would be there.

Yusuf. This would be the last time Liam paid the Turkish barber a visit, that was for sure.

Donovan strolled over to the door of the shop where another customer was just about to enter. Donovan held the door shut with one hand, turning the sign from *open* to *closed* with the other and locked the door. The customer outside gave an angry look, then retreated down the street as he took in the loan shark's menacing appearance.

Liam twisted his head to keep Donovan in view in the mirror, but Buzz Cut gave him a slap on the face and pushed him back into position.

'This is one of my shops, did you know that?' said Donovan, returning to stand beside Liam. 'I own a number of businesses in Scarborough in addition to my payday loans company. I like cash businesses. No paper trails. No excessive bureaucracy. Keeps everything nice and simple.' He nodded to Buzz Cut, who picked up the cut-throat razor that Yusuf had left on the worktop. Donovan took it from him and held the blade up to the light, angling it so the metal flashed. Meanwhile the henchman began cracking his knuckles, as if limbering up for some action.

Liam didn't know where to look – Donovan, his henchman, or the razor? He tried to keep all three in view in the glass of the mirror.

'So, Liam, how is your construction project going?' asked Donovan.

Perspiration was gathering on Liam's skin and it wasn't from the hot towel. 'Good. Coming along nicely.'

Donovan leaned in closer, the naked blade in his raised hand. 'That's not what I heard, Liam. And so, I'd like to bring forward your next repayment date. As a gesture of good faith.'

Liam gripped the armrests on the chair, wishing he could escape but knowing there was no possibility of that. 'But Donovan, we agreed all this. The first repayment is due at the end of the month.'

'I know.' Donovan studied the edge of the blade, watching the way it caught the light. 'But circumstances change. We have to be adaptable, eh, Liam?'

Liam did the sums in his head, but that took no longer than an instant. There was no way he could pay Donovan before the end of the month, and even that was going to be a stretch. 'When do you want it?'

'By the end of this week.'

'But–'

Buzz Cut seized hold of Liam's head, wrapping a thick arm around his neck.

'It seems we have a little problem,' said Donovan. He lifted the razor and brought it to Liam's throat, tickling the skin with the edge of the blade.

The henchman pulled Liam's head back so he could no longer see what was happening in the mirror. Perhaps that was a mercy. He stared at the ceiling, his eyes wide. Sweat trickled down his back.

'Perhaps I didn't explain clearly enough,' continued Donovan in his friendly drawl. 'A payment is due to me when I say it is, and when it's due, you give me the money. On time. In full. Without exception.'

The razor's edge pressed against Liam's throat. He could hardly breathe for fear of the blade cutting into his flesh. He sat rock still as Donovan spoke.

'Do you hear me, Liam? Is it clear what I'm saying? Say yes if you understand.'

Liam made a gurgling sound that was halfway between *yeah* and *urgh*.

'So,' said Donovan, 'I'll expect to receive eight thousand pounds from you by the end of the week.'

Eight thousand pounds. How was Liam going to get his hands on that sort of money in four days? He had no idea.

Donovan was a crook. Liam had known that when he went to him. But he'd thought that even crooks kept their word. Honour among thieves and all that.

'We have a deal?' asked Donovan.

'I'll get the money,' croaked Liam. What else could he say if he wanted to leave here with all his body parts still attached?

Donovan dropped the razor in the sink and Buzz Cut released his grip. Liam breathed more easily.

'Good man,' said Donovan, patting him on the shoulder. 'You made the right choice.'

The two men left the shop through the front door and Yusuf returned from the back, holding a fresh towel.

'Is all okay?' mumbled the barber, unable to look Liam in the eye.

'No, is not all okay,' snapped Liam. He grabbed the towel from Yusuf's hands and wiped the shaving cream from his chin. He stood up, heading for the exit. He'd had quite enough of barbers and wouldn't be back here again.

★

Fish and chips again – the daily diet of a police officer was a tasty one, although not necessarily the healthiest or most varied. Raven inhaled the sharp scent of vinegar and enjoyed the taste of salt on his tongue before setting about the serious business of taking in carbs, fat and protein. Becca seemed hungrier than the previous day and didn't offer to share her chips with him. Jess, on the other hand, had far too much to say to focus on food.

'So, I found the craft shop easily enough. RHB isn't such a big place, is it? And guess what – the girl who runs the shop with her mum is an old schoolfriend of Anna's. And when I say friend, she comes across more like her arch-rival. Who do you think her new boyfriend is?'

Raven hazarded a guess. 'Connor Hepworth?' It wasn't as if there were many candidates on the shortlist.

'Exactly,' said Jess.

They had found a quiet spot on the quarterdeck behind the old coastguard station and were sitting on a bench looking out to sea. The tide was in, the water lapping at the rocks just below the sea wall. Gulls wheeled and swooped overhead, lured by the prospect of free food.

Jess ate a chip and licked her fingers before speaking again. 'Fern didn't know why Anna had come back to Robin Hood's Bay, although she obviously suspected her of wanting to steal Connor away from her. She wasn't very sorry that Anna was dead. Anyway, a couple of things to note. Anna came to the shop at four thirty pm and left before five. She had her phone with her at the time, but the reason we didn't find the necklace she bought was because she left it at the shop.'

'Good work,' said Raven. 'That fills in some of the gaps in Anna's movements.'

'But there's more,' said Jess excitedly, her blonde hair bobbing. 'Fern went to the pub at closing time to look for Connor and she saw Anna again.'

'At closing time?' said Raven. 'This would have been at eleven pm?' Now they were really starting to narrow down the time Anna might have met her death.

'That's right. Fern saw Anna leaving the pub. But guess who Anna was with?'

Raven offered up his palms in a gesture of surrender. 'No idea.'

'Connor's dad, Joe Hepworth. And guess what they were doing?'

Raven was growing tired of Jess's guessing games. But she was quick to give him an answer.

'Embracing.'

Becca leaned in to join the conversation. 'This is the second time we've heard Joe Hepworth's name this morning. We weren't able to speak to Kate Capstick earlier, but Sid, Anna's grandfather, mentioned Joe too. He accused him of knowing more than he was letting on.'

'For such a small village,' said Raven, 'Robin Hood's Bay is holding a lot of secrets. It's time we got to the bottom of them.' He pulled out his phone and called Tony at the station, putting the phone on speaker so that the others could hear. 'Tony? How are you getting on?'

'Some progress, sir,' said Tony. 'I've got twelve months' worth of calls from Anna's mobile phone provider. Most of her contacts are people in London. Friends, work colleagues, and so on. Looking at the calls she made on Saturday, there was only one. Joe Hepworth on Saturday morning, about the time her coach arrived at Scarborough. She seems to have called him sporadically throughout the year.'

Raven exchanged glances with Becca and Jess. 'What about calls or texts she received?' he asked Tony.

'Just one, sir. A call from her friend Lexi at 9:34 pm on Saturday evening. I've spoken to Lexi about it. She said she phoned to ask Anna when she was heading back to the youth hostel. Anna told Lexi she still had a couple of things she wanted to do in Robin Hood's Bay.'

'Anything on Davy Capstick?' quizzed Raven.

'That's my next job, sir, along with chasing up Anna's bank statement.'

'All right, Tony. We'll let you get on with it.'

Raven dropped his empty fish and chip carton into a nearby bin. 'Looks like we have our work cut out for us. Becca, let's go back to the pub and speak with Joe Hepworth again. Jess, can you head over to the youth hostel and talk to Lexi? Find out if Anna ever mentioned Joe.'

CHAPTER 13

This time, Sarah Hepworth was behind the bar at the Waterfront when Raven and Becca entered the pub. She looked no more pleased to see them than she had before. In fact, her scowl could have given even Davy Capstick a run for his money.

Raven walked up to the bar, ignoring the drinkers whose heads swivelled in his direction. Some of them had been here on Sunday too. Didn't they have anything better to do than drink at lunchtime? 'Mrs Hepworth, we'd like a word with your husband.'

'With Joe?' Sarah eyed them suspiciously. 'I'll give him a shout.'

She called through to the kitchen and Joe appeared a minute later, drying his hands on a tea towel. 'Can I help you?'

'Perhaps we could sit outside,' suggested Raven. He might have added, *out of earshot of your wife.*

'All right,' said Joe, 'it's not a bad day for September.'

Sarah watched them go outside to the small pub garden, her eyes on her husband's back, the glower never leaving her face.

They sat together at a metal table next to the sea wall, facing out across the bay in the direction of Boggle Hole. A sun umbrella extended upward through a hole in the middle of the table, its canopy folded away. A loose bit of material flapped in the cool breeze. The sea roared gently and waves threw spray over the wall. The clouds were thickening overhead. Raven buttoned his coat and turned up his collar. He didn't share Joe's optimistic assessment of the weather, but at least they couldn't be overheard out here.

'Nice view,' he said. 'I bet it's fabulous on a clear day. How long have you been managing the pub?'

Joe smiled broadly, cheerful despite the dismal weather and happy to engage in conversation even though he was a suspect in a police inquiry. He really was ideally suited to his role of pub landlord. 'It's a family business. My old man ran it before me and I took over when he died. I grew up here and can't imagine living anywhere else. For me, you can't beat the Bay, and you can't beat the life of a publican. The Waterfront's a special place for sure, there's nowhere like it.'

Raven lifted his gaze to take in the grey horizon of the sea that stretched as far as the headland at Ravenscar. He envied Joe's unbroken connection with this place. Being anchored so firmly to one location gave you a strong sense of identity. Becca had it, and so too did Jess and Tony. But Raven had turned his back on his hometown at the age of sixteen and had been a nomad ever since. A brief spell in the army followed by so many years in far-off London, a city of anonymity and displacement where everything was fluid and no one truly fitted. Now he was back in Scarborough but still he felt like an outsider. He didn't really belong anywhere and probably never would.

He had lapsed into silence and Becca cleared her throat, stepping in to keep things moving. 'A building as old as this must have a bit of history behind it, Mr Hepworth.'

Joe smiled. 'It's one of the oldest in the village, dating

back to the sixteenth or seventeenth century. Baytown was prosperous in those days, largely thanks to the fishing industry. At one time the catch here was bigger than at Whitby. Then in the eighteenth century, smuggling became the most lucrative endeavour because of the high duties imposed on goods like rum, tobacco and tea. Boats arrived on the beach in the dead of night, loaded up with contraband. It's rumoured that a former owner of the Waterfront led the smuggling operation from the pub itself.' He leaned in conspiratorially as if the ghost of the old smuggler might be eavesdropping from the shadows. 'In those days, smuggling was considered a very serious offence, punishable by transportation to America, or even hanging. But nine times out of ten, the smuggling gangs spirited away their goods before the authorities knew what was happening. They say that the old town is riddled with secret passageways, hidden cupboards and cellars even to this day.'

'And what's the origin of the name, Robin Hood's Bay?' enquired Raven.

Joe laughed. 'The tourists who visit us like to imagine that Robin Hood of Sherwood Forest came here once, stealing from the rich and giving to the poor, but there's not a scrap of evidence to support that. The first written reference to Robin Hood's Bay dates back even further than the legend of Robin of Sherwood, so perhaps our Robin Hood travelled south to Nottingham. The reality is that nobody really knows.'

It seemed as if Joe would happily spend all day talking about the past, but Raven's concerns were about more recent events. 'We've been checking Anna's phone records.'

'Oh, have you?' Joe did his best to look relaxed, but couldn't stop a slight wariness from entering his voice.

'She called you from the coach on her way to Scarborough.'

Joe nodded. 'She did. Just a quick call. She asked how things were in the Bay and I told her everything was just the same as always. She said she'd be arriving later that day and she might call in at the pub to see Connor.'

'Connor didn't seem to be expecting her.'

'Well,' said Joe, 'I probably forgot to mention it to him. Saturday's a very busy day for us.'

It was an unconvincing answer and Raven pressed harder. 'But why did she phone you? Why not Connor? She didn't even tell her mum she was coming.'

Joe scratched his head. 'I guess she didn't want to spook Kate. Anna's mum can be a bit... fragile, you know. And Davy can go off the deep end where Anna's concerned – those two never really got on. Maybe she thought it best just to turn up and catch Kate unawares.'

'I'd have thought it would make more sense for Anna to warn her mum she was coming so that she could arrange to avoid bumping into her father.'

Joe spread his hands wide. 'I can't really say what Anna was thinking.'

It was Becca who asked the next question. 'Connor told us he was very upset when Anna split up with him. Do you know what led to the break-up?'

Joe stared at the decking and shook his head sadly. 'I wish I did. It hit Connor hard and I was sorry to see her go. She was a nice lass.'

'But you kept in touch with her.'

Joe didn't try to deny it. 'Anna didn't get on with her father. I looked out for her, that was all. I wanted to make sure she was all right in London.'

'You spoke to her several times by phone during the year. What did you talk about?'

'Like I said, I just wanted to check she was doing okay. I was reassured when she got a job and moved into a flat with a friend.'

'Did you tell Connor that you were still in touch with her?'

Joe seemed unhappy to be subjected to such intense questioning. The jolly landlord façade was gone, and in its place Raven detected – what? Fear? 'Anna asked me not to. She didn't want to upset him.'

'And your wife? Did you tell her that you were in regular contact with Anna?'

Joe looked embarrassed. 'Sarah was never a big fan of Anna.'

'So in fact,' Becca concluded, 'you carried on a secret relationship with a girl half your age for a whole year? A girl who died in suspicious circumstances when she returned to Robin Hood's Bay? And you didn't think this was worth mentioning to us when we spoke to you on Sunday?'

Joe blanched and turned away. 'You didn't ask me anything. You just asked to speak to Connor. I would have told you if you'd asked.'

Raven took over the questioning again. 'Joe, what would you say if I told you that as far as we know, you were the last person in the village to see Anna alive on Saturday night?'

The bombshell landed hard, just as Raven had intended. Joe's mouth fell open. 'No, that can't be right... I... I was just...'

But there was no explanation forthcoming for what Joe was doing.

'A witness saw you together at eleven pm outside the pub,' said Raven. 'According to the witness, you and Anna were embracing.'

Joe shook his head and leaned forward earnestly. 'You've got the wrong end of the stick. There was nothing inappropriate going on between me and Anna. I was just giving her a hug to say goodbye.' He stopped, perhaps realising that his explanation fell short. 'Connor means the world to me, and I would have loved to have a daughter like Anna. When the two of them became a couple, I was more pleased than I can say. I imagined them getting married and growing up here, raising a family together. When Anna left, it hit me almost as hard as it hit Connor. I was happy when she returned for the day, but when I saw her leaving the pub I got the impression that she never intended coming back. That's why I gave her a hug. I just wanted to wish her well.' He sighed. 'That lass had a hard life. Kate and Davy are as poor as church mice and Davy, well, he wasn't cut out to be a father. I can understand why Anna wanted to get away from here, but I don't think she found the streets of London paved with gold either. I wish I could have done more for her somehow.'

Raven nodded slowly. It was a plausible explanation, not easy to disprove on the basis of the facts. Joe did genuinely come across as a good guy wanting to help.

The door to the lounge bar opened and Sarah peered out, casting her sullen gaze at Raven and Becca. 'Have you finished with my husband yet? Only it's getting busy inside and I could do with a hand behind the bar.'

'I think we're all finished, love.' Joe stood up. 'Was there anything else?'

'Not for now,' said Raven.

Joe followed his wife back inside and Raven turned to Becca. 'Why do I get the distinct impression that Sarah doesn't like us talking to her husband or her son?'

Becca stroked her chin, a faraway look in her eyes. 'I'm starting to get the impression Sarah doesn't like us being here at all.'

*

The quickest way from Robin Hood's Bay to Boggle Hole was on foot. It was only a half mile walk, which was nothing to Jess. The tide was in, covering the sandy beach, so she headed towards the path over the cliff, the same route Anna must have taken when she left the Bay sometime after eleven on Saturday night.

A flight of wooden steps led up from the side of the old coastguard station, which was now a museum. The climb was steep, but Jess soon got into her stride, breathing in the bracing sea air, feeling more alive with every step. This was part of the Cleveland Way, a trail that stretched along the coast from Filey to Saltburn-by-the-Sea before turning inland and crossing the moors, ending in the market town of Helmsley. Over a hundred miles in total, and parts of it challenging, especially in poor weather. But if you were reasonably fit it was well worth the effort, rewarding the walker with stunning and constantly changing vistas across both sea and moor.

Today, however, Jess's eyes were fixed not on the distant views but on the ground before her feet as she kept her eyes peeled for any evidence she might find. The CSI team had searched the path thoroughly close to where Anna had suffered her injuries, but had they examined the entire route? Jess wasn't so sure.

She reached the top of the steps and continued across level ground, following the line of a fence. The path was narrow, with only a few feet or so to the edge of the cliff. Tufts of long grass billowed in the breeze and waves crashed onto the shore below. She reached a patch where a thorny hedge clung to the cliff edge and spotted a cigarette butt lying on the ground. It couldn't have been there for longer than a few days because there had been heavy rain the previous week, which would have washed it into the mud. Slipping a pair of gloves over her hands she stooped down and picked it up, dropping it into an evidence bag.

A few minutes later she descended the steps that led down to Boggle Hole. She paused at the foot of the stairs to examine the spot where Anna had most likely met her death before her body was moved by Rory Gamble to the cave. The steps here were just as steep as the ones she had climbed at the start of the trail and were slick with mud. If anything, they were even more hazardous as they weren't even proper steps, just wooden retaining planks fixed into the bare earth. Thick woodland grew up on both sides of the valley and at night it must get very dark. Was the explanation for Anna's death simple after all – a young woman, possibly the worse for wear after drinking too much, slipping and tumbling down the slope, perhaps hitting her head on a stone? They would have to wait for the post-mortem to find out.

A woman matching the description of Anna's friend was sitting at one of the picnic tables outside the youth hostel. She was huddled over her phone, vaping and sipping from a bottle of Coke in an impressive display of multi-tasking.

'Lexi Greene?'

She made no response but kept flicking one finger lazily across the screen.

Jess moved closer and the girl looked up. She removed a pair of headphones and gave Jess a dirty glare. 'Looking for summink?'

'If you're Lexi, I was looking for you.' Jess fixed a friendly smile to her face, hoping to win the girl's trust. 'I'm Jess Barraclough, Scarborough CID. Okay if I talk to you for a bit?' She slid onto the opposite bench and swung her legs under the table.

'Wotever.' Lexi sucked on her vape then exhaled in a long smooth action. 'That miserable geezer in the coat said I 'ad to stay 'ere even though I told 'im I gotta get back to work.'

'DCI Raven?' Jess smiled to herself at Lexi's characterisation of her boss.

Lexi shivered, clearly feeling the bite of the wind through the thin material of her jacket. 'It's freezing cold and boring as fack.'

'I like it here,' said Jess. 'There are some great places to explore.' She stretched out an arm to take in the stunning woodland and coastal scenery, the small wooden bridge that led across the nearby beck. 'You just need some warmer clothes.'

'Well, I ain't got none,' said Lexi sullenly. 'I fought I was only coming 'ere for one night. 'Ave you caught 'im yet? 'Cause I've really gotta get back to London.'

'Why do you say "him"?' asked Jess.

Lexi gave an exaggerated roll of her eyes as if Jess was an idiot. ''Cause 'e's an 'im, ain't he? Rory. The kitchen boy wot killed Anna.'

'We're not treating Rory as a suspect,' said Jess. 'And we haven't yet established whether Anna's death was foul play or an accident.'

'Well, 'ow long are you gonna take to do that?'

Jess let the question pass and instead asked, 'How close were you and Anna?'

'We were mates. We met at work and found a flat to share together. Nuffink fancy, like, but it was okay. I'd known 'er 'bout a year, ever since she came down sarf.'

'I'm sure she appreciated having you as a mate, especially since you're from London.' Jess couldn't imagine arriving in the capital city, not knowing anyone and having no job and nowhere to stay. 'Did Anna ever talk about why she left Robin Hood's Bay in the first place?'

'Nah, but probably 'cause it's so fackin' boring.' Lexi exhaled a plume of smoke and took another swig of Coke.

'Did she ever talk to you about a man called Joe?'

'Who?' Lexi looked blank. 'She never mentioned anyone from round 'ere.'

'What about her family?'

'Only 'er mum and dad. They didn't get on. Her dad beat 'er, I reckon.'

'Did Anna say that?'

'Nah. She never said nuffink.'

'So why did she come back?'

Lexi fixed Jess with a hard stare. 'Good question. I wouldn't 'ave come back if it was me. Who'd want to live 'ere? It's so fackin'–'

'Yes, you've already said it's boring,' interrupted Jess. She felt like telling Lexi that London was dirty and overcrowded but held her tongue. 'But Anna must have given you a reason for coming.'

Lexi tugged at a piece of loose skin on her finger. 'She didn't say exactly, but I reckon she was 'ere on a mission.'

Jess blinked in surprise. 'A mission? What do you mean?'

'Dunno, like I said. But she came 'ere to see someone

or get summink, I reckon.'

'Do you have any idea what?'

'Nah.'

'So why did Anna ask you to come with her?'

Lexi took a last glug of Coke and lobbed the empty bottle in the direction of the nearest bin. It fell short. 'She just wanted a mate to come wiv 'er. But as soon as we got 'ere she dumped me and went off on 'er own.'

Jess wondered if she was wasting her time with Lexi. The girl knew next to nothing about Anna, her so-called mate. Or if she did, she wasn't going to share it with the police. 'So how did you spend your time on Saturday? What did you do all day?'

'Nuffink. There's nuffink to do 'ere. This place is so fackin'–'

'–You must have done something,' said Jess impatiently.

Lexi sighed as if this was all a waste of her valuable time. 'I already told the other geezer, we walked to Robin Hood's Bay then Anna went off on 'er own to see 'er mum. I saw 'er go over to the pub a bit later, then she went down to the beach. This fit-looking guy followed 'er down. Then she went into a shop that sold all kinds of crap. I went in myself to 'ave a look round, but I didn't buy anyfink 'cause it was all just tat. Anyway, the girl who worked there was on the phone the whole time. I fink she must 'ave been talking to the guy on the beach 'cause she was like, *You said she wasn't coming back*, and, *Don't let me see you with that bitch again*. She was going fackin' mental.'

So now the truth was coming out. Lexi had secretly followed Anna around all day, watching her every movement. Jess suppressed a shudder of excitement. Had Lexi witnessed something that would unlock the mystery of how Anna had met her death?

'Where did Anna go after she left the shop?'

'Dunno.'

'What do you mean, you don't know?'

Lexi shrugged. 'I dunno where she went after she left

the shop. I never saw 'er again. I wandered around a bit on my own. But you know wot? There was really nuffink to fackin' do.'

Jess stared at Lexi in disappointment. After all that coaxing, she had seen nothing that the police didn't already know about. 'So what did you do?'

Lexi picked at her loose skin again. 'Came back 'ere.'

'You took the clifftop path?'

'Nah. Walked along the beach, innit? Got back 'bout ten o'clock. Tell you wot, it gets dark as fack 'round 'ere at night.'

At that, Jess smiled. 'It certainly does.'

It seemed like the interview had come to a natural end. Jess couldn't think of anything else to ask Lexi, so she let her get back to her phone and her vaping and set off back to Robin Hood's Bay.

Lexi was right about one thing – there was nothing to do around here if all you did was sit and stare at your phone all day.

CHAPTER 14

A short report, printed on crisp A4 sheets, was sitting at the top of Raven's in-tray when he and Becca returned to Scarborough. The post-mortem results, fresh from the examination that had taken place that very morning.

'That was quick work,' said Raven grudgingly. He had no liking for Dr Felicity Wainwright, the senior pathologist at Scarborough Hospital. He had done his best to be friendly towards her, but she'd repelled his efforts from their very first meeting. He had concluded she was a sociopath and had given up trying to get on with her, and instead now did his best to keep out of her way.

'What does it say?' asked Becca.

Raven skimmed the report, stopping to read various details that caught his attention. 'The cause of death was blunt force trauma to the skull. Other injuries were consistent with a fall. Anna's blood showed a concentration of 20 milligrams of alcohol per 100 millilitres.'

'So she'd had a drink, but she was well below the legal limit for driving. What's Dr Wainwright's conclusion?'

'The worst kind,' said Raven. 'Inconclusive. *Based on the available evidence, it is not possible to determine whether death was accidental or the result of foul play.*'

'What was the time of death?'

Raven flipped to the relevant page in the report. 'Midnight, or one hour either side.'

'Well, that gives us something,' said Becca.

'Does it?' Raven tossed the report onto his desk, sank into his chair and rubbed his temple. What had he been hoping for? Proof that Anna Capstick had been murdered? Of course he didn't want that, but not knowing was even worse. The coroner would likely return an open verdict, leaving no one satisfied and the family forever haunted by uncertainty.

An image of the dead girl as he had seen her on the beach was lodged in his mind. Blonde hair, skin pale in the early morning light, her slim arms at her side. At nineteen, she was only a couple of years younger than Hannah. He didn't know how he would cope if something like this happened to his daughter.

At the very least, he would need to know the truth.

The door to the office opened and Gillian appeared in the doorway. She brandished a report in her hand, one that looked very similar to Raven's copy. 'Seen the PM report, Tom?'

Raven nodded. 'Just read it, ma'am.'

'Blunt trauma to the head, and injuries consistent with a fall. Maybe not what you were hoping for, Tom, but often the simplest explanation is the right one. No need to go looking for complications. It's time to wrap this up.'

'I don't think so, ma'am. Not just yet.'

Gillian's lips thinned in displeasure. 'You've found something, then?'

'Not exactly.' He knew he was sticking his neck out. Not just sticking it out, but placing it on the headsman's block, poised for the axe to fall. 'I'm just not ready to call it yet.'

Gillian narrowed her eyes. 'Really? What makes you say

that?'

'There are still too many unanswered questions.'

'I was hoping you'd have wrapped those up by now.'

She stared at him and he stared back. Gillian could be a bully, he realised for the first time. He wondered why it had taken him so long to work that out. She had pushed her weight around in the past, and he'd mostly stood up to her. His tactic had worked, and he didn't intend to back down now, not when the truth was out there.

'I agree,' said Becca, and Raven felt the warm glow of gratification. 'Something's not right.'

Gillian shifted her weight and turned to look at Becca. 'Seems like I'm outnumbered. Well, if you both think there's more to this than meets the eye, I'll give you another day to come up with something concrete.' She turned on her heel and left the room.

Raven let out a sigh. 'I feel like I've been twelve rounds in the ring with her.'

'Gillian can be a bit... forceful.'

'I think you mean brutal.'

'I would never say that.'

'Not to her face.'

They looked at each other and burst out laughing. It cleared the air, and Raven felt more in control. He had been granted one more day. It was up to him to make it count.

'You got any plans for this evening?' he asked Becca.

'No, why?'

'I thought we might try to find out who was driving the car in 1991.' It had been preying on his mind all day. The revelation that the car was registered to the police wasn't the end of his inquiry, it was merely the beginning.

'Sure,' said Becca. 'Have you got any ideas for how to proceed?'

'One or two.'

★

The police archives were kept in dusty boxes in the basement. The temperature dropped a couple of degrees as Raven descended the stairs and his nose wrinkled as it detected the smell of dust, mildew and age. He had the curious sensation of entering a church, although the documents here were of a very different kind to the Bibles and hymn books you'd find in a place of worship.

The basement wasn't a place Raven had spent much time in, but Becca seemed to know her way around. Her fingers reached for a switch and soon fluorescent lights flickered on, bathing the room in a cold uniform light. Floor-to-ceiling metal racks packed with dusty boxes and files ran the length of the basement. How far back in time the archive stretched, Raven had no idea.

'What are we looking for?' Becca asked.

'There should be logbooks. Whenever a police vehicle is taken out, it has to be recorded. The logbooks must be here somewhere. They should tell us who was driving the car on the night of the hit-and-run.'

It took them a while to track down the relevant section amid the labyrinth of shelves, but eventually they found it. The books were filed in chronological order, with file dividers separating them by date. Raven thumbed through them, struggling to read the faded ink labels. 'Here we are: October to December 1990, January to March 1991... shit!'

'What is it?' asked Becca.

'There's a gap. April to June 1991 is missing.' He searched further along the row in case it had been misfiled, but it was simply gone.

Becca stepped closer, standing beside him in the narrow gap between the stacks. 'Someone must have taken it.'

'The bastards covered their tracks.' The disappointment hit Raven harder than he'd expected, although he really should have seen this coming. The hit-and-run incident had been covered up at the highest level. Of course the relevant document would have been removed. Whoever was responsible wouldn't have left such an obvious paper trail behind.

Becca touched his arm, brushing him briefly with her hand. 'We'll find a way. Hang in there.'

★

There was just enough time before it got properly dark for a walk along the North Sands with Quincey. It was on days like this, when nothing seemed to go right, that Raven most appreciated the simple pleasure of throwing a ball for his dog and watching the animal bound after it with undiminished enthusiasm. Hannah readily agreed to join them.

'So how was your first day at the restaurant?' Raven asked her as they strolled along the beach together.

'The bistro,' corrected Hannah. 'It was great, actually. There's a lot to learn and it kept me on my toes, but Ellie's dad's really nice.'

'Keith Earnshaw. He's a good bloke.'

Hannah shot him a look of surprise. 'You know Keith?'

'I met him once. On a case.'

'Really?' Hannah turned to face him, her face lighting up at this unexpected piece of news. 'What happened?'

'Oh, it was... a bit complicated. It involved Keith's brother Greg and his family. Becca was going out with Sam, Greg's son. It was a tragedy, really. You'd best speak to Ellie if you want to find out more.'

'I will,' said Hannah. 'What happened to Sam? Ellie's never mentioned him.'

'He left the country. Went to Australia.'

'Didn't Becca want to go with him?'

'I believe he asked her,' said Raven. 'But she chose to stay here.'

'With you?' Hannah punched him playfully on the arm.

Quincey returned with the ball and dropped it at Raven's feet. He picked it up and threw it as far as he could. Quincey disappeared into the growing dusk.

'I'm sure I had nothing to do with Becca's decision to stay. I don't think she wanted to leave her family.' But Raven was glad she hadn't gone to Australia with Sam, whatever her reason for staying in Scarborough.

'Talking of families,' said Hannah, 'I've been thinking a lot about our family.'

'What, you, me and Lisa?' Raven's ex-wife, Hannah's mum, still lived in London. She was practically allergic to the north of England. It was unlikely she would ever pay them a visit.

'No,' said Hannah. 'I mean your parents, my grandparents. I never met them. But now that I'm living in their house, I can't help wondering what they were like.'

Raven looked ahead, watching Quincey's dark shape flitting across the sand, the ball once more locked between his jaws. Behind him, on the headland, the outline of the castle stood proud against the sky.

He wondered what he should tell Hannah about the past – about his own past. It was only natural she should be curious. Lisa's parents had been a big part of her life growing up, showering their granddaughter with gifts and quietly siding with their daughter in their disapproval of Raven's unsociable working hours. Raven always felt they had never really liked him. But Hannah had adored them, won over by pretty dresses, fancy homemade birthday cakes, and days out at London Zoo.

'They were very different to your other grandparents – your mum's parents. They seemed much older, like they were from another age. My mum died when I was only sixteen.'

'But your dad died just last year,' pointed out Hannah. 'That's why you moved back to Scarborough.'

'Yes, but he was dead to me for a long time before that.' Raven sighed, knowing that the time had come for him to give a proper account to Hannah. He had put it off for too long, but she deserved to know the truth at last. 'Mum was a very kind person. We didn't have much money, but she showed her love in little things, like treating me to an ice-cream on the beach, or helping me build sandcastles.'

'What was her name?'

'Jean.'

'Was she from Scarborough originally?'

'Yes, she lived here all her life. She did all the cooking and cleaning and laundry and supplemented the family income by working as a chambermaid in the Grand Hotel. She was a hard worker.' In truth, there were times when Jean's meagre income had been the only money they had, when the fishing dried up or when Alan Raven had been too drunk to go out on a boat. 'Sometimes she used to take me to the hotel and sneak me in by the back door so that I could have a nose around. It really was grand in those days, like a palace out of a fairytale.'

'And she was killed in a hit-and-run?' Hannah linked her arm through his.

'Yes,' said Raven. It had been simply the worst day of his life. His world had come crashing down, his childhood suddenly over. 'They never caught the person responsible.'

'What about your dad?'

Raven inhaled sharply. He had done his best to shield Hannah from this, but who was he really shielding? His grown-up daughter or himself? There was nothing to be gained from continuing to bury the truth inside himself.

'He was a fisherman,' said Raven. 'But there wasn't much work. Times were tough for the fishing industry, although that doesn't excuse my father.'

Hannah was listening quietly. 'Excuse what, Dad?'

'The way he treated my mum.' Raven's fists had clenched as he said the words, and he took a moment to consciously relax them again. He could see this through, and he needed to. What had he told Becca just the previous day? *Fear is the true enemy. And the only way to defeat it is to face it.*

He took a deep breath and tried again. 'I guess it was the anger that came first. Anger at the way the fishing industry had tailed off. My dad came from a long line of fishermen, including his own father before him. I suppose he'd grown up expecting a job for life. But things change and my father couldn't or wouldn't move with the times.'

Quincey returned and Hannah scooped up the ball, tossing it ahead of them again. The dog's legs kicked up sand as he sped away after it.

'Some of the anger was no doubt directed at himself,' continued Raven. 'He'd been taught it was a man's role to put bread on the table. But often it was my mum who did that. He ought to have appreciated her help, but he turned in on himself. And then came the drinking.'

Raven breathed out, doing his best to stay calm. He had never spoken to a soul about these things, but had kept them bottled up inside. His friends at school, the army psychiatrists, Lisa – not once had he taken the opportunity to unburden himself.

'My father went drinking every night, down at one of the pubs along the foreshore. And every night he came back drunk. I don't know how old I was when I first realised that. Pretty young. Sometimes he would just stagger up the stairs and crash onto the bed. Those were good nights. Other times...'

'He was violent?'

Raven nodded, feeling sick. 'He hit my mum. Never so badly that anyone took notice. In those days – this might be hard for you to understand – people turned a blind eye to that kind of thing. As a child, it was just a fact of life for me. I knew it was wrong, but I was a child. What could I do?'

Hannah slipped her hand into his, her eyes shining with tears in the failing light. 'Nothing, Dad. There was nothing you could have done.'

Quincey returned with the ball and this time Raven picked it up and put it away in his pocket. 'Come on, it's getting dark. We should head back.'

*

Davy Capstick bided his time, waiting until there was a

good crowd in the pub and everyone was distracted by the football on the large screen. Both Joe and Sarah were behind the bar and Connor was collecting empties and taking them to the kitchen to wash. Just as the striker scored and a loud cheer went up, Davy slipped away from the other drinkers and stepped through the door marked *Private*.

He climbed the stairs to the Hepworth family's quarters, thinking about what his father-in-law had told him earlier that evening. Sid had been in touch with the boss, who had told them to lie low until the investigation into Anna's death was sorted.

Well, even Davy had worked that one out. They couldn't carry on their business with Scarborough CID crawling all over the place. The boss seemed to think that Anna's case would be wound up pretty quickly and then they could all get back to work as if nothing had ever happened.

What the boss didn't know – and hopefully would never need to know – was that they'd screwed up. Big time. Sid's words to Davy had been crystal clear: 'For fuck's sake, find it.' Davy was now trying to do just that.

He found Connor's room easily enough at the top of the building. There was no mistaking it. Connor still lived like a teenager – games console, unmade bed, dirty clothes piled high in the corner of the room. Mind you, Anna had been like a teenage girl in some ways even though in others she was all grown up. Before she'd left town, her room had held remnants of childhood – photos of boy bands pinned to the wall, fairy lights strung along the shelves, a few toy animals lingering on her desk – paired with more recent additions – shoes with towering heels, cosy throws and cushions on the bed, and a bewildering array of makeup and skincare products. All that crap was gone now, cleared out after Anna disappeared to London. 'She's never coming back!' he'd yelled at Kate as he chucked it all away. But he'd been wrong about that. Anna had come back after all, and look what a mess she'd made.

Focus, Davy. Don't lose your grip now.

He flung open the doors of an old pine wardrobe and began rummaging, pulling out smelly trainers from the top shelf, searching through piles of jeans, reaching inside each pocket. At first, he was careful to conceal evidence of his search, but when he didn't find what he was looking for, he threw caution to the wind, pulling stuff from hangers, giving everything a good hard shake. Nothing.

He turned his attention to a chest of drawers, pulling out each drawer and dumping its contents onto the floor, searching through mounds of underwear, socks, and T-shirts. He reached under the bed, running his hand along the wooden slats in case anything was taped to them.

Still nothing.

After fifteen minutes of fruitless searching, he had to admit that what he was looking for wasn't here. But where the fuck was it?

CHAPTER 15

Becca dumped Liam's dirty plates from the night before into the sink – he could load them into the dishwasher himself – before dropping two slices of bread into the toaster and making herself a mug of strong Yorkshire tea with a splash of milk. When the toast popped up, she spread the slices with marmalade and sat down at the breakfast bar to scroll through a property website on her phone.

She hadn't said anything to Ellie yet, but Becca was thinking of moving out of the flat. Had been for a while now, ever since her brother moved in. She hadn't left the family home just to have Liam follow her here. Ellie seemed blind to his faults, believing his decision to move in with her proved that he was committed to the relationship. But Becca knew her brother better. Liam was simply taking advantage of Ellie's generous nature. He never did his fair share of the housework. It was just like when he used to take his dirty laundry round to the guest house for his mum to wash. Now Ellie did his laundry for him. *Unbelievable*. And he didn't even seem grateful. He'd been so moody lately, Becca didn't know how Ellie put up with him.

She narrowed her search to one-bedroom apartments and scrolled through the results while munching her toast. Of course she wasn't expecting to find anything as flashy as Ellie's North Bay apartment. Luxury kitchen and bathrooms; huge windows looking out across the beach. That was well out of her budget. But somewhere with a sea view would be nice.

A little place on Castle Terrace caught her attention. The row of terraced houses was high up on the headland overlooking the South Bay, not so far from her mum and dad's guest house. One of the houses had been converted into apartments and the tiny top floor flat offered sloping ceilings and a view over the rooftops to the sea. It looked charming. Her finger lingered over the *Contact* button, but then she realised that Castle Terrace was directly above Raven's house in Quay Street. Did she want to live so close to her boss? But the flat was ideal and just within budget. She pressed *Save* instead, adding it to her favourites.

The door burst open and a bleary-eyed Liam blundered into the kitchen. Couldn't he just open doors quietly like normal people? He always had to burst in. Becca ignored him, continuing to work through the search results and munch her toast.

Ellie had already gone into work to meet a client interested in stocking the beer that Ellie's company brewed. It was time Becca headed off to the station too. She finished her tea and took her plate and mug over to the dishwasher, making a show of loading them inside, in the slim hope that Liam might learn by example.

He was unwashed and unshaven. He leaned against the kitchen counter, chewing his lip. 'Becca?'

'What?' He seemed hesitant, so she rearranged the badly stacked dishes so that she could fit her plate in.

'If there was someone who... I mean if you found yourself in a situation... not that you ever would, obviously.'

She wondered if he was still drunk from the night

before. That was another thing: his alcohol consumption had gone through the roof recently. She slid the racks back into the machine and rummaged in the cupboard under the sink for a dishwasher tablet. There was only one left. 'What situation?'

'What I'm trying to say is...'

She inserted the tablet into the machine, selected eco wash and closed the door to make the dishwasher start.

'If you got involved with someone who...'

Whatever he was trying to tell her, she really didn't have time for it now. She straightened up and turned to face him. 'I really need to get into work, so just tell me what your problem is.'

He shook his head. 'It's nothing, don't worry about it.'

She looked into his eyes, but he turned away, putting his back to her.

'Are you sure?'

'Yeah, I was just... no, it's nothing.'

'Right, okay then. I'm off.' She picked up her phone. 'You'll have to do those dishes by hand.' She pointed to the pile in the sink and headed out of the door.

★

Tuesday morning. Day three of the investigation and Raven still didn't know exactly what he was investigating.

An unexplained death. In Gillian's view, a death that would forever go unexplained. But Raven couldn't accept that. He had to give it his best shot, if not for Davy Capstick, then at least for Kate. And if there was any kind of domestic abuse going on behind closed doors at the Capsticks' house, he was determined to bring that to light too. At the morning briefing, he invited Tony to update everyone on what he'd found out the previous day.

'After I spoke to you about Anna's phone records, sir, I got onto her manager at the coffee shop where she worked. He told me something interesting. Anna was sacked ten days ago.'

'Did he say why?' asked Raven.

'Some stock had gone missing. He couldn't prove it was Anna who'd taken it, but he strongly suspected her. And it wasn't the first time she'd come under suspicion. He let her go on the grounds that they weren't so busy now the summer rush was over.'

Raven thought about this. 'If she'd just lost her job then she must have been short of money. Was that what precipitated her return to Robin Hood's Bay?'

'Possibly,' said Becca. 'Connor bought her lunch because she was skint. But she made it clear she wasn't planning to stay. And Kate and Davy haven't got much money anyway.'

Raven acknowledged the truth of that. 'Anything else, Tony?'

'So next I checked Anna's bank account. She was overdrawn to her limit. She really didn't have a penny left. I think she must have spent the last of her money on the coach ticket travelling up here.'

'That smacks of desperation,' said Raven, 'so we can't rule out a financial motive for coming back home. What about Kate and Davy? Did you find anything on them?'

Tony shook his head. 'I know that you were expecting to find something, sir, but Davy Capstick has never been involved with the police and Kate has never reported him for domestic violence.'

'That's often the way,' said Becca. 'Doesn't mean it isn't happening though.'

Raven nodded his agreement. Sadly, that was very much his own experience. But without some tangible evidence, there was little the police could do. He turned to Jess. 'How did you get on with Lexi Greene?'

'I walked over to Boggle Hole, following the route along the Cleveland Way that Anna must have taken the night she died. I found a cigarette butt on the path so I bagged it and sent it off to the lab, just in case it's relevant.'

'Okay,' said Raven, sounding a note of caution. 'I don't think that Gillian is going to authorise the cost of a DNA test, but maybe the forensics team can tell us something.'

Jess nodded her understanding. 'So I found Lexi at the youth hostel and had a chat with her. She's bored out of her skull hanging around Boggle Hole, desperate to get back to London. But she did reveal something interesting.'

'In that case you did better than me,' said Raven, recalling the way the foul-mouthed young woman had virtually refused to speak to him at all. 'What did she tell you?'

'Well, after she and Anna split up, Lexi seems to have spent most of Saturday hanging around Robin Hood's Bay, watching Anna from a distance. She saw Anna meet Connor on the beach and then go into the craft shop. Eventually she got fed up and went back to the youth hostel at ten o'clock, so she can't help us with Anna's movements after she left the pub at eleven.' Jess paused for breath. 'But the most interesting thing was that Lexi went into the craft shop for a nose around after Anna left. While she was there she overheard a phone conversation between Fern and Connor. Fern was angry that Anna had shown her face in Robin Hood's Bay again. Lexi got the impression that Fern was really jealous.'

'You already gathered that from speaking to Fern, didn't you?' said Raven.

'Yes,' said Jess, 'but'– she consulted her notes – 'according to Lexi, Fern's exact words to Connor were, "You said she wasn't coming back," and, "Don't let me see you with that bitch again."'

Raven leaned on his desk. 'Some pretty intense sentiments. So now we've got a disgruntled ex-boyfriend *and* a jealous girlfriend to contend with. We'll follow up this phone conversation with Connor. See what he has to say for himself.'

He straightened up again and approached the whiteboard. At the centre was a photograph of Anna taken from Lexi's phone. Youthful, bright, seemingly without a care in the world, although a darker picture was now emerging of a deeply troubled young woman. Pinned in a circle around her were the persons of interest in the case: Anna's parents, Kate and Davy Capstick and her grandfather, Sid Sutcliffe. Her ex-boyfriend, Connor Hepworth and his parents, Joe and Sarah. Rory Gamble, the kitchen lad who had moved the body. And Fern Adams, Connor's new girlfriend. Not to mention Lexi Greene, Anna's friend from London. Between them they had woven a web of intrigue, but none remained more mysterious than the person at the heart of it all – Anna herself.

He summarised the results from the post-mortem for the benefit of Jess and Tony. 'The pathologist concluded that Anna died of head injuries, possibly as a result of a fall, and consistent with accidental death. She noted that Anna had consumed a modest amount of alcohol, but she certainly wasn't drunk. The time of death was midnight, plus or minus one hour. So that tells us little we didn't already know.' He cast a steady gaze at his team, signalling the importance of what he was about to say. 'At present, Anna's death is likely to be recorded as accidental. If there are any grounds for suspecting murder, then we need to find them as soon as possible. Detective Superintendent Ellis has given me one more day before writing my final report for the coroner.'

CHAPTER 16

Raven knew that Becca shared his feelings of frustration, both with the ongoing inquiry into Anna Capstick's death and the off-the-books investigation into his own mother's death. But as they headed back to Robin Hood's Bay in the M6 that morning, he sensed that something else might be distracting her. She scrolled through her phone, keeping the screen to herself, and stared out of the side window. He contemplated asking her if everything was all right, but decided Becca's personal life was none of his business.

'You going to drive all the way into town again?' she asked as they entered the village.

'Well, I'm not walking up and down that hill. My leg won't thank me if I try.'

'Sorry, I didn't think.'

'No worries.'

It was easy for people to forget about his injury, he supposed, even someone like Becca who was used to working with him every day. It wasn't like he advertised his difficulties, he always did his best to disguise them. And for the most part they were easy to hide.

He manoeuvred the car down the steep hill into the village and parked once again by the dry-docked boats near the slipway. Today, there was no sign of Davy or Sid. No wonder they struggled to make ends meet if their work was so sporadic.

It was another breezy day, cool yet dry and bright. After climbing out of the car, Raven took a moment to enjoy the warmth of the sun on his face.

'Catching the rays?' enquired Becca.

He returned her smile with a grin of his own. 'You know me. Normally I dodge them, in case they turn me into dust. But there aren't so many around at this time of year.'

The Waterside wasn't yet open for business, but the front door was unlocked and they found Connor in the lounge bar, polishing the tables.

Raven scanned the room quickly for signs of the boy's parents, but thankfully they were nowhere to be seen. 'Got a moment?' he asked Connor.

The lad ceased his work with a wary look. 'Er, yeah, what's this about?'

'Let's sit down by the window, shall we?'

Raven chose a seat at a table looking out across the bay and waited for Connor to join him. The sea was choppy today and maybe that explained why Davy and Sid's boat was out of action. But the view across the bay was clear, the surface of the water a pale blue instead of the previous day's grey. The sea was different every time you looked at it, and Raven knew he would never grow tired of it, however long he lived.

The young lad seemed a bit out of sorts. 'Is there news about Anna?'

Raven studied his face, seeking to read the thoughts and emotions that simmered beneath the skin. But years as a detective had taught him that people rarely gave away their secrets so easily. 'A witness has reported overhearing a conversation between you and Fern Adams. It seems Fern was angry that Anna had come back to Robin Hood's

Bay.'

'Oh yeah,' said Connor. 'But that was nothing. Fern just got a bit upset, that's all. I told her everything was over between me and Anna. That was a year ago. Anna coming back didn't change anything between me and Fern.'

'Did she believe you?'

'Yeah, I think so.'

'And was it true, that everything was over between you and Anna?'

Connor looked less sure of himself. 'Of course.'

'We've also heard that Anna returned here around eleven o'clock on Saturday night. You told us previously that you didn't see her after meeting her on the beach that afternoon. Did you see her again later?'

Connor flushed bright red and Raven knew he'd been caught out. 'Oh God, I should have told you about that.'

'Told us what, Connor?'

'I did see her,' he admitted. 'But only briefly. It was literally just for one minute.'

'All right,' said Raven. 'Tell us what happened. And don't leave anything out this time.'

Connor lowered his voice, glancing over his shoulder even though there was no one else in the room. 'Anna came to the pub just around closing time. She said she hadn't planned to, it was just a spur of the moment thing. She was going to leave the Bay that night, but she couldn't go without saying goodbye to me. The way she was talking it sounded like she was never coming back, so I asked her and she said no, she would never see me again. I kept asking her why not, but she wouldn't tell me.'

'And how did you respond to that?' Raven knew there was more to the story than this.

'I got cross with her. Told her she'd already upset me and that she should have just stayed away and not come back at all.' His shoulders sagged. 'I could tell that my words had hurt her and I regretted them instantly. But how was I supposed to behave? She never told me why she left me in the first place, and now it felt like she'd just come back to rub salt in the wound. I told her to go, but even then she couldn't just leave. She said she needed my forgiveness.'

'Your forgiveness?' probed Raven. 'For what?'

'She didn't say. I thought she was just winding me up.' Connor's shoulders began to tremble as he sobbed.

Raven studied the lad thoughtfully. He felt sympathy for sure, but was the story true or just an elaborate act? 'Connor, did you hit her? Did you hit Anna?'

'No!' The cry was heartfelt and Connor looked at Raven, an appeal in his eye to be believed. 'I could never do anything to harm Anna! You have to believe me!'

The boy looked genuinely shaken and Raven decided not to push it further. 'All right, Connor, but is there anything else you need to tell us?'

The lad opened his mouth to speak, but then the door to the kitchen opened. Sarah appeared behind the bar and came over when she saw Raven and Becca.

'I didn't know you were here,' she said accusingly. She glanced at Connor, immediately registering his red eyes. 'What on earth have you been saying to my son?'

Raven rose to meet her. 'We've just been asking a few questions, that's all, Mrs Hepworth.'

Sarah studied Raven suspiciously and then turned to Connor. 'Have you told them yet?'

Connor shook his head.

'Told us what?' asked Raven.

'About last night.'

Raven looked at her in confusion. 'Last night? What happened last night?'

'Someone broke into Connor's room, that's what happened.' Sarah was most indignant, seeming to hold Raven responsible for the incident. 'They went through all his stuff, turned the place upside down. It was a right mess, I can tell you.'

'How did they get in?' asked Raven.

Sarah shrugged. 'Easily enough, I suppose. They must have sneaked in while the pub was busy. We don't keep the door to our private quarters locked. Normally you can trust people around here.' She glared at Raven as if he had personally brought shady characters to the village.

'Have you reported it to the police?' asked Becca. 'Was anything taken?'

'Sergeant Fields in Whitby came over last night and had a look. He said he'd send someone round to take prints, but it didn't sound like there was much more he could do,' said Sarah resentfully.

'In any case,' added Connor quickly, 'nothing was taken. I had a good look through all my stuff. There's nothing missing.'

'Well,' said Raven, 'I doubt that someone broke into your room just so they could leave a mess. They must have been looking for something. Do you have any idea what that might have been?'

'No,' said Connor.

'Something connected with Anna?'

'Her mobile phone for example?' suggested Becca.

'I don't know,' said Connor. 'I don't have her phone. Why would I have her phone?'

'Anyway,' said Sarah. 'We know who did it.'

'You do?' said Raven.

'It'll be one of them from over there.' She pointed to Kate's house. 'Sid or Davy. Davy probably, because Sid's getting a bit old for that sort of thing now.'

Raven studied her, wondering if this was just sour grapes – some long-held smalltown resentment playing out – or if there was reason for Sarah's suspicions. 'Why would Davy do that?'

'Because that family is no good and never has been! Let me tell you something, Chief Inspector. Sid killed Joe's dad. No, don't interrupt, let me finish,' she said as Connor tried to interject. 'Everyone from around here thinks the same, although it was never proven.' She placed her hands on her hips, daring Raven to contradict her.

Raven exchanged a look with Becca. More sour grapes? Or was there substance to this accusation? How could something this big have been missed in their background checks?

'That's a very serious claim, Mrs Hepworth. Perhaps you could elaborate.'

'I'd be more than happy to,' said Sarah. She took a seat next to Connor, as if settling down to tell a good story. 'Joe's Dad, Roger, ran the pub before Joe, and he enjoyed a spot of fishing on his days off, not that a publican ever truly has a day off. Anyway, he and Sid used to go out together on Sid's boat. One day, not long before I met Joe, Roger and Sid went out in the boat but only Sid came back.'

She stopped, as if that proved everything.

When Raven failed to respond, she continued. 'Sid claimed that Joe's dad had fallen overboard drunk. It's true that Roger was a bit of a drinker – it's a hazard of running a pub, not that Joe has any problems in that regard – but by all accounts he could hold his liquor, and he knew the dangers of the sea well enough. But there was no one else onboard to contradict Sid's version of the story. The body washed up a couple of days later at Ravenscar.'

Raven pressed a finger to his forehead, trying to process the details. 'When exactly did this happen? You said it was just before you and Joe got together?'

'Twenty years ago, almost to the day,' said Sarah.

'But surely this was investigated by the police at the time?' said Becca.

Sarah shrugged dismissively. 'Accidental drowning was their conclusion. No one in the village ever believed that. Another case of police incompetence.'

So this was the reason for the grudge – you might even call it a feud – between the Capsticks and the Hepworths. Or at least between the older generation. Connor and Anna had clearly felt no qualms about getting together. And strangely enough, Joe had only ever expressed his fondness for Anna and a certain affection for Kate. But it was becoming clearer to Raven why Sarah Hepworth was so implacably opposed to the Capstick family and in particular, the relationship between Anna and Connor. And also why she was so clearly hostile towards the police.

'Well,' said Raven, 'that may all be true, but I don't see what the death of Joe's father twenty years ago has to do with Anna's death or why you think Davy would have broken into Connor's room.'

Sarah folded her arms. 'I can't explain it all. But the three things must be connected, don't you think? Can't you arrest Sid and Davy and question them?'

Raven shook his head. *If only it were that easy.* 'I can't arrest anyone on the basis of speculation, but I will certainly bear in mind everything you've told me.' He stood up. 'Thank you for your time, both of you.'

He beckoned Becca to join him outside. They stood by the boats near the slipway, watching the oncoming waves lap against the shore. Seaweed glistened in the sunlight and gulls soared on high. 'What do you make of that?' asked Raven.

'They're just like the Capulets and the Montagues, the two families in *Romeo and Juliet*. I expect you missed that lesson at school,' Becca added, when he looked blank. 'They hate each other. Sid pointed the finger at Joe for Anna's death, and now Sarah is blaming Davy for breaking into Connor's room. Neither has any proof, they just distrust each other so much that they jump to conclusions.'

'Unless there's something in what they say,' said Raven. 'It turned out that Joe did have something to hide after all. He'd been communicating with Anna secretly all the time she was in London. Maybe this business with Sid and Roger has a grain of truth in it too?'

Becca shrugged. 'I don't know how we're going to establish that. If the police investigation concluded that it was accidental death, then what are we going to find to contradict that, twenty years on? And even if we did, how does that relate to Anna's death? We're supposed to be wrapping the investigation up today, not embarking on a new one.'

Raven nodded, acknowledging the truth of her words.

Yet at the same time, he could hardly ignore the parallel with his own mother's death. Covered up more than three decades ago now, yet still top of his agenda. If Jean Raven deserved justice, then why not Roger Hepworth too?

Assuming there was any justice to be had. Maybe, like Sid claimed, he had simply fallen into the sea after one drink too many.

'Let's get Tony to look into it,' he concluded. He dialled Tony's number and explained what Sarah had told them.

'Twenty years ago,' repeated Tony, 'and the man's name was Roger Hepworth?'

'That's right,' Raven confirmed. 'See what you can find out.'

'I'll get onto it,' said Tony. 'I was going to call you anyway. Since we spoke this morning, the lab have got back to me about that cigarette Jess picked up on the path to Boggle Hole. Apparently it's a Polish brand.'

'Polish?' said Raven. 'Thanks, Tony.'

He eyed Becca thoughtfully. 'Who's Polish?' she asked.

'Not who. What. Do you remember the cigarettes that Davy dropped on the floor during our first visit to the house?'

'I remember.'

'They were a Polish brand too.'

'What a coincidence,' said Becca. 'Sounds like it's time for another chat with Davy Capstick.'

*

It was just shy of midday when Liam arrived at Salt Castle Brewery where Ellie worked – well, she ran the place, to be precise – and rapped on her office door.

She looked up from her paperwork in surprise. 'Hiya. What are you doing here?'

He strolled into the office doing his best to appear casual and leaned against her desk. He didn't want her to think anything was up. 'Are you busy?'

'A bit. Why?'

'I thought I'd take you out for a bite to eat. My treat?'

She closed the file she'd been working on and gave him a smile. 'How could I possibly refuse?'

Liam grinned. That charm of his. It never failed to work. And he couldn't afford for it to fail. Not today. Not now.

Ellie picked up her phone. 'I'll shoot Dad a message and ask him to keep a table free for us. We can see how Hannah's getting on.'

'Oh, okay.' Liam's heart sank but he did his best not to show it. For what he had in mind, somewhere discreet would be better, certainly not Keith's restaurant. But Ellie's thumbs were already flying over the keyboard and if he objected she would know something was up.

'Done,' said Ellie when she'd finished. 'Let's go, then. I'm starving.'

The restaurant was quiet on a Tuesday lunchtime in September, just a solo diner reading a book while eating a bowl of spaghetti, and a retired couple occupying the table in front of the window.

Hannah greeted them and showed them to a table against the far wall. 'It'll be nice and quiet for you here,' she said, taking Ellie's coat and Liam's leather jacket.

'Perfect,' said Liam. He glanced around but Ellie's dad was nowhere to be seen. He was probably working in the kitchen. Liam hoped he would stay there.

'How are you getting on with the new job?' Ellie asked Hannah.

'Great. At least, I haven't dropped anyone's food in their lap yet. Or muddled up the orders.'

'I knew you'd be good at this,' said Ellie.

Liam waited for Ellie and Hannah to finish chattering. He was on edge and just wanted to have Ellie to himself.

'Shall I give you a few minutes to look at the menu?' asked Hannah.

'No need. I already know what I'm having,' said Ellie. She hadn't even opened her menu. 'Seafood linguine. And a glass of Pinot Grigio, please.'

'Liam?'

'Oh, yeah.' He didn't know if he'd be able to eat a thing until he'd put his proposal to Ellie, but he needed to choose something. 'Steak and chips, please. And a beer.'

'Coming up.' Hannah disappeared into the kitchen.

'Well, this is nice,' said Ellie. 'We should go out more often on the spur of the moment. Live dangerously.'

Liam swallowed. 'Um, yeah. But perhaps not too dangerously...'

He glanced over his shoulder, half expecting to see the bald head and big nose of Donovan Cross in the company of his rent-a-thug henchman in dark glasses. But of course there was no one there apart from the diner engrossed in the book.

'What is it?' said Ellie. 'Are you expecting someone?'

'No, of course not.' Liam managed a smile. 'Just the two of us.'

'Good. You know I've been meaning to talk to you alone.'

'You have?' He wondered if she had picked up on his financial difficulties. He'd done his utmost to conceal them, but Ellie was highly perceptive. It wasn't for nothing she was the managing director of a brewery.

She ran a hand through her rainbow-coloured hair. 'About Becca.'

'What about Becca?' Liam was confused by the direction the conversation was taking. This wasn't how he'd planned it.

'Haven't you noticed?'

'Noticed what?'

'She doesn't seem very happy in the flat at the moment.'

Liam let out a sigh of relief. Was that all? His sister wasn't very happy? Well, thank God it was nothing more serious than that. 'Doesn't she?'

'No,' said Ellie, 'I think she preferred it when it was just us two girls in the flat.'

Liam's stomach lurched. Was Ellie going to ask him to move out? He couldn't possibly afford to get a place of his own. Not now. He gulped nervously. 'Do you want me to leave?'

'No, of course not.' Ellie gave him one of her sweetest smiles. 'But I wouldn't be surprised if Becca decided to move on. I think she really wants to be on her own.'

'Yeah, probably.' Liam thought back to his morning's encounter with his sister over the breakfast bar. He had tried to ask her for advice. He'd come *that* close to telling her about his dealings with a loan shark. Confessing everything to a police sergeant. But she'd been like a bear with a sore head, telling him to wash his dirty dishes.

A man threatened to cut my throat, he'd felt like saying. *And all you care about is dirty dishes.*

That was sisters for you.

'Can she afford it?' he wondered aloud. It was galling to think that Becca could get her own place and he, a property developer and landlord, had to scrounge off his girlfriend.

'I don't see why not,' said Ellie. 'She is a detective sergeant, after all.'

Hannah returned with the drinks and placed them on the table. 'A Pinot Grigio and a beer.'

'Thanks,' said Ellie, giving her a big smile.

'Yeah, thanks,' said Liam distractedly. Once they were alone again, he reached across the table and took hold of Ellie's hands. He needed to take charge of this conversation and steer it back in the right direction.

She gave him a look of surprise. 'Something on your mind?'

'There's something I wanted to say. I wanted to ask you a question, in fact.'

Her eyes widened. 'Oh really?'

Shit. She'd got the wrong end of the stick. She probably thought he was about to propose marriage or something. 'It's a business proposal.'

'Oh, right.' If she was disappointed, she handled it well.

'You mean your property business?'

'Yes. It's um...it's going well and I wondered if you'd like to invest some money?' He watched her closely for any signs of suspicion. She must be wondering why he'd sprung this on her. 'What do you say?'

'I'd need to see your accounts first, of course.'

'My accounts?' Shit, he hadn't anticipated that. But naturally she would want to see the books. She was a company director, after all. He thought quickly. He could show her the accounts for the most recent financial year. Everything had been going swimmingly until he'd embarked on this latest project. If it wasn't for this damned Victorian house bleeding him dry, his profits would still be soaring. 'Sure, I can get my accountant to send you the latest report.' He swallowed a gulp of beer.

Ellie fixed him with a serious look. 'In that case, I'd be very interested. Very interested indeed.'

Liam felt the tension in his stomach unwind.

Hannah arrived with the food and Liam plunged his knife and fork into the steak with relief. The meat was cooked to perfection – brown on the outside, pink and juicy on the inside.

'How's your pasta?' he asked Ellie.

'Excellent, as always.'

She had a few more questions for him over the course of the meal and he answered them deftly – he knew his business inside out. These were just details now. The deal was done. Ellie would put a much-needed injection of cash into the business, enough to see him through these short-term bumps in the road. He'd clear his debts with Barry and pay off the loan to Donovan, and get the work completed. Ellie would see a good return on her investment and all would end well.

'How's the food?' Keith had appeared from the kitchen and come over to say hello. Ellie's father made an intimidating impression. With a heavy build and a deep booming voice, his dark grey hair and thin lips cemented his forbidding appearance.

'Great, thanks,' said Liam, chewing through his last mouthful.

'Hey, Dad,' said Ellie, 'pull up a chair and hear what Liam's got to say. He's got a business proposal you might be interested in.'

Liam almost choked on his steak. This was *not* part of the plan.

Keith took a chair from a nearby table and sat down between them just as Hannah came to clear away the plates and ask if they'd like to see the dessert menu.

'Of course they would,' said Keith indulgently. 'So what is this business proposal, then?'

'Liam's asking if we'd like to put some money into his property business,' explained Ellie. 'He says things are going really well at the moment and he wants to take advantage of all the opportunities.'

We? That wasn't quite what Liam had said. It was one thing accepting money from his girlfriend, quite another being in debt to her father too.

A deep frown appeared across Keith's brow. 'You're asking for a loan?'

'Well,' said Liam hurriedly, 'only if you have some spare cash to invest…'

Keith fixed him with a grave look. 'I'm not made of money, Liam. I have my own business to think about. The bistro, you know?'

'Of course,' said Liam. 'No worries.'

Keith's craggy face broke into a broad smile. 'But if your business is good enough for Ellie to invest in, it's good enough for me.' He gave Liam a hearty slap on the back. 'After all, perhaps one day before long, you'll be my son-in-law!'

CHAPTER 17

'There he is now,' said Becca. She pointed, and Raven saw that Davy Capstick had just emerged from his house, in faded jeans and jacket, and was making his way across the square to the boat. He was lighting a cigarette – a Polish one, no doubt – as he walked and didn't look up.

'Perfect timing.' Raven set off to intercept him and Becca followed. 'We need to talk,' he called when Davy was still twenty yards away.

Davy looked up at them, gave one of his trademark scowls, then set off at a run, the lighted cigarette still clamped between his teeth.

'Shit,' said Raven. 'What's the silly bugger playing at?'

Davy dashed off down the alleyway where Raven and Becca had bought fish and chips, and by the time Raven reached it, he had disappeared into a maze of narrow lanes that led off it.

'You go after him,' said Becca. 'I'll head up the hill and try to cut him off. He can't get far in a place this size.'

She started running up the road so Raven had no choice but to head down the alley and follow the route Davy had taken.

The lanes here were narrow – far too small for vehicles – and sloping in places, with steps in the steepest bits. Even smaller paths, no larger than ginnels, led off in a tangle of ever-narrowing passageways. Davy was nowhere to be seen, but Raven took the first turning he came to and set off along the rear wall of a public house called the Smugglers Ale House. The route led down uneven flagstones and then up a flight of steps. *Bloody hell.* Raven placed his foot on the first step, grabbed hold of a railing and braced himself for pain.

Familiar territory.

At the top of the stone steps he took a sharp left, figuring that if Davy turned back onto the main street, Becca would nab him. The ginnel took him past a terrace of small cottages, huddled together in a cleft of the valley. Bright displays of hanging baskets greeted him cheerfully as he grunted his way along the path, a burning pain in his thigh as he headed higher up the valley.

The further he went, the more crowded the houses and cottages became, tucked closely together. There were hidden passages everywhere, nooks and crannies where someone could easily hide. It was possible that he had already passed Davy and hadn't seen him. Or that the man had run in the opposite direction altogether.

This is futile!

Raven tried to run faster but his right leg protested, jarring him to a halt. He paused to rub at it and caught a glimpse of denim jacket disappearing round a corner. He set off in pursuit again.

'Give it up,' shouted Raven as he ducked beneath a hanging basket, avoiding an oncoming pedestrian by a whisker. 'There's nowhere to go!'

But Davy wasn't buying it and vanished down another side alley.

Raven hauled himself along in his wake, hoping for some reprieve but not finding any. Davy was a few years younger than him and not in great condition, with that smoking habit not doing him any favours. But unlike Raven, he hadn't taken a bullet to the leg in a war. It was an unfair advantage and gave him the edge. Not to mention the fact that he'd lived in this village his whole life and probably knew these narrow lanes like the back of his hand. What had Joe Hepworth said? *The old town is riddled with secret passageways.* He hadn't been kidding. Raven had never seen a town quite like it.

He pushed on, ignoring the pain in his leg and the knowledge that it would be ten times worse in the morning. Davy had run for a reason and couldn't be allowed to escape.

He dashed past picture-perfect scenes of stone cottages, pot plants and old-fashioned streetlamps. But they were all just a blur. The path took him straight past the front doors of houses, virtually in and out of people's gardens. From inside one home, an old man looked out of his window in surprise as Raven rushed past just inches away.

He turned a corner, puffed up yet another flight of steps and caught a glimpse of Davy. 'Stop!' Raven yelled, though he might as well have saved his breath. Davy kept going, but he was running out of steam.

You and me both, mate.

Raven put a final spurt on up the hill just as Becca appeared at the very top. Davy stopped, spinning round in a panic before diving into a back alley.

Not again.

But in his haste he had made a serious mistake.

It was a dead end.

Raven caught up with him just as he was trying to scrabble over a stone wall into someone's garden. He grabbed hold of Davy's legs and held on as the man kicked and squirmed like an unruly toddler.

'Fuck off!' yelled Davy, but Raven had him now and wasn't letting go. He pulled him to the ground.

Davy landed in a heap, struggling to get away, but Becca had arrived too, blocking his escape. Raven twisted his arm behind his back, pushing him face-down onto the cobbles, and snapped on a pair of cuffs.

'Davy Capstick, I am arresting you on suspicion of the murder of Anna Capstick. You do not have to say anything. But it may harm your defence if you do not mention when questioned something which you later rely on in court. Anything you do say may be given in evidence. Do you understand?'

'Yeh bastard!'

Raven took that as a confirmation.

'Are you all right?' asked Becca.

'I'll be fine,' said Raven. But he already knew there would be a price to pay after this kind of action.

Davy spat on the ground.

Raven hoisted him up. 'In the car. Now!'

*

Jess was pleased when Raven asked her to supervise the search of the Capstick home in Robin Hood's Bay. It was a responsible job, documenting and logging the evidence to maintain the chain of custody and make sure the search complied with all legal requirements.

Raven and Becca had taken Davy back to Scarborough for interviewing, and Jess had been joined by Sergeant Fields from Whitby who had brought along a couple of uniformed cops to secure the premises. The presence of one of them in his hi-vis vest, standing by the open front door of the house was certainly attracting the attention of passers-by. Visitors and locals lingered by the boats on the square, eager for a glimpse of some real-life drama. Meanwhile, Kate and her father, Sid, had agreed to stay out of the way and had retreated to a local pub, although not the one directly opposite.

The white CSI van pulled up in the square and Holly clambered out. Erin and Jamie followed, then disappeared around to the back of the vehicle to fetch their gear. An excited murmur rippled through the gathered watchers, no doubt speculating about the arrival of the newcomers.

Holly nodded a greeting and zipped up her white coverall. 'Right then, Jess, what are we looking for today precisely?'

'Anything linking Davy Capstick to the murder of his daughter, Anna.'

'Oh good,' said Holly, deadpan. 'I do like specific instructions. Makes my job so much easier.' She turned to bellow at her young assistants. 'Erin! Jamie!' The pair emerged from the van, carting their box of tricks between them. 'Okay, you two, let's get started. I want to be home in time for the kids' bedtimes. Our brief for this afternoon is to look for "anything". Got that?'

Erin gave a wry grin. 'Got it, boss.' She was clearly used to Holly's particular brand of sarcasm.

'Right then,' said Holly, her hands on her wide hips. 'What are you waiting for?'

The CSIs dispersed into the house and began the job of turning the place upside down. Jess wasn't exactly sure what Raven hoped to find. Anna hadn't lived there for a year, had only popped back for a flying visit, and had been found dead half a mile away near the youth hostel in Boggle Hole.

But that was often the way with physical clues. You didn't know what you were looking for until you found it.

It didn't take long before a shout from Holly summoned Jess into the kitchen. She made her way past the uniformed constable on the doorstep and stepped gingerly into the small, dark room at the back of the house, being careful where she trod. She peered into the gloomy space, unsure what she was supposed to be looking at.

'If this kitchen belonged to a restaurant, I'd rate it zero for food hygiene,' declared Holly critically. 'Not that I'm too hot on culinary matters myself. My husband usually does the cooking at our place. But even I would be ashamed of this setup.'

Jess was inclined to agree. The kitchen looked like it dated back to the 1960s. It had probably never been installed properly and had been patched up many times over the years. The kitchen cabinets were stained and chipped and the work surfaces were sticky with all manner of unidentifiable substances. Used tea bags had fallen onto the floor and found their way into the gaps and crevices between the badly fitted units. Jess wouldn't have been surprised to spot a mouse peeping out from beneath the cupboards.

'Look here,' said Holly, pointing to one particular stain on a cupboard door. 'This is blood.'

Jess edged nearer to take a look. The red mark appeared to be a fingerprint. 'How can you tell it's blood and not just ketchup or something?'

'Oh,' said Holly, exchanging a weary look with Jamie, 'I expect that would be down to my years of training and experience.'

'Sorry,' said Jess quickly. She was never quite sure when Holly was joking or when she was about to bite your head off. She had seen what happened when someone annoyed her. It was best to err on the cautious side. 'I only meant—'

'Let's prove it for certain.' Holly took out a bottle of luminol from her bag and sprayed it evenly across the cupboard door, the worktop above, and the floor of the surrounding area. 'Yank those curtains shut, will you, Erin? And Jamie, get ready with the camera. Close the door, please, Jess.'

The three of them scurried around doing Holly's bidding and soon the room was even darker than before.

'There you go,' said Holly, standing back to admire her handiwork. Jamie moved in to photograph the result.

A faint blue glow was appearing where the luminol had been sprayed. As well as the fingerprint there were a few splashes on the cupboard doors and a substantial pool on the floor beneath.

'Someone tried to clean up but they didn't put a lot of effort into it,' said Holly. 'My husband would have done a much better job. Mark my words, Jess, if I ever get bumped off in mysterious circumstances, there'll be nothing to incriminate him, you can be certain of that.'

Jess watched as Jamie continued photographing the blood stains, her mind spinning.

This changed everything. Could Anna have been killed here, in this very kitchen, and her body carried over to Boggle Hole?

'This is amazing, Holly. Raven isn't going to believe it when I tell him.'

Holly tapped the side of her nose. 'They don't call me the bloodhound for nothing.'

Jess had heard the head of CSI being called a few other names, but she thought it best to keep that to herself. 'Can you get a sample sent over to the lab asap? If we can get a DNA match to Anna, and if that fingerprint is Davy's, then I think we've got all the evidence we need for a conviction.'

Holly puffed out her cheeks. 'The trouble with you detectives is that you're never satisfied. Isn't that right, Jamie? Give them one thing and they say, ta very much, can I have two more?' But Jess could see from the twinkle in her eyes that this was definitely intended in good humour.

'Boss?' Erin was standing in front of the old chimney breast that had once housed a large cast-iron stove. At one time it had probably supplied hot water for the house as well as providing somewhere to cook. Now the place that the stove had occupied was blanked off with a steel plate. Erin rapped on the soot-black metal with the end of her flashlight. A hollow clang rang out. 'Reckon there's something behind here?'

Holly marched across to the chimney and gave the cover a closer inspection. 'Anyone got a screwdriver handy? Ta.' She accepted the tool that Jamie had handed her and began to poke around the edge of the metal plate. It didn't take her long to find a gap to slot it into. With a gentle pull, the steel cover hinged open, revealing a small hollow behind it.

Erin turned her flashlight on and shone the beam into

the space that had once enclosed the cooking stove. 'Got you!' declared Holly. She reached her white-gloved hand inside and pulled out a small package. 'This of any interest to you, young Jess?'

Jess gaped in amazement at Holly's discovery. It was a small mobile phone, a cheap model from a brand Jess hadn't heard of. 'Anna's missing phone!'

Holly showed it triumphantly to her two assistants before popping it into an evidence bag and handing it over. 'The thing to remember, Jess, is that at CSI we tackle hard challenges for breakfast. Need a miracle? Just give us till teatime!'

CHAPTER 18

Raven switched on the recording equipment and introduced himself and Becca, giving the date and time. It was late now on Tuesday afternoon and Raven was keen to get cracking with the interview. The fact that the suspect had tried to run away from him in Robin Hood's Bay meant there would be some serious explaining to do. His leg was already playing up after the chase around the Bay, and Raven stretched it out beneath the table, rubbing it with one hand as he spoke.

'Also present is the suspect, David Capstick, known as Davy, and his legal representative' – Raven checked the name in his notes – 'Mr Brian Moody, duty solicitor.'

Moody coughed into his fist – a smoker's cough – and cleared his throat with a loud rattling noise. He had been the only solicitor available at short notice willing to do the job for legal aid money. He'd make a couple of hundred quid for showing up today. And that was before the overheads of running a law firm. Not a great incentive to put on a suit and do your best work.

'Mr Capstick,' continued Raven, 'please could you confirm your name, date of birth and address for the tape.'

In the unfamiliar surroundings of Scarborough police station, Davy Capstick looked like a caged animal. He was clearly unused to sitting at a table for any length of time. He scraped his chair back, stretching out his muscular arms and twisting his head from side to side as if seeking an escape route.

He wouldn't much enjoy the confines of a prison cell.

'Mr Capstick?' prompted Raven.

'Oh, yeah.' Davy gave the details he had been asked.

'We are here today to interview you in relation to the murder of Anna Capstick.' There was no longer any trace of doubt in Raven's mind that Anna's death had been murder. He had known it all along, despite Gillian's scepticism, and he was determined to prove it. 'Before we begin, I must remind you that you are under caution.' He repeated the words he'd spoken to Davy in Robin Hood's Bay. 'Do you understand?'

Davy shook his head. 'I didn't do it. I swear.'

Raven ignored the remark and proceeded to state his case. 'On Sunday morning, the body of your daughter, Anna Capstick, nineteen years old, was found at the entrance to a cave in Boggle Hole near Robin Hood's Bay. From evidence collected at the scene and the statement of one witness, it appears that she sustained her fatal injuries at or near the bottom of the steps leading down to the beach from the Cleveland Way. Davy, can you account for your movements between eleven o'clock on Saturday night and the early hours of Sunday morning?'

Davy spread his fingers out on the desk, showing coarse, hairy hands calloused from hard work. The tattoos on his arms were clearly visible. 'Saturday night? I were out drinking with Sid. You can check that. There were plenty o' witnesses.'

'Until what time?'

Davy shrugged his broad shoulders. 'Don't remember exactly.'

Raven leaned in closer. 'Closing time is eleven o'clock, Davy. I'm asking you where you were after eleven.'

Davy's eyes wandered around the small room. He looked like he wanted to be anywhere but here, and to do anything but answer Raven's questions.

'If you don't wish to answer a question,' remarked Moody, 'you can say "no comment".'

'Well, no comment then,' said Davy.

'On the other hand,' said Raven, 'it may harm your defence if you do not mention, when questioned, something which you later rely on in court.' He produced the evidence bag containing the cigarette stub that Jess had found. 'Do you recognise this, Davy?'

Davy gave the stub an unwilling look. 'A cigarette. Could be anyone's.'

'It could be, Davy, but it's an unusual brand. Polish. The exact same brand that you smoke. Is it yours?'

'Hard to say, in't it?' said Davy. 'Where'd you find it?'

Raven smiled. 'Glad you asked. It was found on the clifftop path leading from Robin Hood's Bay to Boggle Hole. Is it possible that you dropped it there?'

Davy looked to his solicitor for help. 'You can say "no comment",' said Moody, coughing again.

Yet Davy seemed reluctant to say that. 'It's possible that I dropped it. I mean, I do live at Robin Hood's Bay, don't I?' He smiled as if that was a good joke, but his face quickly turned sour when no one else in the room seemed to find it funny.

'Did you walk along that path on the night Anna was killed?' pressed Raven.

Davy seemed to be doing some kind of calculation in his head. 'Well, I might've done. I wanted to clear my head before going to bed. But I didn't see owt, mind you. I didn't see Anna.'

'What time was this?'

Davy shrugged. 'Dunno. I don't wear a watch.'

'Why did you take the clifftop path?'

'The tide was in, so the beach was covered.'

'I see. And how far did you walk exactly? All the way to Boggle Hole?'

'Nah,' said Davy. 'Not that far. Like I say, the tide was in, so there was no point. I just went a little way and then turned round. That's it.' He nodded to himself as if satisfied with his reply.

'Davy,' said Becca, 'where do you get these cigarettes? They're an unusual brand.'

He looked to the ceiling as if for inspiration. 'You know. Just a mate.'

'Can you give us your mate's name?'

'No.' Davy's eyes flashed with something akin to alarm. 'He's not really a mate. Just a bloke I met in the pub one night.'

'You don't know his name?'

'No.'

Raven found this hard to believe. So apparently did Moody, who leaned towards his client and advised him that "no comment" might be a better answer.

'Well, no comment, then,' said Davy, clearly flustered.

It seemed a good time to turn up the heat. 'Why did you run from us when we approached you in Robin Hood's Bay earlier today?' asked Raven.

Davy grinned. His teeth were crooked and yellowed. 'That's what folk do round 'ere when the cops are after them.'

Raven smiled back pleasantly. 'Would it have anything to do with the blood we found in your kitchen?' He produced a set of photographs showing the extent of the blood spatter in the Capstick's kitchen.

Davy's face fell at the sight of them. 'I don't know owt about that.'

'Is this Anna's blood? Did you kill her in the kitchen and then carry her body to Boggle Hole? Is that what happened, Davy?'

'No, I swear, I didn't kill 'er. Not there, not anywhere. I didn't see 'er, I swear.'

'Perhaps she was at the house when you got back from the pub. You'd had a drink, and so had Anna. She said something that made you angry. You hit her. You didn't mean to hurt her, but she fell and hit her head. Is that how it was, Davy?'

Davy's eyes were wide with terror. 'No. Nothing like that. I didn't see 'er. Not then, not anytime that day. She kept well away from me.'

Becca produced the next photo, which was of the phone the CSI team had found at the house. She laid it on the table so that Davy could see it clearly. 'Do you recognise this phone, Davy? Did it belong to Anna?'

Davy gave it a quick glance. 'Dunno. Where'd you find it?'

'It was found in a secret compartment in your kitchen, Davy. Do you know the one I mean?'

'Secret compartment?' Davy's eyes flickered left and right. 'Oh, I know what you're talking about. You mean the nook in the chimney where the old oven used to be.' He grinned nervously. 'That's not secret, just hard to find. We put our valuables there to keep 'em safe.'

'So whose phone is it, then?'

Davy shrugged. 'Just a spare, like. It's never been used.'

'Well,' said Raven, 'it's with our forensic team right now, so they'll confirm whether or not that's true.' He decided to risk a punt. 'So what were you looking for when you broke into Connor's room?' It was guesswork, but one with a decent chance of being true.

Davy's reaction confirmed it. 'I weren't looking for nowt.'

'So you admit that you broke into his room?'

Davy's jaw dropped open. He realised he'd walked straight into a trap.

'What does this have to do with the death of Anna Capstick?' asked Moody. 'I don't see how an alleged break-in is relevant. You can't pin everything on my client.'

There was a knock at the door and Raven paused the interview. He stepped outside and was pleased to see Jess. 'Do you have any news from forensics?'

Jess nodded, but he could tell from her expression that

the news wasn't good. 'We fast-tracked the analysis of the blood found in the kitchen. It's not Anna's blood type. I've spoken to Kate and she says it's hers. She claims she cut herself with a knife when she was gutting a fish.'

'Do you believe her?'

'I don't know,' said Jess. 'You're thinking that Davy hit her? I suppose it's possible, but if the blood isn't Anna's...'

'Yeah, sure,' said Raven despondently, 'then our kitchen murder narrative has no legs. What about the mobile phone?'

'Sorry,' said Jess, 'but it's not Anna's. It's an unregistered sim-free phone and has never been used.'

'That's what Davy claimed,' admitted Raven. 'Shit.'

It was fair to say that the case was falling apart.

Raven returned to the interview room. 'I think,' he told Moody, 'that in the light of fresh evidence, we will not be holding your client any longer. Davy Capstick, you're free to leave.'

CHAPTER 19

Becca tapped on Raven's open office door and went inside. He was sitting at his desk, his tie loosened, his right leg up on a chair, staring morosely into space. Since the interview with Davy, he had withdrawn into himself and she could feel the waves of frustration rolling off him like sea fret on a cold morning.

Becca felt equally frustrated. After the chase at Robin Hood's Bay, they'd both been sure they had caught their man. Davy Capstick had shown every sign of being a killer. Indifferent to his daughter's death, almost certainly violent towards his wife, he had no alibi, no good answer to any of the questions that had been put to him. And most damning of all, he had tried to scarper from the police.

Yet despite all that, they'd been unable to pin a thing on him. The man had proved as slippery as the fish that Kate claimed to have been gutting when she supposedly cut herself with the knife. All their leads had come to nothing and Gillian's deadline was effectively up.

'Not a great outcome,' she said.

Raven appeared to suddenly register her presence. 'No.'

Becca had been hoping for a little more conversation from her boss. He could be so hard to read at times. She closed the door quietly so that no one would overhear what she was about to say.

'I was thinking about that other matter.'

Raven gave her his full attention now. 'What about it? There's not much we can do with the logbook gone. When I told you I had one or two ideas, I really only had the one.'

'Well, there must be other records in addition to the logbooks. I don't know what exactly, but why don't we grab everything from the archive relating to police vehicles for 1991 and take a look? We might turn up something unexpected. I'm free this evening, if you like.' Becca realised she had no desire to return home to the flat and put up with Liam's moods or the general mess.

Raven gave her a glum look. 'I'm sure you must have something better to do.'

'No, as it happens. My life is null and void without work.' She meant it as a joke, but it struck her as depressingly true.

'Well, in that case, we'd better find you something meaningful to do. But not here. We'll take the stuff back to my house. Is that all right?'

'Sure.' Becca had never been inside Raven's house and was curious to see it. He'd invited her in once, but then his girlfriend at the time had appeared and Becca had thought it best to make herself scarce. But that girlfriend was no longer on the scene. 'I'll meet you there.'

After raiding the archives, they drove in convoy to Raven's house. Becca parked her Honda Jazz next to Raven's BMW at the end of Quay Street. The M6 was too wide for the parking space, but the Jazz was dinky, so there was room for the two of them side by side. Raven was limping after his dash around Robin Hood's Bay in pursuit of Davy, so Becca helped him carry the boxes they'd filched from the archives.

'Come on in,' he said, opening the front door and moving aside to let her through.

'This is lovely.' She stepped into the hallway, admiring the unadorned white walls, the polished wooden floor and the modern runner going up the stairs. Barry Hardcastle had done a good job, but presumably this was Raven's own taste in interiors on display.

Understated and stylish.

She'd probably have brightened it up with more colour and some personal knick-knacks if it had been her place, but it was undeniably a charming old building. Lots of character and original features, but with a clean and contemporary finish. She thought again of the flat she'd seen on the property website. It was just up the hill from here, a stone's throw from Quay Street.

A furry black beast barrelled out of the front room and straight into her legs. She was almost thrown off balance with the large box she was carrying.

'Steady,' said Raven, putting a hand to the small of her back. 'Down, Quincey!' The dog was now jumping up and trying to lick Becca's face.

Laughing, she handed the box to Raven and stooped down to give Quincey the attention he craved. 'Good boy!' She'd always wanted a dog growing up, but her parents had said there was no space in the guest house they ran on North Marine Drive. Perhaps if she had a flat of her own?

'This dog is never interested in me,' said Raven, 'even though I feed him and take him for walks every day. He has no sense of loyalty whatsoever.'

Hannah appeared in the doorway. 'Hi, Dad. I picked Quincey up because I wasn't sure what time you'd be back. Oh, hi, Becca.'

Becca had met Raven's daughter briefly at her own birthday party the previous month, but they hadn't had an opportunity to get to know each other properly. She wasn't sure how best to greet her. Shaking hands seemed too formal, and hugging too intimate so Becca settled on a wave of the hand.

'How are you, Hannah?'

'Good.'

Hannah looked nothing like Raven. Whereas he was dark and brooding, she was blonde with a sunny smile. She must take after her mother instead. But as Becca studied her more carefully, she caught a glimpse of Raven in her brown eyes and in the way she held herself. Hannah was wearing a jet necklace with matching earrings and Becca recognised them as the present she had helped Raven choose for Hannah's most recent birthday.

'There's nothing in the fridge, Dad,' complained Hannah. 'What are we having to eat tonight?'

'I'll phone for a pizza,' said Raven. 'Becca, what toppings do you like?'

'Oh, you don't have to feed me.'

'Nonsense. I think we'll be a while going through those boxes. My treat.'

While Raven ordered food, Hannah showed Becca into the front room. It was decorated in the same unfussy style as the hallway. White walls, a modern sofa and armchairs, a glass-topped coffee table, polished wood floor. Everything was in its place, and the lack of clutter was refreshing. The flat Becca shared with Ellie and Liam was always so full of junk. Unwashed coffee cups, empty wine glasses, boxes of half-eaten takeaway food.

'Have a seat,' said Hannah and plonked herself down cross-legged on a rug in front of the fireplace. Quincey lay beside her, his head in her lap.

Becca sat at one end of the sofa and waited as Raven brought the dusty archive boxes through and placed them on the coffee table. She opened one at random and began to trawl through. The yellowing paper smelled of must and was spotted with age.

'What are you doing?' asked Hannah.

'Looking for evidence,' said Raven, taking a seat next to Becca.

'Of what?'

Becca wondered how much Raven had told his daughter about the circumstances of her grandmother's death. It would have happened long before Hannah was born. It was a shame to grow up not knowing your grandparents. Becca's grandparents lived just up the road in Scalby and she was always popping in for a cup of tea and a chat. She couldn't imagine not having them around.

'We're investigating a historic crime,' said Raven.

'Sounds intriguing,' said Hannah. 'A murder?'

'Hit-and-run,' said Raven.

Hannah's eyes widened. 'Not your mother's death?'

He nodded.

'Will you find anything?' asked Hannah. 'After all this time?'

'That remains to be seen.'

Becca lifted out a brown cardboard folder and studied its contents. Index cards, each one punched, dated and stamped. But quite what they were for, she couldn't tell.

The doorbell rang and Hannah sprang to her feet. 'That'll be the food. I'll get it.'

A moment later the smell of melted cheese and oregano wafted into the room.

They took a break from sorting through the boxes to eat their food.

'So, what are you doing these days, Hannah?' Becca asked. She might have added, *after you jacked in your internship with a local law firm.* That was a decidedly delicate matter. Becca wasn't privy to all the details, but Hannah had uncovered some dubious legal practices and had shopped the firm to the National Crime Agency. It was the same law firm where Becca's ex-boyfriend, Daniel, worked. And the senior partner, Harry Hood, had some connection with Raven. From what Becca had heard, Harry Hood might be needing a lawyer of his own.

'I'm waitressing in Ellie's dad's bistro while I figure out what to do next. In fact, Ellie and your brother were in today having lunch.'

'Nice for some.' Becca hadn't eaten anything much since breakfast. She'd been too busy at work and the chase around Robin Hood's Bay had given her a raging appetite. She was making light weather of her pizza which was already more than half gone.

'I know I shouldn't gossip,' said Hannah, 'but I couldn't help overhearing. Liam asked Ellie to invest some money in his latest building project. He even got Keith interested too.'

Becca scooped another slice of pizza out of the box. 'Liam never misses an opportunity for a bit of wheeling and dealing. He probably told them he's making a ton of money and they'd be crazy not to get involved.'

Raven was listening to the discussion with a frown across his brow. 'Ellie needs to be careful. I ran into Barry this morning when I was dropping Quincey off with Vicky. He was having a bit of a moan about Liam not paying his bills.'

Becca wasn't surprised to hear that. Liam's philosophy was always to get paid on time but put off paying his own bills for as long as possible. It was good business sense, she supposed. In any case, she really didn't want to get involved in her brother's affairs. She was sure Ellie could make the right decision on her own – after all, she ran a successful business herself.

When the pizza boxes were empty, Raven and Becca got back to work. They sifted through piles of old maintenance records, looking for anything relating to the Vauxhall Cavalier involved in the incident. By now, Becca could recite the number plate more easily than she could that of her own car.

Suddenly she froze. The number plate – now branded forever onto her memory – leapt out at her. She pulled a sheet of paper from the pile and studied it carefully, re-reading it twice before showing it to Raven. If this was true, it was a bombshell.

'Look at this,' she said.

She watched his face as he absorbed the details, a deep furrow creasing his forehead. The document she'd found was a form authorising the repair of a broken headlight and cracked windscreen of the vehicle involved in the hit-and-run. It was dated two days after the incident took place.

She waited for his reaction when he saw who had signed the car in for repair.

'Bloody hell,' said Raven. He tossed the piece of paper onto the coffee table and stood up abruptly.

Quincey whined.

'What is it, Dad?' asked Hannah.

Becca picked up the document and read it through one more time to make absolutely sure.

There was no doubt about it. The car had been signed in for repair by Gillian Ellis.

★

It was nearly midnight when Rory Gamble slipped out of the youth hostel and made his way down to the cove, a pair of binoculars slung around his neck. They'd been a present from his dad for his thirteenth birthday.

Rory loved his dad, though not as much as he'd loved his mum. He tried to recall her face now, but she'd been gone so long he couldn't really remember what she looked like. It was her smell he recalled, the fresh smell of summer meadows, and her gentle touch. Her voice too. 'I love you, Rory,' she'd said to him as she held him close in her soft warmth. 'When I'm not here anymore, you remember that.' And he had.

After she was gone, his dad had done his best, but it was hard for a man to bring up a child on his own – at least, that's what his dad told him whenever he got cross and shouted. He would always give Rory a big hug afterwards and say he was sorry, he shouldn't have lost his temper. 'It's all right, Dad,' Rory would tell him, but he knew it would be better if his mum was still alive.

The moon was out, casting broken light across the water, and Rory walked across the sand and rocks to the cave entrance on the shore. On Saturday night, when he'd returned to the youth hostel, the mouth of the cave had been underwater. But the tide came in an hour later each day and hadn't yet reached the spot where he'd put Anna's body on Sunday morning. He'd known, deep down, that there weren't really any goblins in the cave who would make Anna better, but he'd wanted to believe it so badly he'd been prepared to chance it. The kids at school would have made fun of him, but Anna would never have laughed. She had always been kind to him. She trusted him. And he had let her down.

He didn't like Lexi, Anna's friend from London. She talked funny, always saying "innit" in that horrible screechy voice. He felt like putting his hands over his ears whenever she opened her mouth. He could tell that she looked down on him. She thought him stupid, like the kids at school had done. Perhaps he was stupid. Even his dad said so sometimes. But Lexi was stupid too. She was staying in a place as beautiful as Boggle Hole, and all she did was moan about how she wanted to go back to London.

Rory had never been to London and didn't want to, if all the people there were like Lexi.

He liked coming down to the beach with his binoculars. He liked being able to see things he couldn't see with his bare eyes. Birds in the daytime, turnstones and oystercatchers hard at work on the sand, kittiwakes and gannets along the clifftop. At night, he looked at the stars in the sky and the shimmering reflection of the moon as the waves rose and fell.

He raised the binoculars and looked out across the ink-black sea. A light blinked on the horizon. A boat. Rory didn't really like boats, despite living by the sea. He didn't like the way they rocked beneath his feet. He preferred the solidity of firm ground.

An orange glow lit up the sky to the north and a faint smell of smoke carried on the breeze. He turned towards it and saw the unmistakable signs of a fire in Robin Hood's Bay.

His first thought was for Anna, for her safety. He set off along the beach, drawn like a moth to the flame, but he didn't get far because the tide was coming in, the water lapping at the foot of the cliffs.

Then he remembered that Anna was dead. He turned and headed back to the youth hostel.

★

Jackson Webb enjoyed his work. His employer, Donovan Cross, could be a bastard at times, but that was all right. Jackson could be a bit of a bastard himself. In fact, being paid to be a bastard was the part of the job he liked most. Roughing up a punter, a sharp punch to the gut and a few kicks when they were down on the ground. He'd done that kind of thing for fun in the old days. Now he got paid for it. Result.

He liked the way they squealed helplessly, asking for a few more days to find the money, begging for a bit of leniency, a chance to make it all good. Another kick was usually enough to shut them up. Not that Donovan let him go too far. A dead punter was no use to a loan shark.

Just the other morning, he'd watched as Donovan pressed a razor to some guy's neck, making unreasonable demands, changing the terms of the loan without warning. Guy had nearly shat himself. That was Donovan all over. Absolute bastard.

Jackson had a lot of respect for that.

But as he steered his black Audi – Donovan's car, an RS7 Sportback, aggressive styling and a menacing profile, another aspect of the job he appreciated – down the steep hill that descended into Robin Hood's Bay, he soon realised that something was up. It was supposed to be quiet in the sleepy village at midnight. That was why he came and went at this hour. *Incognito.* But tonight there were far too many people about and they were all carrying buckets. It seemed a bit late in the day to be building sandcastles.

Jackson proceeded down the hill anyway. There was nowhere to turn the car around, and his instructions from Donovan had been unambiguous: meet Davy Capstick and pick up the goods. Jackson had last been here on

Saturday night, dropping the money off. That business with the girl had been a bit of a problem but she was out of the way now. Donovan had given him the all-clear to return.

When he rounded the corner at the bottom of the hill and entered the square, he saw straight away what all the fuss was about.

A boat was on fire. Davy and Sid's, if he wasn't mistaken. People were desperately trying to put the fire out with buckets of water filled from a standpipe. In a place as old and tightly crammed as Robin Hood's Bay, a fire would decimate the town if it wasn't put out quickly. No wonder the townsfolk were mucking in with buckets.

Jackson wasted no time. It was far too dangerous to hang around. He couldn't afford to be seen. He spun the car around and sped back up the hill as quickly as he could.

Why someone had torched the boat, he had no idea, but one thing was certain. Donovan would not be happy when he learned about this. Jackson gritted his teeth in anticipation of delivering the bad news. There were parts of his job he did not enjoy.

CHAPTER 20

Raven stared out of the steamy window at the grey, drizzly morning. The weather had taken a turn for the worse again, the way it did in September. The dreary atmosphere reflected his mood.

'Do you actually think Gillian was driving the car when...?' Becca tailed off, unable to finish her sentence.

It was the question that had kept Raven awake half the night. Had his boss killed his mother and then destroyed the evidence? Gillian could be tough and single-minded, but Raven had always believed she would stand up for justice, even if it proved harmful to her own interests. Was he romanticising his image of her? Portraying her as a noble guardian of truth, willing to fall on her own sword if necessary? It was naïve, and not the kind of courtesy he should extend to a suspect in a police investigation, even if that investigation didn't officially exist.

Besides, he knew her only in her present role as detective superintendent. Back in 1991, she had been a different person entirely – a lowly police constable, still in uniform. Admitting to involvement in a fatal accident might have ended her career before it had barely begun.

And Gillian had gone on to enjoy a flourishing career.

'There's a countersignature on the form,' said Becca, cutting open her croissant and spreading it generously with butter and jam. They had arranged to meet before work at a café just around the corner from the police station. Last night's revelation that Gillian had signed the hit-and-run car in for repairs had shocked them both. They needed to take stock and review their next move.

Becca slid the document across the table towards him, and Raven eyed it with circumspection. Beneath Gillian's signature was a countersignature where another person had authorised the repair. It looked as if a senior officer had scrawled his or her name on the document without giving it a second glance. They probably had no idea what they were signing. 'It's illegible,' Raven grumbled.

He wasn't really a breakfast person. He had ordered toast and coffee, but the rounds of toast sat untouched on their plate, and he had barely sipped his coffee. This morning, his appetite was particularly weak, and it didn't help that his leg still ached like the devil.

Becca didn't seem to share his aversion to food. 'I've got an idea,' she said through a mouthful of croissant.

'Go on.'

'Why don't we ask someone who was around at the time to identify the countersignature?'

'Do you have someone in mind?' asked Raven, although he already knew what was coming.

'DI Derek Dinsdale.'

Raven groaned. Derek Dinsdale was his least favourite person in all of Scarborough, unless you counted Dr Felicity Wainwright. Or Harry Hood, criminal lawyer and one of Raven's teenage associates in the days before he ran away to join the army. Or possibly Darren Jubb, dubious nightclub owner and another former friend of Raven's – the one who had stolen his first girlfriend away from him.

Come to think of it, there were a lot of people in Scarborough he didn't much care for.

'I was hoping we could keep this between ourselves,' he

told Becca, 'at least until we know what's what.'

'Well, how are we going to identify the signature, if we don't speak to anyone who might recognise it?'

Raven grunted. Just because he was wrong, it didn't mean he had to admit it. He turned the plate of toast around to see if it looked any more appetising from the other side. It didn't.

Becca took another bite of buttered croissant and chewed it thoughtfully. 'If you don't want to ask Dinsdale, then you'll have to ask Gillian herself.'

'I can't do that. Not yet. I need to know more first.'

'Then Derek it is.'

'I'll think about it.' He pushed the toast towards her. 'Do you want this? I don't have any appetite.'

Becca cast it a suspicious glance. 'Not really. I'm trying to watch my weight.' She looked at it a second time. 'Oh, go on then.'

Raven had no further desire to discuss Gillian Ellis. 'In the meantime, we still have an unexplained death on our hands, and I'll have to write up my report for the coroner this morning.'

Becca was enthusiastically spreading butter over the toast, all the way up to the edges. So much for watching her weight. 'We did our best, Raven. But you can't find evidence if it's not there.'

'There's Anna's missing phone.'

'Which is still missing,' she replied.

'And the fact that Davy broke into Connor's room to search for something.'

'Which is not technically a break-in,' she countered, 'since he seems to have just walked in through an open door and not taken anything.'

'The ambiguous post-mortem...'

'Which stated that Anna's injuries were consistent with accidental death.'

'Plus this business about Sid killing Joe Hepworth's father twenty years ago.'

'Which we have no hope of investigating after all this

time.' She took a large bite of toast, leaving a smear of jam on her lips.

Raven paused. 'And finally, the clear and obvious signs that Davy Capstick is abusing his wife.'

That wasn't so easy for her to parry. 'What can we do, though? Even Kate refuses to admit that anything's happening.'

'So are you happy to leave things at that?'

A look of defiance flashed across Becca's face. 'I hope you know me better than that.'

'Good, because I don't want to drop the case either.'

'There are too many loose ends.'

'I agree.'

'But what about Gillian?' asked Becca. 'She wants the case closed.'

'I think,' said Raven, 'that after last night's revelation, I'm less inclined to do what Detective Superintendent Gillian Ellis wants.'

He downed the last of his black coffee and rose to his feet. Becca crammed the last of the toast into her mouth and wiped away the crumbs with a paper napkin.

'Come on, then,' said Raven. 'We've got work to do. And you ought to watch your weight. That was two breakfasts you just polished off.'

Becca pulled a face at him. 'Pig!'

Raven nodded. 'You said it.'

*

'There's been a development,' said Tony, speaking up as soon as Raven called the morning briefing and asked if anyone had new information to share before they were obliged to wrap things up. 'Although whether it's related to Anna's death remains to be seen.'

'What is it, Tony?' Raven didn't like to be on the back foot.

'There was a fire at Robin Hood's Bay last night. Sid and Davy's boat was set alight. The emergency services were called out shortly before midnight, but by the time the firefighters arrived, the townspeople had already doused the flames. But the boat's a wreck. She'll never sail again.'

Raven pictured the boat that Davy had been fixing on the dry dock. Could his repair work have accidentally caused the fire? Or had something more sinister occurred? With all the other goings-on at the Bay, arson seemed a more plausible explanation.

'We'll drive over and check it out,' said Raven, glad that the incident had given him the perfect excuse to defy Gillian and head back to Robin Hood's Bay. More than ever he was convinced that the investigation needed to continue. 'Anyone else got anything?'

Jess raised her hand. 'We put out an appeal on social media for sightings of Anna around Robin Hood's Bay on Saturday. We didn't get a huge response at the time, but this was emailed in this morning.'

She pinned a photo to the whiteboard. It was an outside shot of the church that Raven and Becca had visited to speak to Rory.

'It was taken by a woman describing herself as a taphophile.'

'A what?'

'A cemetery enthusiast,' explained Jess, 'also known as a tombstone tourist. Her hobby is visiting graveyards, searching for unusual or famous gravestones, making rubbings of epitaphs. Her Instagram is full of churchyards.'

'First, a fossil collector,' grumbled Raven, 'now a gravestone tourist. Who's next? A ghost hunter?' He signalled for Jess to continue.

'If you look closely you can see two figures in the background on the edge of the shot. I've enlarged them here.' She pinned a second photo to the board – a close-up of the original. 'One of the figures is Anna and the other must be the vicar. They appear to be having a conversation.'

'When was this picture taken?' asked Becca.

'Six o'clock in the evening,' said Jess. 'There's a digital timestamp on the image.'

'We spoke to the vicar the day after Anna's body was found,' said Raven, recalling his unsatisfactory encounter with the Reverend Mark Taylor, 'so why did he not tell us he'd seen Anna on Saturday? That's another thing that needs following up.' He reached for his coat.

'Just one more thing before you go,' said Tony. 'I looked into the death of Joe Hepworth's dad.'

Raven paused. 'What did you find out?'

Tony referred to his written notes. 'Twenty years ago, Roger Hepworth was out on a fishing trip with Sid Sutcliffe when he fell overboard. Roger was an experienced sailor, but Sid claimed there'd been an unexpected surge that caused the boat to almost capsize. Roger had been standing by the bow, but by the time Sid righted himself and stabilised the boat, Roger was nowhere to be seen. Obviously, there was a police investigation but nothing was found to contradict Sid's account of what happened. Likewise, the post-mortem examination found no evidence of anything untoward and so the coroner concluded it was accidental death.'

'Accidental death,' mused Raven. 'For a place as small as Robin Hood's Bay there are rather a lot of fatal accidents, don't you think? Especially involving the Hepworth and Capstick families.'

CHAPTER 21

A charcoal hull was all that remained of the fishing boat, together with the scorched engine block that Davy had been repairing. A pungent, acrid smell, thick enough to taste at the back of your throat, lingered behind. At every gust of wind, flakes of charred wood rose into the air, settling like black snowflakes on the ground. A few visitors had stopped to stare at the unexpected sight, and Sid and Davy stood to one side, gazing mournfully at the wreck, as if wishful thinking could raise her like a phoenix from the ashes.

Sergeant Mike Fields was on hand to manage the situation. He raised his hand wearily as Raven emerged from his car. 'Raven, Becca.'

'That's a sorry sight,' said Raven. 'What can you tell us about it?'

Mike Fields's face was grim. 'The Whitby fire engine was called out at midnight but the fire was already out by the time it arrived. The cause isn't yet known but the Fire Investigation Officer has sent samples off to the lab for analysis. Sid and Davy are convinced it was arson.'

'Is it safe to have a closer look?'

'Safe enough, but I wouldn't try to climb onboard.'

Raven walked up to the blackened hull and carefully placed one hand against its side. The blistered wood was still warm to the touch.

'What are yeh going to do about this, then, eh?' demanded a familiar voice from behind. 'Our livelihood gone up in smoke!'

Raven turned to see Davy Capstick, a look of unbridled fury on his face. 'This is what you lot ought to be investigating. Not arresting me for nowt!' He pointed at the ruin of the boat. 'This were deliberate! Someone is trying to ruin us!'

'The fire *is* under investigation,' said Raven, seeking to calm him down. 'But what makes you so sure it was arson?' He wouldn't put it past Sid and Davy to torch their own boat and claim the insurance.

'Do you think I'm stupid?' bellowed Davy. 'What else would it be? It stank of petrol out 'ere last night. Ask anyone who were 'ere! And that's half the village.'

Sid joined them. 'Davy's right. The flames went up like that.' He clicked his fingers. 'Someone's trying to put us out o' business, and we know who.' Sid's manner was more measured than his son-in-law's but Raven could sense the anger boiling beneath the surface. He began to doubt that they had burned their own boat.

Davy's features twisted suddenly into a look of absolute hatred and he balled his hands into fists. 'You!' he shouted across the square. 'You've got a nerve, showing yerself!'

Raven spun to see Joe Hepworth on the other side of the cobbles, standing at the entrance to his pub. Joe gazed across the square to the men by the boat. His expression was difficult to read, but he stood his ground, perhaps reassured by the police presence. 'Keep your distance, Davy Capstick.'

Mike Fields moved to interpose but he was too slow. Davy charged across the square, his fists clenched. 'Yeh fucking burned our boat last night, yeh fucking–'

But whatever he'd been about to say, he'd clearly

decided that actions spoke louder than words. Before Fields could reach him he landed a punch on Joe's face.

There was a loud crack, and blood spurted from Joe's nose, spattering both men in a fine spray.

Mike Fields reached Davy a moment before Raven and dragged him away. 'Cool it, Davy!' he shouted. With Raven's help, he managed to pin Davy's arms behind his back.

Davy resisted, trying to break free. His face was spattered with Joe's blood. 'You arresting me again, yeh bastards?' he cried. 'You should be arresting him!'

Raven forced him into a kneeling position and held him still. 'Unless you calm down, Davy, I'll have no choice but to arrest you again.' He held the man still until the heat had gone out of his anger.

Becca attended to Joe, pressing a wad of tissues to his face. 'You should go to the hospital,' she advised him. 'That nose might be broken.'

Joe shook his head. 'I'm a pub landlord. It wouldn't be the first broken nose I've suffered. But I had nothing to do with the fire. I was in bed when it started, and I got up to help put it out.'

'Liar!' shouted Sid.

'Forget it,' said Joe. 'You two' – he levelled a finger at Davy and Sid – 'are banned from my pub.'

*

The Reverend Mark Taylor was just getting out of his car when Raven and Becca arrived at the church on the hill. The altercation in the village square had been defused at last, and both Davy and Joe had been persuaded to return to their homes. Yet now there was a punch-up to add to the growing list of resentments between the two families, not to mention the possibility that Joe really had set fire to the boat. There was enough animosity for almost anything to happen next, and Mike Fields had promised to keep a close watch on the situation.

'Chief Inspector Raven, wasn't it?' said Taylor. 'What brings you back to the church?'

Raven studied the vicar more closely than he had the first time. He wasn't wearing his cassock today, just a grey shirt with his white clerical collar. He was probably in his thirties, although his rapidly receding hairline made him look older. But there was a boyish look to his features, a shine to his eyes, as if the world he saw was brighter than Raven's. He moved with an eagerness that Raven instinctively distrusted.

'We'd like a word, please, vicar.' Raven cast his gaze around the churchyard, singling out the spot where Anna had been caught on camera in conversation with Taylor on the day she died. The churchyard made a tranquil setting, the lichen-stained graves and weathered stone crosses clustered beneath a canopy of trees. He could understand the attraction of taphophilia, if that was a word.

'Well, yes, all right then. Come with me to the vicarage.' Taylor retrieved a leather briefcase and locked the car door with a key. The vehicle was an ancient one, a Ford Focus that had seen better days. 'I've been in Fylingthorpe all morning,' he explained. 'Deathly dull parish matters.' He grimaced, inviting them to sympathise with his plight.

Raven thought he seemed rather jumpy. He was talking too much. Perhaps he had already guessed why the police had suddenly turned up on his doorstep. Raven followed him into a modest bungalow near to the church, holding the door open for Becca.

'Make yourselves comfortable in here.' The vicar indicated a study on the ground floor that looked onto the back garden. 'Be with you in a mo.'

The room was furnished with a couple of shabby armchairs that looked as if they had been picked up at a house clearance. A laptop computer sat on a desk surrounded by mounds of documents and manuscripts. Raven lifted a sheet of paper to study. It was a letter addressed to the church warden and went on for many pages. The Reverend Mark Taylor was clearly not a man of few words.

Raven peered out at the garden. It was mostly laid to lawn with a handful of neatly clipped shrubs. Like the house itself, it seemed rather suburban in comparison with the timeless beauty of the church and graveyard next door. But perhaps that was the intention – a clear separation between sacred and secular.

Yet as if to puncture that idea, the bookshelves against the wall were laden with different editions of the Bible and an assortment of books on prayer, meditations and reflections on the Psalms, as well as biographies of religious figures. A painting of Jesus adorned the wall above the fireplace.

Raven shuddered. He distrusted religiosity in all its forms. He wasn't an atheist as such, just a natural sceptic. But he disliked being reminded of the possibility – however remote – that he might one day burn in hell.

Mark Taylor returned, all smiles and bonhomie, as if he had read Raven's mind and was determined to show there would be no burning lakes of sulphur on his watch. 'Would you like a mug of tea? I won't have any myself, I've been drowning in tea all morning, but if you'd like an Earl Grey or –'

'–there's no need for tea,' said Raven. 'Please have a seat.'

The vicar sat down at his desk chair, swivelling it round to face them. His smile was beginning to flounder under the onslaught of Raven's steady rudeness, but he seemed steadfast in his desire to put on a brave face. 'So, what can I do for you?'

'We're here about the death of Anna Capstick. Again.'

'Ah yes,' said Taylor. 'I guessed as much. Is there any news with regard to that?'

'When we spoke to you on Sunday, you didn't mention you'd spoken to Anna the previous day.'

'No. I – ah...I didn't actually... That is...' the vicar's voice trailed off. The smile had definitely run its course now.

Raven waited, the best tactic when faced with silence. He didn't want to accuse a man of the cloth of lying, although this wouldn't be the first time. Better to give him a chance to come clean.

But the reverend tenaciously held his peace. He folded his hands in his lap and waited.

'Maybe this will help jog your memory, Reverend Taylor,' said Becca, presenting a copy of the photograph showing him with Anna.

The effect was dramatic. Mark Taylor took one look at the picture and seemed to collapse in on himself. 'What must you think of me? I can't deny it anymore or the cock will start crowing.'

'What happened?' asked Raven.

Taylor sighed and closed his eyes for a moment as if seeking divine guidance. 'Anna came to the church to look for me. It was on the Saturday.'

'What time was this?'

'About six o'clock in the evening. I was in the churchyard at the time, as you can see from the photograph.'

'What did she want?'

The vicar's features contorted, as if the mere act of saying it caused him pain. 'The short answer is money. The long answer is a bit more complicated than that.'

'We have time,' said Raven, settling back in his armchair. 'Go on.'

Taylor cleared his throat. 'You have to realise that this is extremely embarrassing for me. If this got out, well... my parishioners wouldn't be best pleased, let's put it that way. Can what I'm about to tell you stay between us, in confidence?'

'I can't promise anything,' said Raven. 'We are investigating a suspicious death.'

'Yes, yes, of course.' He seemed to come to a decision. 'Anna threatened to expose me.'

'For what?'

'It all began a long time ago, more than a year ago, before Anna left home. Her mother, Kate, started coming to see me. She was unhappy. More than unhappy, she was deeply dissatisfied with her marriage. Well, you've seen for yourselves what Davy's like.'

'Does he beat her?' asked Becca.

'He gets a bit rough from time to time, especially after he's had a few to drink. Which is most nights.'

And there it was. The same old story. The one Raven had lived through himself. A different man, a different woman, but the facts as banal and yet horrifying as ever. The unspoken hurt. The pain. The shame. Raven sat in silence as the vicar continued his account.

'Kate came to me seeking solace, or advice, or perhaps just a friendly ear. I encouraged her to go to the police, but she didn't want to. She was afraid of the consequences of taking action. She was really just looking for comfort, I think.'

'Comfort?' queried Becca. 'What kind of comfort did you offer her?'

Mark Taylor squirmed in his seat. 'Look, I'm not proud of what I did, in fact I'm deeply ashamed. In my defence, it only happened the once, and it was Kate who initiated it. The Lord knows we are all weak and fallible. I've asked God's forgiveness ever since.'

'You slept with her,' said Becca coldly. 'You abused your position of trust and exploited a vulnerable person in your care.'

The vicar looked like he'd been physically slapped. Perhaps he'd told himself a different story, one in which he wasn't so culpable. To his credit, he hung his head in shame. 'It was unconscionable of me.'

'And so, Anna came to you demanding money?' said Raven. It was hard to feel much sympathy for the Reverend Mark Taylor. Anna was desperate for money, and he had set himself up as a blackmail victim.

'She had somehow found out about me and Kate. I don't know how, perhaps Kate confided in her. Anyway, she tried to use it against me. She knew how things would go for me if word got out. I might face serious consequences. And if Davy ever heard about it, I'd be pulp. That possibility alone was enough for me to take her threat seriously.'

'What exactly did she demand?' asked Raven.

'She wanted money, right then and there. Cash. She asked for a thousand.'

'And what was your response?'

'Well, I was taken completely unawares. I had to think on my feet. I told her I couldn't possibly give her that much money, and in any case I didn't have more than a few pounds on me.' He showed his empty palms as if to illustrate his point. 'I mean, no one really uses cash these days, do they? The nearest bank machine is in Whitby. I gave her eighty quid, which is all I had in the house. She said she'd come back the following day but I warned her that I wasn't going to keep paying her. She said she'd see about that. Frankly, after she'd gone I was at my wit's end.'

'So it was convenient, then,' said Raven, 'that she didn't return the next day.'

The vicar's face paled, his expression one of absolute horror. 'But you can't think... I mean... you can't...' But it seemed that on this occasion, he was quite unable to find words to express his feelings.

CHAPTER 22

Liam was feeling flush. It was a nice sensation, one that he hadn't experienced in a long, long time. Both Ellie and Keith had given him money and he was going to pay off that greedy bastard Donovan Cross once and for all. Then he'd be free of his debts and able to visit the barber's without fear of getting his throat slit.

Not that he was ever going back to Yusuf's shop again.

Before setting off, he paused for a moment to admire his car, which he kept in the underground parking bay beneath Ellie's flat. A Chevrolet Corvette C7, Torch Red, it was his most cherished possession and his pride and joy, a symbol of everything he'd achieved. The Chevy was a masterpiece of style – a miracle of smooth curves and sharp angles. After clearing his first hundred grand profit in the property game, he'd had the car specially imported into the UK. Not many guys his age could boast of owning such a car.

Becca's boss had a nice set of wheels too. But Raven's German-made Beemer was more of a grand tourer, intended for eating up long journeys on the autobahn. The Chevy, by contrast, was an all-American muscle car, built for the track and made for pure performance. He started it up and experienced the same thrill as always at the animal roar of the six-litre supercharged V8 engine. Music for the soul.

It made him believe he could do anything, and on a day like this he knew he could.

On his way to Donovan's, he decided to call in at the house renovation to see how work was progressing. Barry should have started replacing and repairing the old timbers by now.

He stopped the car outside the grand building and looked up. Now that he had fresh funding, he could get the job back on track, complete the ruinously expensive structural work that had derailed the project, split the building into separate units and sell them on for a nice chunk of change. With Ellie and Keith on board, he might even be able to keep one of the apartments and rent it out at premium rates. Executive rental was the way to go.

He unlocked the door and went inside.

'Barry? Hello? Reggie? Anyone?'

It was uncannily quiet in the house. Normally Barry had his radio blaring, classic hits of the nineties livening up the workplace. Today, nothing. Only the echo of Liam's voice off the bare brick walls where the plaster had crumbled away. He climbed the stairs to the top floor, where the rotten old ceilings had been taken down, and peered up into the empty roof void.

There was no trace of Barry. Not even his ladder or his tools had been left behind. Celine Dion wasn't belting out one of her greatest hits, and the Backstreet Boys were conspicuously absent. What the hell was Liam paying his builder for if not to get on with the job? He whipped out his phone and dialled Barry's number.

'Where are you, mate?' he said as soon as Barry answered. 'I'm round at the house now and there's nothing happening. You were supposed to be making a start on those joists this week.'

'I'm doing a job in Cayton Bay,' said Barry. 'A kitchen

extension. They've been waiting for me to start for a while now. I said I'd fit them in while I had a little space in my schedule.'

Liam couldn't believe what he was hearing. 'Space? What space? You're supposed to be here. You know how much work needs doing on this place!'

There was an awkward pause, and in the silence Liam thought he could make out the vocal strains of Celine Dion proclaiming that her heart would go on. Then Barry said, 'I work where I know I'm going to get paid. I have bills to pay. And Reg too.'

Liam felt like he'd been punched in the gut. He had always paid Barry on time. Always. At least until this current job. And if things had slipped recently, it wasn't his fault. It was that bloody loan shark bleeding him dry.

'Mate, listen,' said Barry in a more conciliatory tone. 'I don't want any trouble. If you can ping me that thirty grand you owe me, I'll be back on the job in a couple of days, say one week tops.'

'A whole week? Do you know how much a delay like that will cost me?'

'Best I can do,' said Barry.

In the background, Celine was still singing about love lasting a lifetime, but all Liam could think of was the ominous mass of the approaching iceberg and the two miles of cold water immediately beneath him.

'I've got the money,' he said. 'I'll wire it to you now.'

'Ah, cheers, mate. Speak soon.' The line went dead.

Shit! Liam kicked the wall in frustration. He would have to hand over all his new money to Barry, leaving nothing for Donovan Cross. There'd be hell to pay, and he couldn't see a way out.

*

'We need to speak to Kate,' said Raven as soon as they were back in the BMW. 'I want to corroborate Mark Taylor's story and see if we can persuade her to open up about Davy.'

'Agreed,' said Becca. 'Do you think she will?'

Raven slid the car into drive and set off down the hill. 'We can't force her, but we can try our best.'

He knew from experience there were many reasons a woman might be unwilling to accuse her own husband or partner of abuse. Fear of retaliation, worries about how she would get by on her own, emotional dependence, concerns about not being believed. Many of the most vulnerable women had been emotionally undermined for years by their abusers. Building the bridge of trust necessary for Kate to speak frankly to the police could be a long haul, and Raven didn't have the time or the resources to embark on that journey. Hell, he shouldn't be here at all. Gillian's deadline to close the investigation into Anna's death had already expired.

Yet here he was.

He parked in his usual spot and walked with Becca to Kate's house. He was pleased to see that Davy and Sid were still moping over the wreckage of their boat and made no moves to cross the square.

'Do you have time to talk to us, Mrs Capstick?' he said when Kate answered the door. She looked tired and dishevelled. She was clearly deep in mourning for her daughter, and no doubt the previous night's fire hadn't helped. Who knew how Davy might have taken out his rage on her after the destruction of his boat? At least there were no fresh bruises on her arms.

She showed them into the front room and sat down at the table, hugging a baggy cardigan around her thin frame.

'How are you doing, Kate?' asked Becca. 'Is it all right if I call you Kate?'

Kate shrugged. 'Of course. I'm all right, I s'pose.'

'Do you have friends or family nearby who can offer you support?'

Kate's eyes gazed unseeingly at the flagstone floor. 'I have Sid and Davy.'

'Anyone else?' pressed Becca.

'I suppose there's Mark.'

It was the opening Raven had been hoping for. 'You mean Mark Taylor, the vicar?'

Kate nodded. 'He's a good man. I can talk to him.'

'That's good,' said Raven. 'We've actually just been to see him. In fact, he told us all about you.'

Kate shot him a scared look. 'What do you mean? What did he tell you?'

Becca bent forward encouragingly. 'What is it you think he may have said, Kate? Is there something you'd like to tell us?'

A shiver ran through her thin body. 'You know, don't you?' she said miserably. 'We had sex, but it were just the once and I'd hate him to get into any trouble over it. Davy mustn't find out. If he did–'

'What?' pushed Becca. 'What would Davy do? Would he hit you, Kate?'

But Kate was saying nothing more. She rocked back and forth, her lips pressed together.

'If Davy is abusing you,' pursued Becca, 'we can provide protection for you. There's no need to be afraid of him. Did he cause those bruises on your arm? Did he cut you with that knife?'

Kate's expression was resolute. 'No. He's a good husband. He's never done owt wrong.'

Becca looked over at Raven but they both knew it was hopeless. Kate wouldn't point the finger at Davy, even now.

'We'd like to ask some more questions about Anna, if you don't mind,' he said.

She nodded her assent.

'Were you aware that Anna had lost her job in London?'

Kate nodded. 'She told me about it when she came to the house. Said she'd got the sack. Said it weren't her fault, but there was nowt she could do.'

'What was her financial situation, in that case? Could she afford to stay in London, or is that why she returned home?'

'Dunno,' said Kate. 'Anna never told me much. If she were thinking about coming back to live here, she didn't mention it.'

'Did she ask you for money?' asked Raven.

Kate gave a hollow laugh. 'Well, she asked, but you can see for yourselves we haven't got owt.' She waved her hand around the sparsely furnished room. 'No point coming here for cash. She'd have been better off staying in London and saving her coach fare.'

Outside, Raven heard raised voices in the square. He went to the window and saw that Sid and Davy were engaged in a heated conversation with another villager. The topic of debate was, inevitably, the burning of the boat. Sid was loudly blaming Joe Hepworth for arson. Davy was calling the pub landlord a *fucking liar*.

'What do you know about the break-in at the pub on Monday night?' Raven asked Kate. Someone went into Connor's room and turned the place upside down. It's been suggested to us that Davy may have done it.'

He wasn't going to say that it was Connor's mother who had told them that, but Kate clearly had her own ideas. 'Sarah said that, did she? She's a right bitch, always stirring.'

'Why do you say that?'

Kate shrugged. 'It's just how she is. Some folk are made that way.'

The resentment between the two families ran deep and kept resurfacing. But Kate still hadn't answered Raven's question. 'So, could Davy have done it?' he asked.

She made no attempt to deny it. 'He might have. I can't vouch for him, if that's what you're asking.'

'What might he have been looking for?'

'No idea.'

'Anna's mobile phone is still missing.'

'Is it? I don't know anything about that.'

'Has Davy said anything about it to you?'

'No.'

Raven sighed. Was he going to get anything useful out of this visit? It seemed unlikely. 'What about the boat?' he asked. 'Davy accused Joe of setting it alight.'

Kate seemed to find that amusing. 'I'm sure Joe had nothing to do with it.'

'Who could have done it then?'

But once again she shook her head. 'Search me.'

Becca leaned forward one last time. 'Kate, if you're afraid of your husband, just tell us now. There's no need to be afraid. We can help you.'

Kate gave them a sad smile. 'You don't need to worry about me and Davy. Everything is just fine.'

Raven looked to Becca. There was nothing more they could do here. He stood up. 'Thank you, Mrs Capstick, and if you need anything, feel free to call us at any time.'

CHAPTER 23

'Ah, there you are, Tom. I was wondering what had happened to you.'

Raven had hoped to avoid meeting Gillian Ellis until he'd found out more about her possible involvement in the hit-and-run, but she nearly collided with him as he was making his way slowly up the stairs at Scarborough police station. His leg was almost back to normal after chasing Davy, but it liked to remind him every now and again how badly it had been treated and that it wouldn't stand for that kind of behaviour again.

'Just tying up some loose ends, ma'am.'

She greeted his remark with a glare. 'Not at Robin Hood's Bay, I hope. I thought that investigation was over. Accidental death.'

'There's been a case of suspected arson now too.'

'One for the Whitby constabulary, surely. So when will I have your report on the Anna Capstick death?'

'Be with you tomorrow morning, ma'am.' Raven had no intention of delivering any such report, but he needed to buy himself time, and agreeing to his boss's request was the easiest way to do that.

He hauled himself up the remaining flight of steps with the help of the banister and went to track down Becca. He found her in the tearoom. 'Got a minute? About that other matter?'

She followed him back to his office and pulled the door closed behind her. 'You're going to try Dinsdale, then?'

'Might as well. Want to come with me?'

'You bet.'

Raven wasn't surprised she was keen to witness the encounter. Everyone at the station knew that he and Dinsdale had been shadow boxing ever since Raven had arrived in Scarborough the previous year. At times, they had come within a razor's edge of exchanging physical blows. At others, they had found a way to cooperate. But even at the best of times, they had never fully worked in unison, and Raven found it galling that he needed to ask Dinsdale for help on a matter of such personal importance.

They found the older detective inspector in his office. 'What's this?' said Dinsdale, looking up crossly as Raven and Becca knocked and entered. 'A delegation?'

'Just wondering if you could help us with something, Derek?'

Dinsdale's eyes immediately narrowed in suspicion. 'Oh, you did, did you? And why do you think I would want to help you?'

'It'll only take a moment,' said Raven.

Dinsdale leaned back in his chair and patted his belly. 'Well, a moment is all I can spare. I'm a busy man, you know.'

'I'm sure you are, Derek. I won't waste your time.' Raven pulled out the vehicle repair form that he and Becca had recovered from the archive and placed the yellowing document on the desk.

Dinsdale immediately snatched it up to peruse. 'What's this about, then? Broken headlight? Cracked windscreen? This document is dated 1991! Are you having a laugh, Raven?'

'Not at all.' Raven eyed the man sullenly. He should

have known that Dinsdale would give him the runaround. 'I just wanted to know whose signature this is down the bottom.'

Dinsdale's eyes ran down the length of the form, stopping as soon as he encountered the first signature. 'Gillian Ellis? Is there something you're not telling me, Raven? I think you'd better explain yourself.'

Raven pursed his lips, struggling to restrain his rising sense of anger. Had this been an almighty error of judgement, coming to Dinsdale for help? He had half a mind to snatch the form back and walk away.

It was Becca who came to his help. 'It's not that signature we were interested in, Derek. It's the one below it, the countersignature.' She pointed helpfully to the illegible pen marks near the foot of the page.

Dinsdale cast a sulky glance at her, perhaps because she'd referred to him by his first name. He was precisely the sort of person to take offence at that, Becca being his junior. But his curiosity seemed to overcome his sense of pride and he slipped his reading glasses on and followed the direction of her finger.

'Ah, yes. I know exactly who that handwriting belongs to.'

'Well?' said Raven gruffly. 'Who?'

Dinsdale gave a thin smile and tossed the form back onto the desk. 'What's it worth, then, Raven?'

Raven could hardly believe his ears. 'What do you mean, what's it worth? You're supposed to be a colleague. Show some professionalism!'

But Dinsdale refused to be goaded. 'Colleagues, is it, Raven? Professionalism, you say? Well, something tells me you're not being straight. If you want my help, you'd best tell me what this form is all about, what Superintendent Ellis's name is doing on it, and what you're up to.'

Raven knew this had been a mistake. They should never have involved Dinsdale. 'I can't tell you what it's about,' he admitted. 'You're right, it's off the record.'

Dinsdale laughed. 'Are you sneaking around behind

Gillian's back, DCI Raven? And you too, DS Becca
Shawcross? I'd have thought better of you.'

'Are you going to help or not?' asked Raven. He'd had
just about enough of this.

'Depends what you can offer me in return.'

'What do you want?'

'A favour. Not now, but in the future. I'll come to you
when I need it.'

This had to be a bad idea. A blank cheque, that's what
Dinsdale was demanding. But what choice did Raven
have? 'Agreed,' he growled.

'Well then,' said Dinsdale, picking up the form again.
'1991. That *was* a long time ago. John Major was prime
minister. Operation *Desert Storm* liberated Kuwait from
Saddam Hussein. And a certain Vauxhall Cavalier got
itself into a bit of a scrape, it seems.'

'The signature, Derek?'

'A very familiar one, as it happens. I'd recognise that
anywhere. Chief Superintendent William Seagrim. Long
retired now.'

The name wasn't one that Raven recognised. 'Is he still
alive?'

'Just about, last I heard.'

'And where can we find him?'

Dinsdale scribbled an address on a Post-it note.

'Cheers, Derek,' said Raven. 'You've been very
helpful.'

'I have, haven't I?' gloated Dinsdale. 'So just be sure to
stick to your half of the bargain.'

★

Becca recognised the estate agent as soon as she got out of
her car. He'd shown her around other properties at the
beginning of the year when she was contemplating moving
out of her parents' bed and breakfast. That was just after
Sam had gone to Australia, and she had come to the
realisation that her life needed a new direction. Now she

needed to change course again. Dr Felicity Wainwright had advised her to live alone, and the attractions of that lifestyle were becoming obvious, but it was still a daunting step to take. It would be a lot more expensive than sharing the apartment with Ellie, but it might be worth it for her own peace of mind.

'Miss Shawcross, how lovely to meet you again.' He extended a hand. 'I do hope we can find somewhere you like this time.' So he remembered her. Back in February, he'd shown her round a flat that on paper was perfect in every respect – shiny new appliances, built-in wardrobes, a reserved parking space, just within budget – but it had left her cold. At first she hadn't been able to work out why she wasn't more excited, and then the reason had hit her like a thunderbolt. That flat didn't have a sea view.

This time was different.

The flat on Castle Terrace might not be as smart as the one she'd seen before, but it had a view to die for. Or so Becca hoped.

The agent handed her a sales brochure and invited her to follow him inside. 'Watch the stairs,' he cautioned. 'They're quite steep.'

The entrance wasn't very prepossessing. The hallway and stairs were badly lit and in need of a fresh coat of paint. Becca climbed the steps carefully, holding onto the banister. The narrow terraced house had been converted into three small flats, one on each floor. The flat in question was at the very top. A daily climb up these stairs would certainly help to get her in shape.

The agent opened the door to the flat and flicked the light switch. Nothing happened. 'Oh,' he mumbled, 'the bulb is missing.' He treated her to a forced smile. 'Obviously we'll make sure that's replaced before you move in.'

Before you move in. That was taking a lot for granted. First impressions weren't good.

He ushered her into the kitchen area, where fortunately the light did work. 'As you can see, the kitchen has everything.'

Becca peered around the cramped space with a growing sense of dismay. It had looked poky in the photographs. In real life it was miniscule. But at least the essentials were all present – a gas hob, a compact oven and an under-the-counter fridge. 'Is there a dishwasher?' she asked. But she knew without being told that the answer was no.

'Let's move on to the bathroom.' The agent pulled a cord to turn on the light, and a noisy extractor fan clattered into action, sounding like a helicopter about to take off. He raised his voice. 'In here, there's a shower over the bath and, well, pretty much everything you could want.' His smile was increasingly strained.

She peeked into the confined space with trepidation. 'Mmm,' she said. 'It's a bit tired.' The less time she spent in here, the better. 'I'd really like to take a look at the view.'

She gravitated to the window in the sitting room. It was a dormer window built into the sloping roof and, unlike everything else in the flat, looked new. She pushed open the top sash which tilted upwards and the bottom sash which moved outwards and suddenly she was standing on a makeshift balcony looking out across the South Bay.

She caught her breath.

The view was stunning. Below her, hugging the steep hillside, were the rooftops of Overton Terrace and, at the foot of the hill, the tall, narrow houses of Quay Street. Reaching out beyond them was the harbour with its lighthouse at the end of the pier. To her right, the Grand Hotel rose proudly above the South Sands. Directly opposite across the bay stood the spa buildings and rising above them the green hill of Oliver's Mount. The coastline curved in an elegant arc, stretching all the way to Flamborough Head. Gulls screeched and the music from the fairground rides at Luna Park floated towards her on the breeze. Becca breathed in the fresh, salty air and felt herself come alive. Standing here, she would be able to drink her morning tea while watching the waves roll across the bay beneath the ever-changing sky. The sea would be the first thing she saw in the morning and the last thing she saw at night.

'I'll take it,' she said.

★

Police Superintendent Brandon Holt spotted Donovan Cross's black Audi as soon as he pulled up at the top of Oliver's Mount opposite the café. He parked his Mercedes as far away from it as he could and set off in the direction of the war memorial. He had taken time out of his busy schedule to come here today and was acutely aware of the risk he was running. He couldn't afford to be seen with the likes of Donovan Cross. Any taint of association with the seedy loan shark could shatter his career into a million pieces. But this was an emergency and needs must.

He stopped when he reached the war memorial to admire the view across to the harbour and to pay his respects. His own grandfather's name was inscribed on one of the plaques at the foot of the cenotaph. Arthur Holt, died June 1944, Normandy. Twenty-eight years old. A hero.

The familiar figure of Donovan Cross appeared from around the side of the cenotaph, sporting tight designer jeans and a black leather jacket, a cigarette clamped between his lips. Holt's own lips curled in distaste at the sight of the man, strutting about like a gangster, his bald head brown despite the September haze. Self-importance oozed from his skin like grease. Characters like Donovan Cross thought they could do as they pleased, and to some extent they could. But only for as long as Brandon continued to provide him with protection.

Donovan tossed his cigarette aside and ground it into the stone at the base of the war memorial.

'Show some fucking respect,' said Brandon.

But the only response he got was a broad-shouldered shrug. 'You asked to meet?'

'We'll walk.' Brandon didn't want to hang around the

cenotaph with the likes of Cross. He set off around the large, flat plateau that formed the top of Oliver's Mount. It was a cold day and there was no one else about, but he wasn't going to take the chance of being spotted.

'You want to tell me what's going on?' said Donovan.

'Tell me what you know, first.'

Donovan slid a second cigarette out of his pocket and lit up, cupping his big hand around his lighter. 'Jackson went to Robin Hood's Bay last night to collect the goods. Only, the boat was on fire. Sid and Davy couldn't go out to meet the delivery vessel.'

'And the money?'

Donovan shrugged again in that infuriatingly arrogant manner of his. 'Jackson didn't hang around to find out.'

'Fucking brilliant,' said Brandon. 'So you're telling me that not only has our smuggling operation gone up in flames, but the goods are missing and the money could be anywhere.'

Donovan took a long drag on his cigarette and blew smoke into the wind. 'You promised it was safe now, Brandon. You said the investigation into the girl's death was over. Accidental death, you said.'

'That's what I heard.'

'So what went wrong?'

It was the question Brandon had come here to find out, but it seemed as if Donovan knew no more than he did. Or at least he was saying nothing. 'It could be that someone is targeting the smuggling operation. Or else Davy did something stupid and made an enemy in the village.'

Donovan blew more smoke from his nose. 'Davy can't open his big gob without making an enemy. He's a fucking liability.'

'Who else can we work with?' asked Brandon.

'No one we can find in a hurry. What's the old man going to say when he hears?'

Brandon gave Donovan a thin smile. Seagrim would probably have a fucking seizure when he found out what had happened. But the problem wasn't Seagrim, it was the higher-ups. They must never find out about this almighty clusterfuck. 'Don't worry about the old man,' he told Donovan. 'I run the show now, and don't forget it.'

They started walking back towards the war memorial. 'Do you reckon Sid and Davy set the boat alight themselves for the insurance money?' Donovan asked.

That was funny. Brandon gave a hearty laugh. 'That pair of gormless numpties have never had insurance. The fact is, the boat's gone and it's not coming back.'

Donovan ran a thick thumb across his smooth scalp. 'Look, if the problem is just the lack of a boat, then we could buy them a new one.'

'Don't be stupid,' said Brandon. 'That would leave a trail.' This was the problem dealing with numbskulls like Cross. 'The problem is not the bloody boat. The problem is Sid and Davy.' He turned to Donovan and jabbed his finger in his chest. 'You need to fix them before anything else goes wrong. I'm sure that Jackson knows what to do.'

CHAPTER 24

Raven looked up from his desk when Becca returned to the station from wherever she'd been. She had a noticeable spring in her step and a smile on her face. 'You're looking very pleased with yourself,' he told her.

'Just getting something sorted.'

Enigmatic. He waited for her to say more, but when she didn't, he stood up and lifted his coat off the hook on the door. 'I'm ready to knock off. If you're not doing anything special this evening, how would you like to pay a visit to retired Chief Superintendent William Seagrim?'

'Tonight? Absolutely.'

There was nothing more that Raven could do about the investigation into Anna's death. But there was definitely a way forward with the case of the hit-and-run. Dinsdale's revelation of a name opened up a fresh line of inquiry. Gillian Ellis may have been the one who took the Vauxhall Cavalier in for repair, but a senior officer had authorised it. Could this be the same officer who had shut down Lesley Cartwright's efforts to follow up the sighting of the car back in 1991? There was only one way to find out.

'Come on then,' said Raven. 'Let's get moving.'

Twenty minutes later they were ringing the doorbell of a house on Wheatcroft Avenue. This was the posh end of Scarborough, far from the fish and chips and amusement arcades of the old town. Far from the sands and the holidaymakers, but with a nice sea view over the cliffs. This was a land of broad, quiet streets lined with well-tended hedges and smooth, rolled lawns. Your neighbour here was likely to be a doctor or the senior manager of a local firm. Or perhaps a retired police superintendent.

The door was opened by a woman in a nurse's uniform. She looked them up and down before enquiring about the purpose of their visit. Raven showed his warrant card, yet still she seemed disinclined to let them cross the threshold. 'Chief Superintendent Seagrim's not a well man.'

'I'm afraid I have to insist,' said Raven. 'We're here on police business.' He had hoped to gain entry more informally but was prepared to use his rank and position if necessary.

The nurse seemed unimpressed by his credentials but conceded defeat eventually. 'Very well, my patient can probably manage a short visit. If you'd like to come this way.'

They followed her to a room at the back of the house that had been converted into a sick bay. Raven noted the hospital bed, oxygen tank and intravenous drip that had been set up to keep its occupant alive for as long as possible.

Raven hated hospitals, and this place had the look, feel and smell of one, even though it was masquerading as a dining room.

The nurse marched up to the bed. 'Two visitors for you,' she said to Seagrim, fussing over him, plumping his pillow and checking the drip. She turned to Raven. 'No more than twenty minutes.' Raven had no doubt she would keep them to the allotted time. She went out, closing the door behind her.

Now Raven looked properly at the man in the bed.

Seagrim was shrivelled, his face as lined and wrinkled as driftwood. His chest wheezed with every laboured breath, but his eyes were as sharp as a bird of prey. He scrutinised the newcomers with the sagacity that came from years of experience in the police force. Raven knew he was assessing them, trying to work out if they were friend or foe, honest or with criminal intent.

Becca went to stand by the window and Raven approached the bedside, taking the high-backed dining chair. 'Chief Superintendent Seagrim, thank you for seeing us. I'm Detective Chief Inspector Raven and this is my partner, Detective Sergeant Becca Shawcross. Do you mind if I sit?'

Seagrim waved a bony hand at the chair. 'You won't wear it out by sitting.' His voice was a hoarse whisper. 'I doubt this is a social call, so I presume you are here on official business?'

'Neither.' Raven wondered if Seagrim had any idea who he was. If so, he wasn't letting on.

'Ah, I see,' said Seagrim. His face contorted into a grimace, and Raven realised he was chuckling. He showed Raven a toothless grin. 'It's like that is it? This visit is off the record. What would your boss say to that? Who is your boss, by the way?'

'Detective Superintendent Gillian Ellis.'

'Ooh, she's a feisty one.' The effort of speaking made Seagrim cough, but he seemed to be enjoying the banter. Maybe the worst thing about his illness was the boredom. His nurse didn't look a whole lot of fun. 'I remember young Gillian in uniform. A fine woman.' Another coughing fit ensued and Raven waited patiently for it to die down. When he recovered his composure, Seagrim's mood seemed to have turned sour. 'What do you want with me?' he snapped.

Raven extracted the document from the folder he was carrying and showed it to Seagrim. 'Could you confirm that this is your signature?' He pointed to the scrawl at the bottom of the page.

Seagrim studied the paper eagerly, squinting at the signature. '1991. This is going back a bit. Vehicle repair request. Not the most interesting document ever to cross my desk, but it's my handwriting, sure enough. Never did win any prizes for calligraphy.' He clutched the paper tightly to his chest and levelled a hard stare at Raven. 'Why have you been digging around in the archives? On *unofficial* business, I might add.'

'As you can see from the form, this car had a broken headlight and a cracked windscreen. I want to know how it sustained that damage.'

'Cars get damaged all the time. What's special about this one?'

Raven felt sure that Seagrim knew perfectly well which car he was talking about and what had caused the damage. He was just playing for time. The allocated twenty minutes were ticking away. 'I believe that this car was involved in a fatal collision with a pedestrian two days before the repair was authorised. By you.'

Seagrim pushed himself up a little straighter in his bed. 'You believe? Is this how police work is done these days? What proof do you have?'

Raven shrugged. 'I'm still gathering evidence. The incident in question led to the death of a member of the public. I want to know who was driving the car. Was it Gillian?'

The old man's eyes glinted, but there was no mirth in them anymore. 'You expect me to remember that kind of detail from over thirty years ago? Why don't you just ask Gillian? Why don't you show her your *evidence*?'

Seagrim knew, Raven was certain of it. The old man was taunting him, in the knowledge that he had no evidence of anything. The police investigation into Raven's mother's death had been covered up and a witness statement put aside. The logbooks had been stolen. There was only this one scrap of paper, and it proved nothing.

Raven could feel his temper starting to rise. Seagrim was enjoying this game of cat and mouse. He glanced at

Becca who indicated with a downward gesture of her hand that he should stay calm.

Raven glared at the former chief superintendent, barely able to contain his fury. 'I'm asking you because it's your signature on the form.'

Seagrim shuddered and began to cough again. The bout was worse this time, shaking him from head to foot as he struggled to regain control over his own body. The nurse would be back any moment, Raven knew.

'The hit-and-run incident was investigated at the time,' Raven continued, 'and a witness reported a car speeding away. The registration plate in the witness statement confirms that this was the vehicle involved. But the lead was never followed up. A senior police officer ordered the inquiry to be dropped.'

'How unfortunate,' said Seagrim. The old man sank back into his bed, seeming exhausted by the exchange.

'Were you the senior officer in question?'

Seagrim shook his head. 'I need to rest now. You've worn me out.'

Raven knew he was being played. But short of shaking the truth out of the old man – which would probably finish him off once and for all – there was little he could do.

The door opened and the nurse bustled into the room. 'Whatever have you done to him? He looks exhausted!' She gave Raven a hard stare and put her hands on her hips.

Raven cast one last look over the patient in the bed. Seagrim was lying back, his eyes closed, his breath ragged. He looked like a harmless old man, yet Raven was convinced he was the officer who had blocked the investigation into his mother's death.

But there was no proof. Raven had come here for answers and had hit a brick wall.

'Well, it's been nice chatting about old times,' murmured Seagrim, his eyes still closed, his breathing short. 'And I'm sorry about that woman who was killed.'

'Woman?' Raven rose to his feet, scraping the dining chair back on the parquet floor. 'I never mentioned a woman, I said a member of the public. And I'll have that document back, if you don't mind.'

Seagrim kept hold of the form a while longer, before reluctantly letting it go. Raven snatched the precious scrap of evidence back.

There was nothing more he could do. Becca touched him lightly on the arm and he followed her out.

*

Becca had watched the exchange between Raven and Seagrim with growing concern that Raven might suddenly lose his temper and strike the old man. There was no doubt in her mind that Seagrim was hiding the truth and had enjoyed the little game he had played. Raven clearly thought the same. Leaving the house, he stormed down the garden path, and she hurried to catch up with him as he climbed into his car, slamming the door shut behind him. She eased herself into the passenger side and closed the door gently.

'The lying toad,' said Raven, hitting the steering wheel with the palm of his hand. 'I could have wrung his scrawny pathetic neck.'

'I'm glad you didn't. It wouldn't have helped.'

'It would have helped me!'

'Not for long.'

Perhaps this was the best way for her to assist him in his investigation. To keep him on a tether and prevent him from doing any damage to himself, or others. With the stakes so personal, there was a real danger he would take things too far.

He started the car.

'Wait,' said Becca. 'Let's talk this through.' Raven was a hazard behind the wheel at the best of times. She didn't want him driving in this condition or who knew what might happen.

He let out a long breath and switched off the ignition. Outside the car, dusk was gathering, yellow light spilling from the large bay windows of the houses. A black cat sidled past on the pavement. 'Okay. What do you suggest?'

'Seagrim clearly knows more than he's letting on, but the problem is we don't have proof to charge him with anything. The state he's in, he'd never stand trial anyway.'

Raven's grip tightened on the steering wheel. 'We'll find proof.'

'How? The only other person we can speak to is Gillian herself. But she's far too smart to incriminate herself, so the question is how to handle her.'

Surprisingly, Raven smiled at her. 'You leave Gillian to me.'

Becca was glad to.

CHAPTER 25

'Tom, you're in early today. Is something the matter?'

Rattled by his encounter with retired Chief Superintendent William Seagrim, Raven had slept badly, his sleep haunted by the malevolent spirit of the former police officer, taunting him over his mother's death and laying the blame squarely at Raven's feet. He had woken before first light, bathed in sweat. Leaving Quincey in Hannah's care, he had gone into work intent on confronting Gillian before the demands of the working day intruded. He found her seated behind her desk, enjoying a ground coffee from the machine in her office and perusing some early morning paperwork.

He slammed the incriminating repair form onto her desk. 'This is the matter.'

She picked it up and began to read. He had expected her to look at it in horror once she realised what it was, but instead she appeared baffled. 'A document signing a vehicle in for repair in' – her eyes slid to the date at the top – '1991. Why are you showing me this? A car went in for repairs. So what?' She removed her reading glasses and leaned back in her chair, regarding him closely.

He wondered if she had been forewarned by Seagrim. He should have anticipated that. 'It's not just any car. This car was involved in a road traffic accident in which a woman was killed.'

'What are you talking about, Tom?'

'You know damn well what I'm talking about!'

She narrowed her eyes like a cat. 'You'll have to enlighten me. And don't use that sort of language in my office. I don't like your tone, Tom.'

In his mind's eye he saw Becca telling him to stay calm. She would have handled this a lot more serenely than him. But sometimes there was good reason to get angry. 'This car killed my mother,' he said through gritted teeth. 'The registration number was noted by a witness, who gave it to the police, but the investigation was blocked by a senior officer. You signed the car in for repair two days after the incident took place. Chief Superintendent William Seagrim countersigned it.'

'I see,' said Gillian. 'And you think that I had something to do with this apparent cover-up?' Her face clouded over. 'Ah, you think I might have been the one behind the wheel. You think I killed your mother.' Her expression softened, to be replaced by a look of sympathy.

Raven studied her features – the quiver of her lips, the flicker of her eyelashes, the furrow of her brow – as if each subtle signal might offer insight into her thoughts. Was she playing with him as Seagrim had done? If she was, he would lose it entirely.

But all he saw in her face was honesty and compassion.

'I wasn't driving the car,' said Gillian. 'I was simply asked to take it in for repairs. And I swear I didn't know anything about it being involved in an accident. But I do know who was driving the car.'

Raven believed her. 'Who?' His mouth was so dry he could hardly speak.

'Police Superintendent Brandon Holt. Although back in 1991 he was still a lowly constable.'

'Holt?'

The news hit Raven like a punch to the gut. He remembered the officer he'd sat next to at the charity award dinner. *Call me Brandon.* He'd won an award for tackling drug crime. If Raven had known this was the man who had killed his mother, he would have stuffed that award down Brandon Holt's throat before cheerfully kicking the shit out of him.

'But, Tom…'

'What?'

'I can't prove it. You'll simply have to take my word for it.'

Raven snatched up the document. 'We'll see about that,' he said and stormed out of her office.

★

'What an amazing view,' said Jess, scrolling through the photos on the property website.

'Isn't it?' Becca was grateful that Jess had singled out her new flat's best feature and tactfully said nothing about the kitchen or bathroom.

'I'd love to live somewhere with a view of the harbour,' said Jess. 'All I can see from my window is the house on the other side of the street. When are you moving in?'

'As soon as I can,' said Becca, 'but the letting agency has to do a load of identity checks first.'

'To make sure you're not a criminal,' joked Jess, deadpan. 'Do you want me to put in a good word for you?'

Becca laughed. 'I'm hoping I won't need that.'

It felt good to share her news with someone. She hadn't mentioned anything to Ellie the previous night and by the time she'd gone to bed, doubts had started to creep in. She had lain awake for hours, worrying about her snap decision to move. Did she really want to live alone? Was it a good idea to live directly up the hill from Raven? Could she afford her own place? But hearing the positive comments from Jess, she felt the same thrill she'd experienced when the letting agent had shown her around. For all the flat's shortcomings, she would be free and independent and she would never get bored looking at that view.

The door to the incident room crashed open and Raven entered looking as if he was on the verge of exploding.

'What's got into him?' whispered Jess.

Becca said nothing, although she could hazard a good guess. Raven must have gone to his early morning showdown with Gillian. Judging from his air of barely contained anger, the encounter had not gone smoothly. Yet the fact that he was still here indicated that he hadn't completely lost it and been sacked for insubordination. Nor, presumably, had he just murdered the detective superintendent.

So that was all good.

He strode across the incident room, black coattails flying, and disappeared into his office. The door slammed shut behind him, the doorframe shaking.

'Whoa,' said Jess under her breath.

Becca counted to ten before knocking on the door and poking her head inside. 'All okay?'

He was standing with his back to her, glaring at the wall. 'Yeah, good,' he said without turning.

'You've spoken to Gillian?'

'Yep.'

She eased the door closed behind her so that Jess wouldn't overhear. 'What did she say?'

'She said she didn't do it.'

The news gave Becca a huge surge of relief, and she realised how much she'd been dreading hearing that Gillian Ellis was a killer. 'Well, that's good then.'

'Yes.' Yet every ounce of Raven's body language indicated the opposite.

Becca waited to see if anything further was forthcoming, but it seemed that he had said his piece. 'Shall I get everyone together for a briefing?' she asked.

'What?'

'The Anna Capstick case.'

He stared at her as if he had never heard Anna's name before.

'There's been a development,' she explained. 'I'll call the others. Team meeting in five.'

She made herself a mug of Yorkshire tea and a strong black coffee for Raven, although it was by no means certain he would put in an appearance. Jess and Tony took up seats in front of the whiteboard, waiting patiently.

Eventually Raven emerged from his office, still wearing his coat, a scowl darkening his features. 'All right, what's happening?'

'Jess has something to tell us.'

Jess looked uncertain, but Becca gave her an encouraging smile and she began to express her thoughts tentatively. 'There's something that's been bothering me about the case.'

Raven said nothing, so Becca nodded for Jess to continue.

'I've been thinking about Lexi's statement. I think she's tricked us.'

Now Raven started to pay attention. 'What makes you say that?'

'Lexi said that on Saturday night she walked back to the youth hostel along the beach. She told me she got back at about ten o'clock. But I felt that couldn't be right.'

'Why not?'

Jess was growing more excited as she got into her tale. 'Because of the times of the tides. At ten o'clock the beach would have been covered with water, just like when I walked from the Bay to Boggle Hole. I had to take the clifftop route, because the sand was underwater.'

Raven stared at her. 'Are you sure?'

'Jess is right,' said Becca. 'I double checked the times. At the time Lexi claimed to have walked back along the beach, there was no beach to walk on.'

It was obvious once Jess pointed it out. How had Becca and Raven missed such a glaring inconsistency in a witness statement? Had they been so preoccupied with tracking down the driver of the Vauxhall Cavalier that they failed to focus properly on the current investigation? That was unforgivable.

'We need to speak to Lexi again.' Becca looked to Raven, expecting him to take up the suggestion. Normally he would have been halfway out the door by now.

But today his reaction was subdued. 'All right,' he agreed. 'We'll go back to Boggle Hole.'

When they were in the BMW, she decided to have it out with him. 'I know you're disappointed after the meeting with Gillian. But if you've reached a dead end, you just have to accept that. You can't allow yourself to be distracted from the current investigation. You owe it to Anna to find out the truth.'

'I didn't reach a dead end.'

'What?'

'Gillian wasn't the driver of the car. But she told me who was.'

Becca gaped at him. 'And?'

'Police Superintendent Brandon Holt.'

'You're kidding.'

'No.' Raven hadn't yet started the car but he was gripping the steering wheel so tightly his knuckles were white.

'But Holt's a really big deal. He just won an award. He's one of the most senior officers on the North Yorkshire force.

'Not at the time of the accident he wasn't.'

'No, I suppose he wouldn't have been.'

'He was a constable, not long out of police college.'

Becca could feel the raw fury seething beneath Raven's rocky exterior. 'Raven–'

'When I get my hands on him–'

'No wait!' Becca had no wish to hear what Raven intended to do when he got his hands on Brandon Holt. 'I know you want to go after him. I know you need to get justice for your mum. But first we have to focus on Anna Capstick. You've waited over thirty years to find out who was driving that car. It will wait another day. We need to think before we do anything rash.'

He shot her a murderous look, but she held his gaze and he turned away. 'I'm sorry,' he said. 'You must think I'm a monster. I don't want justice, I want revenge.'

Becca looked out of the side window, wondering what she had got herself involved in. She didn't know if she could control Raven, but she knew she had to try.

CHAPTER 26

Raven knew that Becca was right – of course she was. He couldn't just barge into Brandon Holt's office and give him a bloody nose. Nor could he go in with a meat cleaver and slice open his throat.

That would be the wrong thing to do.

But Raven didn't want to do the *right* thing, he wanted to do what *felt* right, and those two things were a world apart.

He brooded silently over the problem as he drove back to Boggle Hole, but he was still no further along in his thinking by the time he reached the car park at the top of the hill. Becca seemed equally caught up in her own thoughts. She had said nothing to him since leaving Scarborough. Perhaps there was nothing more to say.

They left the M6 parked at the top of the cliff and took the long path down to the youth hostel. Raven eased his way down the steep slope, praying that Lexi wasn't about to do a runner when confronted. He hoped she was still staying at the youth hostel. He'd told her to stay put, but he wouldn't have been surprised if she'd already cleared off back to London.

Entering the youth hostel, they found Kevin Brighouse, the manager, on the reception desk. He gave them a dark look. 'Not more trouble, I hope. Have you come to speak to Rory? He's still upset after last time.'

'We don't need to bother Rory again, Mr Brighouse,' Raven assured him. 'We're here to talk to Lexi.'

'That one,' said Kevin with a groan. 'I'll be glad to see the back of her.'

'Causing trouble?' enquired Becca.

'Just generally stroppy.' He leaned across the counter. 'Between you and me, we're all fed up with her moping about. She hates it here. She's in her room now. She never goes out.'

They went to the room and found Lexi sitting cross-legged on the bed, slouched over her phone, scrolling aimlessly. She set the phone down and took her headphones off as soon as they entered. 'Can I go 'ome?' she said petulantly. 'There's nuffink to do 'ere. And that fackin' weirdo keeps giving me funny looks.'

Presumably the "weirdo" she was talking about was Rory. Raven closed the door to the room and leaned back against it. 'No, you can't go home. We have more questions for you. Some of the things you told us don't add up.'

Lexi's eyes narrowed. 'What fings?'

Raven didn't know if he had the patience to endure much more of Lexi's insolence. Although he'd spent a greater part of his life living in London, her whiny south London accent was grating on his nerves. In his current state, he didn't trust himself to conduct the interview with the necessary patience. Instead he nodded for Becca to take the lead.

She shot him a dirty look, but gamely took up the challenge. 'Lexi, when you spoke to our colleague, Jess, you told her that on Saturday night you got back to the youth hostel at around ten o'clock.'

Lexi cast a suspicious look in Becca's direction. 'That's wot I said, yeah.'

'And you also said that you walked back from Robin Hood's Bay across the beach. Is that correct?'

'You callin' me a liar now?'

'No, we're just trying to establish exactly what happened.'

Lexi held Becca's gaze, her face defiant. 'Well I didn't take the bleedin' bus, 'cause there ain't one round 'ere, in case you 'aven't noticed.'

Becca parried the remark deftly. 'Our query is about the route you took, Lexi, and the time. You're sure you got back here at ten?'

'Yeah. 'Bout ten.' Lexi suddenly sounded a lot less cocky. She dropped her gaze, studying a flap of loose skin on her finger.

'And which route did you take?'

'The beach, innit. Like wot I said. I even got my fackin' trainers soaked in the sea.'

'That,' said Raven, 'might be because the tide was already covering the beach by ten o'clock.'

Lexi's face darkened, a mutinous look spreading across her youthful features. 'All right, yeah, the tide was comin' in. I got halfway, then I 'ad to turn back. My trainers are still all covered in salt. Don't know if that's ever coming out.' She sounded indignant, as if she had never been to the seaside before and found the behaviour of the sea objectionable.

'So what did you do then?' asked Becca.

'Well I 'ad to take the path over the cliff, didn't I? Fackin' dangerous in the dark. No streetlights, innit? I could've been mugged or anyfink!'

Raven couldn't be bothered to point out that the likelihood of being mugged in Robin Hood's Bay was next to zero. 'So why did you lie to us, Lexi?'

She pulled furiously at the loose skintag but said nothing.

'Perhaps,' he suggested, 'the reason you lied about walking along the beach was to mislead us about the time you got back to the youth hostel? Can anyone vouch for when you returned?'

'Didn't see no one. There's never anyone about. Apart from that weirdo.'

'You mean Rory Gamble? Did Rory see you get back to Boggle Hole?'

'That's not wot I said.'

'All you've told us so far, Lexi, is a pack of lies.' Raven pointed to a black holdall that was half sticking out from under the bed. It hadn't been there when they'd searched the room on Sunday. 'What's this bag?'

A look of panic gripped the girl. 'What bag? That's nuffink!' She leaned over and stuffed the holdall out of sight.

At a sign from Raven, Becca bent down to retrieve it.

Lexi jumped off the bed as if she'd been stung. 'Oi! Don't touch that, you stupid cow!' She grabbed hold of the bag and held it to her chest.

Raven had reached his limit. He spoke his next words quietly, knowing that if he gave vent to his anger he was at risk of going ballistic. 'Lexi, either you can allow us to search the bag, or we can apply for a warrant and hold you at the police station until it's granted. It's your choice.'

His calm but firm speech had the desired effect. Lexi screwed her features into a sulky glower, then hurled the holdall onto the floor in disgust.

Becca unzipped it and looked inside.

It was full of cash. Rolls of banknotes tumbled out. There must have been thousands of pounds in there.

Lexi slumped, her resolve broken.

'I think you have some explaining to do,' said Raven sternly.

'All right, keep your 'air on.' She took a moment to compose herself. 'So, I wasn't lyin' much. I did walk along the beach at ten, only the tide was in and I 'ad to turn around. When I got back to Robin Hood's Bay, I saw Anna sneakin' about. She was carrying this bag and acting dead shifty. So I followed 'er and saw her give the bag to that weirdo.'

'Rory?' supplied Becca.

'Wotever. Anyway, I 'eard Anna tell 'im to keep it safe. She was coming for it later. So I followed 'im back 'ere and nicked it from 'is room when he was out. I would 'ave been back on the bus to London the next morning if Anna 'adn't gone and got 'erself killed.'

Raven studied the girl's features. The insolent spirit had crept back into her expression as she related her sordid tale. The discovery of the money under her bed seemed to have upset her more than the death of her friend.

'Where did Anna get the money from?' he asked. The amount was far in excess of the eighty pounds that Reverend Mark Taylor had paid her when she visited the church to blackmail him.

''Ow the 'ell should I know? Anna didn't tell me anyfink about no money. She didn't tell me anyfink.'

'But you thought it would be okay to take it for yourself.'

Lexi drew herself up straight and looked him in the eye. 'Don't see why not. That money didn't belong to that weirdo. Anna gave it to 'im, but it wasn't 'is to keep. And it didn't belong to Anna either.'

'How can you be certain of that?' asked Becca.

Lexi laughed. 'Are you for real? 'Cause this is dodgy cash innit. Anyone can see that. Anna never had nuffink. So wherever that money came from, it didn't belong to 'er.'

★

'You think Lexi's telling the truth now?' quizzed Raven. 'About how she came to be in possession of a bag of money?'

'Well,' said Becca, 'she admitted to stealing it from Rory's room, so unless she's hiding something even worse...'

'You think she may have been responsible for Anna's death?'

'We can't rule it out.'

'No.' Raven was grateful to Becca for rekindling his enthusiasm for the investigation. Just when he'd run out of time, run out of leads, and had found himself overwhelmed by the discovery that Brandon Holt had killed his mother, she had put him back on his feet, doing what he did best. His job. 'Do you mind staying with the cash while I speak to Rory? I'll get Kevin to bring you a nice strong cup of Yorkshire.'

Becca gave him a smile. 'You're speaking my language.'

The youth hostel manager was happy to oblige with a hot drink and a pastry, and he was also able to direct Raven in the direction of the kitchen lad. 'Rory's down on the beach. He often goes there after he's finished on breakfast duty. But go easy on him, eh? He's finding it hard coming to terms with Anna's death.'

'I will,' promised Raven. He headed off along the wet sand to where a lone figure stood on the shore, gazing out to sea through a pair of binoculars.

'Hello, Rory. Any boats out there today?'

The lad shook his head, giving Raven a backward glance before returning to his surveillance of the sea and sky. 'Not today.'

'Do you like boats then?'

'Not really. I like birds better. My favourite are the sandpipers. I like to watch them searching for food on the sands.'

Raven's knowledge of birdlife was minimal – he could tell a robin from a crow, and that was about it – but for a moment they contemplated the horizon together before he spoke again. 'Rory, on Saturday night, did Anna give you something to look after?'

The lad let the binoculars fall so that they swung on the leather strap around his neck. 'She told me not to tell anyone.' Raven could hear the panic rising in his voice. 'She made me promise.'

'It's all right,' Raven assured him. 'Anna wouldn't mind if you told me now. She'd want you to tell the truth wouldn't she?'

Rory nodded glumly.

'So what did she give you?'

Rory dug the toe of his shoes into the soft sand. 'A black bag. She asked me to look after it until she got back to the youth hostel. She said I had to be careful with it, that it was really important.'

'Do you remember what time it was when she gave you the bag?'

'Half past ten.'

'Did she tell you what was inside?'

'No, she told me not to open it.' He looked up and Raven could see fear in his eyes. 'But I did. I know that was wrong, but I couldn't stop myself. I looked inside and it was full of money, more than I've ever seen.'

'And what did you do with the money?'

'Just what Anna told me to. I hid the bag in my room. I thought it would be safe. But when I checked later, it was gone.' A tear welled up in one eye and ran down his cheek. 'I let Anna down. She trusted me to keep her money safe, and I lost it. I don't know where it is now. Will I get into trouble for losing it?'

'Don't worry about the money, Rory,' said Raven. 'We found it. It's safe.'

Rory visibly relaxed at the news, his shoulders softening. He wiped the tears from his eyes.

'Just one more question,' said Raven. 'Do you know where Anna got the money?'

Rory shook his head. 'She didn't tell me.' He lifted his binoculars to his eyes once more as a group of birds took noisily to the sky.

Raven left him to watch them.

CHAPTER 27

Brandon Holt sat down in the chair beside the bed, his nose wrinkling at the smell of sickness and decay. Seagrim looked wearier than ever today, his skin tinged with yellow, his cheekbones more pronounced as the flesh caved in. The old man was fading fast. Holt didn't think these visits would go on much longer.

'There's been a hiccup at Robin Hood's Bay. Nothing to worry about, I've got things under control.' When Seagrim said nothing, Holt continued. 'The boat burnt down. Nothing left of it except a pile of charred wood and ash.'

Seagrim's dry, cracked lips moved and Holt strained to hear his words. 'Arson? Who did it?'

'We're not sure at the moment, but it doesn't look like it's connected with the operation. Most likely, Davy and Sid made one too many enemies. They've become a liability, those two. First the dead girl. Now the burnt boat. We can do better than work with those clowns. I've asked Donovan to take care of them.'

Seagrim nodded but didn't ask what "taking care of them" might entail. Some questions were best left unasked.

Holt wondered whether the old man was still interested, now that he was on the verge of meeting his maker. Perhaps his attention was fixed on somewhere over the horizon, a place that could only be seen by those approaching life's finishing line.

He was about to leave when Seagrim suddenly sprang into life. His bony hand seized hold of Holt's wrist with an iron grip. 'We've got another problem,' he rasped.

'What?'

'DCI Raven was here yesterday with his pretty little sergeant, DS Becca Shawcross.'

'Raven? What did he want?' Holt hadn't liked the new DCI when he'd met him at the charity dinner. Too serious by half. Worse, a teetotaller. How could you trust a man who didn't enjoy a drink now and then? And what business could he and his sergeant possibly have with Seagrim?

Seagrim chuckled. 'He showed me a document. A vehicle repair form relating to a certain Vauxhall Cavalier. Don't know how he got hold of it, but bloody good detective work.'

Holt didn't need to ask which Vauxhall Cavalier Raven was interested in. He felt his heart contract. 'I thought you said you'd destroyed all the documentation.'

'Must have missed that one,' said Seagrim with the carelessness of one who had nothing left to lose.

'For fuck's sake!' Holt could have throttled the old man there and then. A pillow over the face and no one would be any the wiser. Only the tread of Nurse Bradshaw in the hallway outside stayed his hand. 'How much does he know?'

'Not so much. He appears to be under the impression that Gillian Ellis was the driver.' Seagrim seemed to find this hilarious but his croaky laugh soon turned into a hacking cough. The old man's chest shuddered as a series of harsh barks clawed their way up from his lungs. His face tightened and his frail shoulders shook until eventually he slumped back, exhausted.

Holt looked away in revulsion. He was beyond caring about his former boss and was simply relieved to hear that Raven was on the wrong trail. More than relieved. Delighted. Gillian Ellis had always looked down on him, as if belonging to CID gave her the right to disdain her former colleagues in uniform.

He stood up. 'Don't worry about Raven. I'll keep a watch on him.'

But Seagrim's eyes had already closed. He made no response as Holt took his leave.

*

'I can only think of one place where Anna could have got the money,' Raven told Becca once the bag of cash had been safely taken back to Scarborough police station and he had briefed her on his conversation with Rory Gamble. 'Rory says she gave him the bag to take care of before going to the pub, so she couldn't have got it from Joe or Connor Hepworth. And the vicar claimed he only gave her eighty quid. So that leaves–'

'–Sid or Davy,' concluded Becca. 'What were they doing with that kind of cash?'

'Up to no good, I'll wager.' Raven didn't know what exactly, but it would come as no surprise to learn that Sid and Davy were caught up in some unlawful activity. How had Davy described the way they earned a living? *Bit o' fishing, bit o' tourism, bit o' this and that.*

The blackened hull of the boat still stood in the village square when Raven and Becca got out of the car. Had Davy and Sid burned it themselves to destroy evidence?

Kate answered the door when Raven rapped on it. She was a mess. Dark rings circled her eyes and her hair hung lank and unwashed. She seemed lost inside the too-large cardigan she hugged around herself.

'We're looking for Davy and Sid,' said Raven.

'They're not here.'

'May we come in?' If they could speak to Kate on her

own they might stand a chance of getting to the bottom of what was going on.

She nodded and they followed her into the front room. The disorder and chaos only seemed to be getting worse. Grey ash from the burnt boat had been trodden into the floor. Dirty plates and used mugs were piled up on the table. Kate pushed them aside and took a seat in her usual place.

'The first time we spoke to you, Kate,' said Becca, 'you told us that Anna came to see you on Saturday at around one o'clock in the afternoon. Did you see her again that day?'

Kate's hands began to tremble and she concealed them beneath the table. 'Anna came back later,' she admitted, 'just to say goodbye.'

'At what time?'

'Her thin shoulders shrugged. 'Not sure. Davy and Sid were down the pub, so it must have been late that evening.'

'Around ten o'clock perhaps?'

'That sounds about right.' A big fly launched itself lazily from the dirty dishes and settled on the wall behind her.

Becca continued, her voice firm but friendly. 'Why didn't you tell us about that earlier, Kate?'

She shrugged again. 'Because we argued, me and Anna. She asked for money again, and I told her we didn't have any.'

The fly began buzzing around the room and Raven swatted it away. 'Did Anna ask for money, or did she demand it?' he asked Kate.

Kate cast him a mournful glance. 'Well, you already know about me and Mark. Anna said she'd tell Davy if I didn't give her some cash. I said I didn't have any to give her.'

'Really?' said Raven.

Kate started. 'What do you mean?'

Becca took up the thread. 'Kate, when Anna left the house, did she take anything with her?'

'Like what?'

'A black holdall, for example.'

Kate was nearly ready to break, Raven could tell. She glanced warily between him and Becca as if trying to work out what the detectives already knew. Raven decided it best to tell her. 'Shortly after Anna left here on Saturday night, she handed a bag of money to someone for safekeeping. Quite a considerable amount of money, in fact. Where did that come from?'

'Oh God.' Kate bit her lower lip. Tears sprang into her eyes and she brushed them away furiously with the sleeve of her cardigan. 'Anna stole the money. It was hidden in the hollow where the old kitchen stove used to be. She knew we used to keep money in there. I didn't say anything before because I was scared of what Dad and Davy might do.'

'Where did the money come from?' asked Raven.

Kate had calmed down now. She seemed almost relieved to be talking. 'Dad and Davy, they do a bit of extra business on the side. You've got to understand, there's no money in fishing these days and the tourist business is seasonal. So they've got a sideline. There's a contact – I don't know his name – but he brings them the money and they go out on the boat and bring stuff back to shore for collection.'

'What kind of stuff?'

Kate shrugged. 'I don't know. They never bring anything into the house. I wouldn't allow it.'

Raven wasn't so sure that Kate had much say in the matter. Sid and Davy seemed to do pretty much as they liked in this house. But the "stuff" in question was obviously contraband. Stolen goods, drugs, firearms, who knew how deep Sid and Davy had got in their criminal venture? Raven had uncovered much more than a suspicious death.

He said, 'What happened when Sid and Davy got back from the pub? They must have discovered that the money was missing?'

Kate nodded. 'I had to tell them what happened. Davy went out looking for her, but he didn't find her.'

'Didn't he?' Raven could already picture the scenario. Sid and Davy rolling home drunk and finding that Anna had stolen the money. Davy setting off along the clifftop path and catching up with her just before she reached Boggle Hole. But Anna had already given the money to Rory for safekeeping. Perhaps Davy hadn't intended to kill his daughter, but a violent shove might easily have sent her tumbling down the slippery steps leading to the cove. If she had struck her head on a rock...

And now Raven guessed what Davy had been searching for in Connor's room. The money. In that case he would have gone away empty-handed. By then, the black holdall was hidden beneath Lexi Greene's bunk bed in the youth hostel. What a mess!

'Where are Sid and Davy now?' asked Raven. 'It's best to be honest with us.'

Kate gave a weary shrug, no longer seeming to care what happened next. 'Dad's probably in the pub up the road. But I don't know where Davy is. He's done a runner.'

CHAPTER 28

There was nothing else for it. Liam was going to have to try his luck with Donovan Cross. Whatever else Donovan was – and whatever dubious methods he employed – he was an intelligent businessman who could surely be persuaded to see sense.

The money that Ellie and her dad had invested into Liam's business had gone straight into the bank account of Barry Hardcastle. But if Liam didn't keep his builder sweet, the work would never get finished and he would never make any of his money back. If that happened, no one, least of all Donovan Cross, would get paid. It stood to reason that you had to see a project through to the end before you could reap the rewards of your investment.

He felt sure that Donovan would cut him some slack once he had laid all his cards on the table.

Liam parked his Corvette in front of Donovan's home on Queen Margaret's Road. The mock-Tudor detached house at the foot of Oliver's Mount was huge and its gardens were immaculate. Donovan must be employing a whole team of gardeners to keep the lawn and flowerbeds looking like that. Well, he could afford to, given the outrageous interest rates he charged. The Porsche 911 on the driveway spoke of the kind of money that the profession of loan sharking could amass, and Liam happened to know that the bright red sports car belonged to Mrs Cross, a peroxide blonde who had once worked as a dancer at a club in town called the *Mayfair*. Donovan's own car was no less shabby – a black Audi RS7 Sportback parked proudly in front of the double garage.

Liam walked around the cars and rang the doorbell.

The door was answered by Mrs Cross. Despite the chilly weather, she was dressed in a thin top that revealed a great deal of tanned skin. Liam tried to not let his gaze linger on her well-displayed curves. She studied him with curiosity, then after a moment her red lips parted in recognition. 'It's Liam, isn't it? Have you come to see Donny?'

Donny. That was a cute name for her menacing brute of a husband. 'Donny, that's right. Is he in?'

'Come on through. He's in the kitchen.'

Sure enough, Donovan was in his enormous kitchen, an ocean of polished wood and black-and-gold marble, helping himself to a snack out of a fridge that was at least as big as the ones they had at the local supermarket. He broke into a broad smile as Liam entered. 'What can I do for you today, Liam my good man?'

'Um...' Liam glanced awkwardly at Mrs Cross. She wasn't exactly helping him to focus on the task in hand and he could hardly break his bad news to Donovan in her presence.

Donovan snapped his fingers rudely. 'Darling, leave us men to talk business, will you?'

She was evidently used to being dismissed in such a way. Giving a brittle smile she withdrew, leaving Liam in the lion's den.

Donovan offered him a plate piled high with a mountain of sausages. 'Fancy a bite to eat? These are made from wild boar with heritage apples. Or were they rabbit with juniper berries?' He scratched his bald head.

'Whatever they are, I've never tasted anything like them. Amazing.'

Liam shook his head politely.

'No? Your loss.' Donovan shrugged and grabbed two for himself, returning the remainder to the safekeeping of the fridge. 'Let's hear what you have to say then.' He bit off half a sausage, his jaws working furiously as he began to chew.

'It's about the repayment schedule,' said Liam.

Donovan's eyes narrowed, his jaws continuing to work at the sausage. 'I hope it's not bad news, Liam. I don't handle bad news well. It tends to spoil my appetite.'

'It's not bad news,' said Liam hurriedly. 'More a case of an opportunity. But it will require some patience.'

'I'm not good at patience either. It's not one of my natural strengths.' Donovan placed the second sausage on a chopping board on the breakfast bar and wiped his greasy fingers on a linen napkin. 'Sounds like you've hit a roadblock with your repayment schedule. I do hope not.'

'It's not a roadblock, just a diversion.' Liam attempted a grin, knowing how weak he sounded. 'The thing is, I've just had to pay my builder a shedload of money – you wouldn't believe how much those guys charge these days – well, maybe you would, you've obviously had a lot of work done here yourself' – he took a deep breath and plunged into what he'd come to say – 'I can't make the next repayment by the end of this week. It's simply impossible. But I can assure you that–' He trailed off when he saw Donovan's expression harden.

The loan shark's mouth drew tight. 'Oh dear. Oh deary me. That is unfortunate. And I was hoping you'd come here today to bring me some money.' He reached for the handle of a kitchen knife and drew the blade from its wooden block. 'How's that lovely girlfriend of yours by the way? Ellie, isn't it? Pretty name. Pretty girl.'

'What?' Liam felt his blood run cold. 'What's this got to do with her?' How did Donovan even know Ellie's name? Had he been keeping tabs on his personal life? His friends and relatives?

Donovan twirled the knife idly in his stubby fingers. 'It would be a shame if anything unpleasant happened to her, wouldn't it?'

'Don't you dare hurt Ellie!' said Liam, his voice raised in anger. But everything he knew about Donovan suggested that the man would dare anything. And if not him, then his thuggish henchman.

Liam cursed his own stupidity, wishing he'd never come here today, wishing he'd never even heard the name of Donovan Cross. He'd been wrong about the loan shark. He wasn't a man you could reason with. He was a lunatic.

Donovan eyed him with the dead-eyed stare of a psychopath. 'It needn't come to that. I have a proposal for you.'

'Oh yes?' Liam listened sceptically. He didn't trust Donovan as far as he could throw him. Which was no distance at all, given the size of the bruiser.

'That car of yours, the Corvette. How about I take it from you as collateral, in lieu of interest payments? You'll still owe me the principal amount of the loan, but it'll be interest-free going forward. You can pay it off when your building project comes good.'

Liam spluttered. Donovan was going to take his car? It was an outrage, but what choice did he have? He couldn't pay the interest and he couldn't risk anything happening to Ellie.

Donovan took a bite of the second sausage. 'Is that a deal then?'

Liam nodded. His mouth was too dry to speak.

Donovan slid the knife back into its block.

Liam would have liked to punch him in the teeth. He knew he'd lost. He'd been backed into a corner. He slammed the car keys down on the kitchen worktop and headed for the door.

'There's a bus stop at the end of the road,' called Donovan as he left.

Liam couldn't bear to look at the gleaming bodywork

of the Corvette as he walked down the drive away from the house. He felt as if he was abandoning an old friend.

Worse. It was like he'd lost a part of himself.

He set off in search of the bus stop, licking his wounds. He had never been so humiliated, not since he'd been bullied at school and had vowed to show those arseholes by making something of himself. He'd done that – the bullies in question were now either working dead-end jobs or behind bars – and he'd built a thriving business.

Now everything he'd worked for was being taken from him. He may have freed himself from the spiralling burden of interest payments, but that still left the original loan and it was only a matter of time before Donovan started pestering him for that. As he waited for the bus, a feeling of utter loathing took hold of him, beginning in his gut and spreading to the tips of his fingers and toes. He now understood at a deep, visceral level what could drive a person to commit murder.

*

After leaving Kate at the house, Raven phoned Tony. 'Davy Capstick's done a runner,' he explained. 'I think he went in pursuit of Anna on Saturday night, looking for a bag of money that she had stolen from the family home. But Anna had already passed the bag into Rory's hands for safekeeping and when Davy didn't find it on her, things turned nasty. At least that's one explanation for what happened.'

'So what do you want me to do, sir?'

'Put out an alert for Davy's immediate arrest. I don't know where he's gone, but he doesn't have access to a car, and he can't have much cash on him either. According to Kate, he doesn't have a passport, so he won't get far. My guess is he's gone into hiding somewhere in the locality.'

'All right, sir. I'll get a trace on his phone and notify all forces in the area to arrest him on sight.'

'Thanks, Tony.' Raven ended the call and turned to

Becca. 'Let's see if we can track Sid down. It shouldn't take long. There can't be many pubs in Robin Hood's Bay.'

They were back on the square, close to the burned boat. The derelict vessel had become a draw for spectators, much like a shipwreck in former times. Crowds stopped to gawp at the destruction and pose for selfies in front of it.

Raven set off up the hill, leaving his car at the bottom. 'I couldn't live here,' he complained. 'This hill would kill me.'

'A bit more walking might do you good,' said Becca. 'Quincey's been good for you. He gets you out more.'

At the mention of his dog, Raven felt a stab of guilt. He'd abandoned both Quincey and Hannah, focusing all his attention on Robin Hood's Bay and the question of who was driving the Vauxhall Cavalier the night his mother was killed. He'd hardly seen either of them in days. When this was over, he would make it up to both of them.

As Raven had predicted, there weren't that many pubs to choose from in Robin Hood's Bay. They found Sid in the first one they entered, sitting on his own in the corner, one empty beer glass on the table and another half empty in his hand. He looked older and frailer than when they'd met him the first time. He regarded Raven and Becca with a doleful expression, as if he'd been expecting them but was disappointed they'd arrived so soon.

'If you don't mind, I'll just finish this,' he said, lifting the glass to his lips and taking a sip.

Raven pulled up a stool and sat down.

'Come to arrest me?' asked Sid. 'Our Kate just phoned. Told me what she'd told you. Silly cow. There was no need to go blabbing about all our doings.'

'She was just telling the truth,' said Raven. 'It would have been much better if everyone had told the truth from the start. We're looking for Davy. Any idea where he might be?'

Sid puffed out his cheeks and exhaled loudly through his mouth. 'Fact is, I don't know and I care even less. He hasn't turned out to be the son-in-law I hoped for when he married our Kate.' He downed the rest of his pint, wiping his mouth with the back of his hand. 'All right, let's get this over with.'

Raven stood up. 'Sid Sutcliffe, I'm arresting you on suspicion of the improper importation of goods. You do not have to say anything, but it may harm your defence–'

'Blimey,' interrupted Sid. 'Is that what you lot call it? Improper importation of goods? In my day, we just called it smuggling.'

CHAPTER 29

It was late afternoon by the time Sid Sutcliffe had been brought back to Scarborough police station, processed and installed in one of the interview rooms where he now sat with a plastic cup of rapidly cooling tea in front of him. The atmosphere in the room was heavy. Sid's breath reeked of beer, but Raven was satisfied that the man was sober enough to be questioned. A hardened fisherman like him could no doubt hold his drink. There was a lot of ground to cover and Raven didn't want to waste time. The accused had declined a lawyer, muttering that he "didn't trust 'em." Raven was more than happy to proceed on that basis. They'd get on a lot quicker without one.

After reading him his rights, he began the interview. Becca sat beside him, silently observing.

'Tell me about the smuggling, Sid. Let's start with your involvement in the operation.'

'Who says I'm involved?' When the old man spoke he revealed yellowed teeth with several gaps.

'Your daughter, for one,' said Raven. 'Come on, Sid. We all know the game's up. Let's not mess about any longer.'

'Fair point,' said Sid. 'So, aye, I do a bit o' smuggling from time to time. A man has to earn a crust somehow.'

'Do you and Davy work together?'

'I like to keep things in the family,' said Sid, flashing a quick grin.

'What kind of goods do you smuggle?'

'I can't rightly say. They come in sealed boxes. I just collect 'em and pass 'em on.'

Raven couldn't say he was too surprised to hear that. If, as he suspected, Sid and Davy's role was simply to pick up goods from an incoming boat and bring them back to shore, there was no need for them to know what was being smuggled. By keeping the boxes sealed, there was less risk of pilfering, by Sid or anyone else along the chain. 'But you must have some ideas? You're not a stupid man, are you?'

Sid smarted at the implied put-down. 'I reckon I'm smart enough.'

'So what's inside the boxes?'

'Drugs, I reckon. But I can't say what sort. That's not my business and I don't want to know.'

'You just take the money, eh?' said Raven. 'Never mind the consequences?'

Sid folded his arms across his chest. 'A man has to put bread on the table for his family. It isn't my problem if some wazzock wants to snort summat or stick a needle in their arm.'

Raven decided to let it go. There was nothing to be gained at this stage by provoking the old man. 'So tell me how it works. What's your role?'

Sid took a sip of cold tea and instantly looked like he regretted it. He pushed the half-empty cup away. 'Me and Davy get a heads-up when a delivery is on its way. A courier brings us cash, and we go out to meet the incoming boat. We give 'em the money, they hand over the boxes and we bring 'em back to shore.'

'And then what?'

'The courier returns, we give him the goods and we get our payment.'

'So where do the boats come from?' asked Raven.

Sid shrugged. 'Nobody tells us. But they're foreign, I can tell you that much.'

'Polish?' queried Raven, recalling Davy's brand of cigarettes.

'Could be. Summat like that.'

The old man was cooperating but wasn't exactly being generous with his answers. If he could be believed, he and Davy were nothing more than the connecting link between a foreign gang and their British counterparts. Their main qualification for the job was that they owned a boat. Or used to.

'So who is the courier, Sid? Is it always the same person?'

Sid ran a hand down his unshaven chin, making a rasping noise. 'You can't expect me to start naming names.'

'Okay,' said Raven, sitting back and assessing his opponent. 'Let me guess how this works and you can tell me if I'm on the right track. I'd say that you and Davy aren't the big shots. You do the grunt work and other people reap the rewards. Am I right?'

A flicker of interest in Sid's eyes encouraged Raven to continue.

'What do you get in return for all your hard work? A small cut of the profits? Some packets of cigarettes? Hardly seems fair, does it?'

'Life's never fair,' said Sid. 'Only a fool expects it to be.'

Raven didn't allow himself to be deflected. 'But then disaster struck. The money the courier had given you, which was supposed to be the payment for the next shipment, was taken by Anna. You had no way of receiving the delivery of goods as planned. Panic set in. Davy went out looking for her but he came back empty-handed. He even ransacked Connor's room at the Waterfront, but he couldn't find the money.'

Sid said nothing but he didn't contradict a word of

Raven's story.

'And now things have taken an even worse turn. Someone set your boat alight and the entire smuggling operation has gone up in flames. Literally. You're going to be in deep trouble with whoever is running this show.' Raven leaned forward. 'Give us some names and we can protect you.'

'No you can't,' Sid shot back, his voice full of scorn. 'You don't know who you're dealing with.'

'Not if you won't tell us.'

But it was no use. Sid crossed his arms and refused to comment, turning his head away. Raven decided it was time for a change of direction.

'Let's talk about Anna, then. She came back to Robin Hood's Bay because she'd lost her job in London and was desperate for money.'

'Don't know why she bothered,' grumbled Sid. 'She knew we had nowt.'

'But that wasn't true, was it? You had the money from the courier and Anna knew where to find it. When Kate refused to give her anything, she took what she needed and fled. Is that what got her killed, Sid? Your own granddaughter died because of your smuggling operation?'

'How dare you!' said Sid.

But Raven pressed on relentlessly. 'Did Davy do it? When he went out looking for Anna on Saturday night, did he take things too far? Was the money more important than his own daughter's life?'

A shudder passed through the old man's body. 'I don't know.'

Raven dropped his voice, adopting a more sympathetic tone. 'What don't you know, Sid?'

'I don't know what Davy did that night. He were in a right state when he found out the money were gone. Kate were saying nowt at first, but he shook the story out of her eventually. Then he went out looking for Anna. He were gone for about half an hour. When he got back, he said there were no sign of her. But I knew summat didn't add up. Then the next day, I heard she were dead.' He began to sob, a single tear running down his wrinkled face.

Raven exchanged a glance with Becca. Here it was. They were on the cusp of discovering the truth.

'Sid,' said Becca, 'is Davy a violent man? Do you believe he's capable of killing someone?'

The old man looked crushed. 'Aye, he's got a temper in him, especially when he's the worse for drink. If someone crosses him...'

'Do you think he killed Anna?'

Sid shook his head slowly. 'I don't know. He told me he never saw her, but...'

'But what?'

'He were gone for over half an hour. How could he not have seen her? She never made it as far as the youth hostel, did she?'

'No,' said Becca gently. 'We believe that Anna met her death on the Cleveland Way just as it descends into Boggle Hole.'

'Then Davy must have seen her,' said Sid, almost as if he were speaking to himself. 'That's the way he walked, along the clifftop path. Dead or alive, he must have seen her.'

Raven left Becca to continue. She seemed to have a knack of coaxing information out of the gruff old fisherman.

'Sid,' she said, 'has Davy ever been violent towards Kate?'

Now that Sid had come clean about the events of Saturday night, his previous reluctance to incriminate his son-in-law appeared to have evaporated. 'Aye.'

'Tell me about it.'

The old man looked very tired under the harsh lights of the interview room. He worked his stubbled jaw from side to side as he mulled over what to say. 'Truth be told, Davy's been nowt but a disappointment all round. Perhaps it's my own fault. When I took him on, I wanted to see the good in him. I encouraged our Kate to take him as a husband. I don't know if she ever loved him, but she did as I asked. But I don't think she's led a happy life.'

'What did Davy do to her?'

'I can't say I know it all,' said Sid. 'Kate keeps tight-lipped and Davy won't talk, but I'm not blind, even if my eyes aren't as strong as they used to be. When he's had a few to drink, he's quick to lash out. It doesn't take much to provoke him. I've never seen him strike her, but I've seen the bruises afterwards.'

Becca's face was like a stone. 'Has there been anything worse than bruises, Sid?'

The old man hung his head and let out another sob. 'He used a knife on her once, I'm sure of it. She said nowt of course, and when I challenged him, he denied it. But I know what I know.'

'Why didn't you report this?' asked Becca quietly. 'You could have gone to the police at any time.'

Sid swung his head from side to side. 'We keep it in the family. That's always been our way.'

Raven had heard enough. 'Where is Davy now?'

'I wish I knew.' Sid looked him directly in the eye and Raven believed him. Sid had nothing to profit now by protecting his son-in-law.

There was one more thing on Raven's mind. 'Tell me, Sid, when did you first get involved in the smuggling business?'

The old fisherman was suddenly on his guard again. 'I don't rightly remember.'

'Ten years? Twenty? Longer? Was Davy your only partner in the business?'

Sid narrowed his eyes. 'I don't know what you're getting at.'

'It's a simple enough question. Were you already involved with the smuggling gang when you took on Davy?' Raven was about to test another theory of his. 'I think that twenty years ago you had a different partner. Roger Hepworth, the owner of the Waterfront Hotel. Joe's father. The two of you used to go out on "fishing trips" together. But perhaps you were bringing back more than just fish, eh, Sid?'

From across the interview table, Sid's implacable face stared back, giving nothing away.

Raven ploughed on. 'But something went wrong between the two of you and after one of your little expeditions, Roger sadly didn't make it back to dry land. What happened that day, Sid? Did he threaten to dish the dirt on you? Did he ask for a bigger share of the profits? Why did you push him overboard?'

'I did not push him overboard! That's a bloody lie!' Sid rose up and leaned across the table, fists clenched. Raven resisted the urge to pull back at the smell of beer on the man's breath. 'There was a full investigation at the time. It was a tragic accident. Nothing more.'

Sid suddenly seemed to realise that he had lost control. He returned to his seat, straightening his collar, breathing hard.

Raven eyed him closely. The old fisherman was as stubborn as the barnacles clinging to the bottom of his boat. Although he had admitted his part in the smuggling operation, he had refused to name anyone higher up the chain. And while he had reluctantly conceded that Davy was an abusive husband, he wouldn't easily admit to murdering Roger Hepworth. Not unless Raven could bring some real evidence forward, and after so many years had passed, he was unlikely to find any.

He called a halt to the interview and asked the custody sergeant to return the suspect to the cells.

But he wasn't done with Sid Sutcliffe yet. Not by a long way.

CHAPTER 30

Becca had followed the intense exchange between Raven and Sid with interest. It had been a battle of wills between two obstinate men and – apart from Sid's admission of Davy's violent behaviour towards Kate – had ended in a stalemate. She knew Raven had been hoping for more, and when Sid had clenched his fists in anger, she had expected fireworks. Under the circumstances Raven had remained remarkably calm. But he was clearly frustrated because as soon as the interview was over he left the room and shut himself in his office without a word.

She hated it when he did that, cutting her off. They were supposed to be a team, but Raven wasn't a team player.

Talking of teams, she decided to check in on Tony on her way back to her desk and see how he was getting on. 'Any luck tracking down Davy Capstick?'

'Nothing as yet,' said Tony. 'His phone is still off and there have been no sightings of him. I'm wondering if we should put out a request to the public for information.'

Becca considered the suggestion. It might well come to

that, but she didn't want to authorise it without Raven's say-so. 'Let's just keep going for the moment. He's bound to surface at some point. Oh, by the way, have you still got the file on Roger Hepworth's drowning incident?'

'It's just here,' said Tony, rummaging through the paperwork on his desk. He unearthed a manila folder, a bit crumpled at the edges and yellowed with age. 'Here you go.'

'Cheers.' Becca took it back to her desk and turned to the first page. She decided she could usefully fill her time with a bit of background reading. Just until Raven emerged from his self-imposed exile.

She scanned the header information. Roger Hepworth had been fifty years old and a resident of Robin Hood's Bay. The accident, or incident, had taken place on a night in March, twenty years ago at approximately ten o'clock in the evening. The reported location was five miles off the coast from Robin Hood's Bay. She was about to turn the page to read the details when something caught her eye.

A shiver ran down her spine as she read the name of the investigating officer who had written the report and the name of the senior officer who had signed it off.

She flicked to the conclusion. 'Freak weather conditions may have contributed to the accident. There is no evidence of foul play. Case closed.'

Raven had to see this. Even if he wasn't in the mood to talk to anyone, he would want to know what she had found.

She scooped up the file and went to knock on his door. When there was no response, she opened it and poked her head around anyway. Raven was sitting at his desk, his eyes dark and unfathomable, a deep frown creasing his brow. He didn't look up.

'I've found something,' she said, closing the door behind her. 'It's the report on the investigation into Roger Hepworth's drowning. Look.' She placed the open file on his desk and pointed to the names that had caught her attention.

Raven sat up straighter then. 'Sergeant Brandon Holt and Chief Superintendent William Seagrim.'

*

Raven looked neither to the left nor the right as he stormed through the incident room, down the corridor, up a flight of stairs and along another corridor. His right leg objected to the sudden burst of energy, threatening to hold him back, but he was having none of it. He marched on, bursting straight into Superintendent Brandon Holt's office without knocking.

The door flew open, crashing against the corner of a metal filing cabinet.

At the sudden interruption, Holt looked up from his computer screen. In a fraction of a second the expression on his face changed from calm to surprise to outright fury before he quickly regained control of himself. 'Don't they teach you to knock in CID these days? Or do you treat every entrance like a raid?' He narrowed his eyes. 'What do you want, DCI Raven?'

Raven approached the desk, panting after his exertion. He took in the sight of the smartly dressed senior officer, all turned out in his pressed white shirt, black tie and rank insignia. He was the picture of integrity, but Raven saw him for what he was. A corrupt policeman. A senior player in a drug smuggling gang. The man who had killed his mother.

He leaned across Holt's desk with both fists. 'What I want is for you to admit that in May 1991 you were driving a Vauxhall Cavalier that was involved in a hit-and-run incident in which a woman lost her life. I want you to admit that you failed to report the incident, and that you were complicit in covering it up and destroying relevant evidence.'

Holt studied him through slitted eyes. 'Is there anything else you want, while you're at it?'

'Yes,' said Raven. 'I want you to admit to your part in

a drug smuggling operation, and also in the cover-up of a murder that took place some twenty years ago, which you investigated and concluded was a boating accident.'

A brief flicker of amusement crossed Holt's face before being replaced by a steely gaze.

Raven noticed that Becca had entered the office and was standing just behind him. Holt addressed himself to her directly. 'Close the door, would you, Detective Sergeant Shawcross?' He waited as she pulled the door shut. 'Have you come to demand that I confess to something too?'

'No, sir,' said Becca. 'I just want everyone to remain calm.'

Holt shot her a thin smile. 'I think that's an excellent idea. Don't you, DCI Raven?'

Raven leaned further across the desk. 'No. A witness reported the registration number of the vehicle involved in the fatal collision. It was an unmarked police car. The officer who interviewed the witness was told to "drop it" by someone high up. Someone who wanted to protect you!' He jabbed a finger at Holt. 'I know you were driving that car–'

'Prove it then!' bellowed Holt. 'Where are the logbooks for the date in question? Show me!'

'You know they've been removed from the archives,' said Raven, raising his voice to match his adversary. 'And it was your mate, William Seagrim, who ordered the inquiry to be dropped.'

'Ha!' sneered Holt. 'You can't prove a thing. I would have thought that someone from CID would know you can't get an allegation to stick without solid evidence. Guesswork and speculation won't get you anywhere. Now get out of my office before–'

'Before I what?' Raven rounded the desk, closing in on Holt. The man was right that Raven had no evidence to support his accusations. The logbook had been removed, the witness statement deliberately not followed up, the repairs to the car deceptively placed in Gillian's name.

Even she had no proof of her claim that Holt had been behind the wheel of the car. As for the allegations of drug smuggling and the cover-up of Roger Hepworth's murder, Raven was even further from the safe harbour of provable fact.

But he knew. And that was enough.

'If I can't prove it, I'll have to take matters into my own hands,' he told the superintendent.

Holt gaped at him, genuine fear registering in his eyes for the first time during their confrontation. Perhaps he could sense that Raven had left all normal restraints behind. 'Meaning what? Are you a vigilante now, setting the world to rights by your own rules?'

'If I have to.' Raven towered over Holt, his fingers curling into fists, the blood coursing through his temples like a boiling river of rage.

Holt lifted his chin in defiance. 'Go on, then. Let's see what you're made of. Let's see if you have the guts to follow through like a real man.'

It was enough. Raven raised a fist, ready to bludgeon Holt's face into pulp, ready to haul him by his collar and drag him along the floor like an animal. The world had turned red and everything was simple at last.

But then a voice rang out. Becca. 'Raven, stop! This is what he wants you to do! If you assault him, you lose everything!'

'What?' Stunned, Raven turned to look into her frightened face. Where had she sprung from? In his anger, he had forgotten she was there.

She moved to stand between Raven and his opponent. Placing her hands on his chest, she gently pushed him backwards. Her eyes were pleading with him. 'Don't do it,' she said more quietly. 'Not like this.'

Raven stood where he was, trembling as the adrenaline seeped slowly away, the fuel that had almost ignited his brain steadily returning to normal levels. He shuddered and took a deep breath.

What had he done? If he had gone as far as even

touching Holt, he would be facing a charge of gross misconduct and all hope of bringing the corrupt officer to justice would have been lost.

His mother's face came to him, hazy after all these years, but beautiful still. She deserved better from her only son. This was his one chance to right the wrong that had haunted him his entire life and he had almost thrown it away.

A tear came to his eye.

Becca's face relaxed as she saw him release the anger. He put his hands up in surrender and she let hers fall from his chest. She too seemed close to tears.

Holt had turned an unattractive shade of red and a vein throbbed in his temple. He must have known how close he had come to being taken away in an ambulance. 'Now, get out!' he snarled. 'And in future, you should listen to that sergeant of yours. She's got more sense in her little finger than you've got in your entire body.'

Raven shot him one final look of contempt before he left the office. 'Don't imagine this is over, Holt. Don't think for a second that this is anywhere near finished.'

*

'You know, I've been thinking,' said Ellie as soon as Liam walked through the door.

Liam groaned inwardly. He was exhausted after his long walk back from Donovan Cross's. He'd waited half an hour for a bus but none had shown up. All he wanted to do was sit down with a cold beer and drown his sorrows. But he recognised the I've-just-had-an-amazing-idea voice that Ellie used whenever she was excited about something, which was quite often. He would have to hear her out or he'd never get any peace.

'What have you been thinking?' he asked, trying to drum up as much interest and enthusiasm as he could.

She gave him a broad smile that lit up her face. 'We should go on holiday somewhere. Get away for a bit. Just the two of us. We've both been working so hard lately. Two weeks in the sun would do us the world of good before winter sets in. I was thinking the Maldives. Or what about the Bahamas?'

She was on her laptop, googling luxury resorts and hotels. Sun-drenched beaches with sparkling blue water, palm trees, and expensive cocktails. When Liam looked over her shoulder and glimpsed the prices his heart sank.

'I don't know,' he told her, stalling while he tried to come up with an excuse that would get him off the hook. He couldn't tell her the truth – that he had no cash, that he was hopelessly in debt to a merciless loan shark, and that the money she and her father had just "invested" had gone to paying Barry with only a vague hope of a profitable return some time in the future.

He came up with the only thing he could think of. 'It would be lovely to get away, babe, but Barry's at a critical stage with the renovation work. I need to be here to keep a close eye on the work. I just don't think it's a good time right now.'

She turned to look at him. 'Couldn't you and Barry message each other? Video call? Technology, you know? Come on, some chillout time would do you good. You've been really tense recently.' She went back to scrolling down the screen.

Tense? Of course he was tense! Anyone would be tense when some gangster was holding a straight razor to their throat!

He wanted to shout at her, 'A loan shark just threatened to hurt you this afternoon! Don't you understand how much trouble I've got myself into?' But what good would that do? None. Instead he said, 'I'll be more relaxed if I know that the work's progressing according to schedule. I don't want to be a long-haul flight away from site right now.'

Ellie folded the laptop closed and came to stand in front of him. She draped her arms around his neck. 'Well if you don't want to go too far away, we could do something closer to home. How about a road trip instead? We could drive anywhere and stop wherever the fancy took us.' She flung her arms wide and tilted her head back, closing her eyes.

Oh God, it was the Celine Dion thing all over again! Liam had a vision of himself and Ellie on the prow of the Titanic. And – spoiler alert – he was the one who would be drowning in the depths.

How was he going to tell her that he had lost his car? That it had been taken from him by an unscrupulous criminal?

'My car...' he began. But the rest of the sentence eluded him.

'What about it?'

'It's at the garage,' he lied. 'It needs some work. A routine service, that's all, but they have to order a part from their supplier.'

'How long will that take?'

'Oh, I don't know. A few days, I guess?'

Ellie's lips parted in triumph. 'And then it will be in tip-top shape for the journey.' She gave him one of her most dazzling smiles.

Liam wished he could die.

★

Darkness was setting in and the first drops of rain were beginning to fall, but Raven didn't turn back. The flat, empty sands of the North Bay stretched out before him and he kept limping along, doggedly putting one foot in front of the other. His leg throbbed, a sharp reminder of his earlier recklessness, but he had no desire to return home. Quincey padded by his side but this evening the dog seemed to sense that his owner wasn't in the mood to play a game of fetch. In fact, Raven was tempted to just walk on and never return. He wanted to leave, but he couldn't escape the person he most wanted to. Himself.

What had come over him back there at the police

station? Some inner demon had taken control. And it terrified him.

He had very nearly pulverised Brandon Holt to a pulp. If he had begun to hit the man, who knew how far he might have taken things. Broken his nose? Put him in an emergency ward? Killed him?

He couldn't rule anything out.

It was exactly how his father would have behaved.

Alan Raven was not a rational man. When he lost his temper, you could never reason with him. He let his fists do the talking. Raven had blamed the drinking for his father's violent behaviour and had made it his golden rule never to touch a drop of alcohol, for fear of unleashing that same demon. He had stuck resolutely to that rule since the day his mother died, even during his army days. Yet what good had it done him?

Stone-cold sober, he had very nearly crossed the line.

He had to face the truth. Alcohol wasn't the problem. Anger was.

The fact was, there had been a violent streak in Alan Raven that had nothing to do with drinking. Had Raven inherited that tendency to violence?

The evidence was staring him in the face.

It had always been his worst nightmare, to become his father. And now the nightmare was a waking dream. A reality.

His mother had shielded him from the worst of the violence, often taking the blows herself. She had shown him a better way to live. But it seemed that he hadn't fully learned her lessons.

Only Becca had saved him today. She was his good angel.

He shuddered in horror when he thought how she had put herself between him and Holt, trying to save him from himself. He felt deep shame and didn't know how he could ever look her in the eye again.

When he reached the rocks at the end of the bay he came to a sudden halt. The darkened mass of Scalby Ness rose up before him and he dropped to his knees, weary to the bone. It was now completely dark, the sky as black as pitch and the sea a fathomless expanse. At the southern end of the bay, the ruined stub of the castle on the headland was no longer visible. Only the glimmer of a distant ship disturbed the blackness.

Quincey lay on the sand and put his head on Raven's lap.

'What am I going to do, Quince?' Raven asked him, stroking the dog's head gently.

The dog had no answer and neither did Raven.

CHAPTER 31

He was going to be fired. Raven knew it was the end as soon as he was summoned to Detective Superintendent Gillian Ellis's office first thing in the morning. Brandon Holt had made an official complaint against him, and he was going to be dismissed from his job with immediate effect, or at the very least suspended before being sacked.

At least he had come in especially early that day. If he could get the humiliation over quickly and leave the building before anyone else arrived, especially Becca, he could at least retain a vestige of dignity. He didn't know what he would do with the rest of his life, but he'd worry about that tomorrow.

He walked with a heavy tread and an even heavier heart to Gillian's office. It was getting on for a year since he'd returned to Scarborough and, despite everything, he was feeling at home here. He had cut his ties with London, divorced his wife, renovated his house and begun to feel settled. Even Hannah had joined him after leaving Exeter, although he didn't know how long she would be staying.

Now he'd screwed up big time. He straightened his tie

and stood a little taller before knocking on Gillian's door. If it was going to end this way, he was determined to take his punishment like a man.

'Enter!' His boss sounded particularly forceful this morning. Raven took a deep breath and went in.

'You wanted to see me, ma'am.' He stood with his hands behind his back, feeling like an army private called in to see his sergeant major for serious misconduct.

Gillian's face was stern. She sat behind her desk, hands clasped together, waiting until he was standing directly in front of her. 'I expect you know why you're here, Tom. I have received a serious complaint regarding your behaviour towards Superintendent Brandon Holt.' She shook her head as if more disappointed than cross. 'What the hell were you thinking?'

'I wasn't thinking,' said Raven. 'I acted on impulse. I'm sorry.'

She studied him through narrowed eyes. 'Is this about your mother?'

He nodded. 'Holt was the driver of the car. I know he was. He killed her.'

Gillian leaned back in her chair, lowering her chin to observe him better. 'We both know that's the truth, Tom, but do you have proof?'

'I do not, ma'am.'

The silence hung heavy between them. Then suddenly Gillian was all business-like. 'Right. In that case, keep a lid on your emotions. If and when you obtain the necessary evidence, I insist that you proceed through the formal channels. I will personally back you in any official proceedings. But any attempt on your part to take matters into your own hands a second time will result in your instant dismissal. Have I made myself understood?'

'Perfectly,' said Raven. 'Will there be anything else, ma'am?'

'Yes, as a matter of fact. What is going on in Robin Hood's Bay? Why is there an arrest warrant out for Anna's father? Are you treating her death as murder now?'

'I am, and I believe that Davy Capstick is responsible. But I've also arrested her grandfather on suspicion of smuggling, and he's admitted under caution that he and Davy were involved in smuggling contraband, probably drugs. Anna stole a sum of money intended to pay for the next shipment. My working hypothesis is that she was killed by Davy trying to get the money back from her.'

Gillian swung her head from side to side. 'What a mess! It seems your instincts were right, Tom.'

Raven nodded in gratitude. It was good to hear it said for once. 'I've informed the regional organised crime unit about the arrest, and I'm holding Anna's grandfather in a cell pending further questioning.' He paused, unsure how much more of his thinking he should reveal.

Gillian cocked her head to one side. 'Yes?'

'There's more.'

'Go on.'

'A second unexplained death.'

She leaned forwards, her face becoming a mask of incredulity. 'I've heard nothing about a second death.'

'It's a historic case. It was investigated at the time and no action was taken.'

Gillian's lips pursed, her expression hardening again. 'And you think that this is suspicious because?'

Raven sighed inwardly. It had been an error of judgement to tell Gillian about his broader suspicions, but now he had no choice other than to tell her everything. 'The suspect I arrested yesterday, Sid Sutcliffe, was involved in a boating accident twenty years ago. His friend fell overboard and drowned. But I think there was more to it than that. The death was investigated by none other than Brandon Holt and signed off by Chief Superintendent William Seagrim, the same pair who covered up my mother's death.'

There, he had said it. But in the cold light of day, the certainty he had felt earlier seemed to be evaporating. Was this simple paranoia?

Gillian clearly felt the same scepticism, but much more

strongly. Her eyebrows shot up and she looked as if she might explode. 'Tom, I understand that you have a personal vendetta against Superintendent Holt, but that doesn't mean you can pin every crime in North Yorkshire on him!'

Raven said nothing more. If Gillian discovered the full extent of his suspicions – that Holt was involved in the smuggling ring too – she might seriously reconsider her decision not to suspend him from duty.

She pinched the bridge of her nose between finger and thumb and closed her eyes. When she opened them again she looked weary. 'I'm warning you, Tom, that this is starting to sound like a conspiracy theory. You need to stick to facts and gather evidence. No more hunches or gut feelings. Do you understand?'

'Yes,' said Raven. 'And thank you.'

She dismissed him with a wave of her hand and a shake of her head.

*

After a broken night's sleep, Becca took her time getting ready for work. She was in no hurry to go into the police station. After that horrible incident with Raven the previous day, she wasn't sure she could face him today. The rage she had witnessed had frightened her. She dreaded to think what might have happened if she hadn't been there to intervene. Even though Raven had refrained from actual physical assault, Superintendent Holt would be fully justified in lodging a complaint for gross misconduct and that could mean the end for Raven.

If he was going to be fired, she really didn't want to be around to witness it. He was a difficult person at the best of times, but the place wouldn't be the same without him.

She would miss him.

She took a long shower, then made herself toast with marmalade and an extra-large mug of tea and sat down, determined to enjoy her breakfast in peace. Ellie had already gone into work and Liam hadn't yet surfaced. Becca was glad to have a moment to herself.

She scrolled on her phone as she took a bite of toast. She was a passive consumer of social media, never posting anything herself. Her profile was a blank. She liked to think it was because of her work, but the truth was she didn't have much of a social life and never did anything worth broadcasting. Still, it was interesting to see what her friends were up to. She hadn't seen most of them in absolutely ages. One of them had a new boyfriend. One had bought her own flat. Another had a baby! Becca couldn't imagine settling down and having kids. Who would she even have them with?

She was halfway through her tea and thinking about making a move when the kitchen door crashed open, banging against the wall. Liam. Her brother looked awful this morning. Unwashed hair, dark circles under his eyes. Not a pleasant sight to witness so early in the day.

'You look terrible,' she told him.

He sniffed, and she thought he was going to ignore her or make some rude remark. That was what brothers and sisters were for, she supposed. Getting on each other's nerves. But he came sheepishly over to her with heavy footsteps and parked himself on the stool next to her at the breakfast bar. 'Got a minute, sis?'

'I need to get to work. Can it wait until this evening?'

'Not really.'

She hesitated. He seemed serious, with no trace of his usual nonchalance. 'Is something wrong?'

And then he did something Becca hadn't seen since he was a small child and he'd broken his favourite toy car. He burst into tears. She sat there watching him in amazement as his shoulders quaked and his face turned to anguish. He gripped the countertop as real tears flooded his eyes and he opened his mouth to cry. The sound that emerged was sharp and raw, and his whole body shook as he gave himself over to despair. She had never seen him so vulnerable.

Now she felt awful for not realising that something was the matter sooner. She'd been so focussed on work – and Raven in particular – that she'd been blind to her own family. She pushed her plate and mug away and drew him into a tight embrace.

'What's wrong?' she whispered. 'Have you and Ellie split up?'

He pulled away, embarrassed, wiping his eyes and nose on his sleeve. 'No, no, nothing like that.'

'Then what?'

'I don't know where to begin.'

'Start at the beginning.'

'Don't you need to get to work?'

'Work can wait.'

Liam hunched forward with his elbows on the worktop. Becca waited patiently for him to speak. 'I've been a complete idiot,' he said.

'Just tell me,' she said sympathetically. 'I won't judge.'

He took a deep breath then turned to her, his face stricken. 'I borrowed some money from a loan shark. His name is Donovan Cross. And now I can't pay it back.'

It was on the tip of her tongue to say, *why did you do something so stupid?* But aloud, she said, 'How much?'

She was aghast when he named the sum. It was far more than her annual salary before tax. She hardly knew what to say. Liam lived in a different world to her, with his property empire and his flashy sports car. She would never have guessed he had financial difficulties.

'I can't tell Ellie what I've done,' he continued. 'I borrowed money from her and her dad, intending to use it for the interest payments, but I had to give the money to Barry instead. When I told Donovan he'd have to wait for his cash, the bastard took my car. He agreed to cancel the interest payments but I still owe him the principal. I'm not even sure he will keep to his side of the bargain.'

Becca nodded in appalled silence. That was the trouble with loan sharks. They were entirely unregulated, operating outside the law. Only a desperate person would turn to one, and that made the borrower extremely vulnerable. 'Has he threatened you?'

Liam's shoulders began to tremble again. 'Yeah. He held a razor blade to my throat, and he has this henchman who looks like he could snap bones with his bare hands. He even made veiled threats against Ellie.'

Becca's jaw dropped open. This was getting really serious. 'He knows about Ellie? Does he know where you live?'

Liam nodded.

Becca's mind whirred into overdrive. If this Donovan Cross knew about Ellie, then he must know about her too. That meant that none of them were safe. 'Right, that's it. You're coming to the station with me immediately and you're going to make a detailed statement. We're going to fix this, you and me together.'

CHAPTER 32

Sid Sutcliffe lay on the unyielding mattress in the police cell and stared at the yellow stain on the ceiling, trying to work out what it reminded him of. It was like one of those tests they did with ink blots. They asked you what it looked like, and then decided if you were a killer or a psycho. To Sid's way of thinking, this stain looked very much like a knife.

He'd been in police custody for sixteen hours already, much of that time spent staring at the ceiling. The custody sergeant had told him they could hold him for another eight hours without charge. That gave him eight more hours to think of something else the stain reminded him of.

He twisted his head one way and then the other.

Still a bloody knife.

The key turned in the lock and the door creaked loudly open. DCI Raven, no doubt, come to charge him at last. What was the maximum penalty for drug smuggling? For a first offence, maybe not so much. Maybe just a stern warning.

'Come to release me?' Sid asked hopefully. 'It's about

time too.' He'd always been one to call a glass half full, even when any bugger could see it was down to the last dregs. How else could you get through life when all the cards were stacked against you?

He pushed himself into a seated position, his bones groaning in protest. He was getting too old for all this larking about. That was why he had taken Davy on, bringing him into the family business and hoping to pass something on to the next generation. But Davy wasn't the sharpest knife in the drawer and things hadn't worked out the way Sid had hoped.

Knives again. He just couldn't get away from them.

He was taken aback when Superintendent Brandon Holt stepped into the cell, closing the door behind him with a loud clang. Holt was the last person he wanted to see right now.

The newcomer leaned against the door, arms folded, saying nothing. He was all dressed up in his shirt and tie, but Sid knew that beneath that veneer of respectability, Holt was as crooked as they came. The bastard was a bully too.

And if you wanted to see what a real killer looked like, Holt was your man.

The superintendent curled his lip into a sneer. 'Where's Davy?'

'No idea.'

'Don't lie to me.'

'I'm not. He's gone to ground. Scared of you, probably.'

Holt seemed to be considering something. He paced up and down the tiny cell like a caged beast. Sid was forced to crane his neck to look up at him.

'You're not going to do anything stupid, are you?' said Holt.

'Like what?'

'You know what I'm talking about.' Holt stopped pacing and raised his hand to strike. Sid ducked back, turning his face away. He had felt the force of that hand before and had no appetite for a second helping. But Holt managed to restrain himself. He stood there, breathing hard, giving Sid a look of pure contempt. 'You don't want to end up like Roger Hepworth, do you, Sid?'

Bastard. Sid felt his guts twist inside him. Despite his better judgement, he said, 'You're the one who should be in this cell.'

The strike fell hard, catching Sid's cheek. Holt seized him by the collar and hauled him to his feet. Pinning him to the wall, he leaned his forearm against Sid's neck. His face was just inches away. 'Breathe a word about what happened to Roger and you'll find yourself six feet under,' hissed Holt. 'You're not going to blab to Raven, are you?'

Sid tried to shake his head, but he could hardly breathe, let alone move. 'You can trust me, Brandon,' he croaked, 'I've kept your secret all these years. I won't tell anyone what you did.'

Holt kept him there for a few seconds longer before finally releasing the pressure. Sid gasped for air, rubbing his neck.

Holt straightened his tie and smoothed down his uniform, glaring at Sid as if this was all his fault. Then he turned and left without another word.

He was a bastard all right.

But there was nothing Sid could do. Holt held all the cards. He always had.

★

'Can I borrow the car?' asked Connor. 'I want to go to Whitby.'

'What for?' His mum was behind the bar, checking the stock.

Connor pursed his lips in annoyance. His mum was so controlling, always wanting to know where he was going. He should have asked his dad instead. 'Just need to buy a few things.'

What he really wanted was to get away from the Bay for

a few hours. Go somewhere that wouldn't remind him of Anna. Take a bracing walk along the east pier and feel the wind against his face. Perhaps he should move away entirely and put everything behind him. But he didn't know where he would go or what he would do. The Waterfront was his home and Robin Hood's Bay was his life.

Sarah looked up, studying him as if she could see right into his head and read his thoughts. 'All right,' she said at last. 'The keys are in my handbag. It's upstairs in the flat.'

'Thanks, Mum.'

He went upstairs and after searching around for a bit found his mum's handbag – a huge shoulder bag with multiple pockets and compartments – by the side of the sofa. He rummaged around for the keys.

The handbag was overflowing with junk. Packets of tissues, assorted pens, a pocket diary, multiple lipsticks, throat lozenges, spare gloves and coins. Seriously, what did his mum need with all this stuff? She was always prepared for everything.

But no keys. He unzipped an inner pocket and reached inside. He froze.

His fingers closed around an object, but it wasn't a key. He carefully retrieved it, turning it over in his hands, examining it closely.

No. It wasn't possible.

But there was no mistaking it. The shiny pink cover, the cracked screen. He'd seen it six days earlier. Anna's phone.

He cradled the device in his hands, letting the bag fall to the floor. Then he ran back downstairs. His mother was crouched behind the bar, counting bottles in the fridge.

'What are you doing with this?' he shouted.

Sarah stood up quickly. 'Oh God, Connor, you gave me a fright. What's the matter?'

'This.' He thrust Anna's phone towards her. 'I found it in your handbag. What's it doing there?'

She paled a little, then pulled her shoulders back in that

gesture of defiance she used when dealing with difficult customers in the bar. 'I found it on Sunday morning when I was cleaning the tables. Anna must have left it behind when she came to say goodbye to you.'

Connor shook his head. 'You found it? And you didn't think to hand it in to the police when they came calling? Or mention it after my room was broken into?'

Sarah shrugged, her face hardening into that familiar expression he knew so well. 'What good would it have done, Connor? Anna's gone and you're better off without her. I hid it to protect you and your dad. I didn't want either of you getting blamed for Anna's death if the police found out her phone was here.'

Connor could barely believe what he was hearing. 'Why would you even think that? You can't imagine that me or Dad had anything to do with her death! The fact is, you just never liked Anna. You're glad she's dead.'

Sarah didn't even try to deny it. 'She was no good for you!'

'Yes, she was! I loved her. Why did you hate her so much?'

'Because she was your half-sister!'

'What?' Connor reeled backwards as if he'd been punched in the gut. 'You're lying!'

Sarah moved towards him and laid a hand on the side of his face. 'I'm sorry, Connor. I didn't mean for you to find out this way, but it's the truth.' Her voice was gentle with no trace of malice.

'I don't understand.' Connor couldn't think. Nothing made sense. Anna couldn't be his half-sister. She was a Capstick, not a Hepworth.

'Come and sit down. We need to have a proper talk.' Sarah took two beer bottles from the fridge, prised the lids off both and led him to a corner table. The pub was still closed and there was no one else around.

He followed her to the table, his head spinning. Nothing felt real. He wondered if he would wake up in a second and find this was all a dream.

She waited for him to sit, swigging a mouthful of beer as if she needed alcohol to give her the courage to speak. Connor didn't touch his. He was feeling dazed enough already.

'When I first knew your dad,' she began, 'he was going out with Kate, Anna's mum. They'd been girlfriend and boyfriend ever since school. Your grandfather, Roger, who you never knew, was pals with Sid Sutcliffe, Kate's dad. They used to go out together on fishing trips.'

'I know all that,' said Connor. 'Dad's told me before. That's how Grandad died. He fell overboard.'

'That's one version of events,' said Sarah, 'though a lot of people in the village didn't believe it. Your grandmother blamed Sid for her husband's death. Nothing was proven and the case was dropped. But the damage was done. The two families fell out. Your dad split up with Kate – he could hardly continue to date the daughter of the man who murdered his father – and soon afterwards, she married Davy. Seven months later, Anna was born. Kate told everyone that the birth was premature, but it doesn't take a lot to work out that your dad was Anna's father.'

Connor shook his head. His own father was Anna's dad? He couldn't believe it. 'That's just speculation. There's no proof!'

His mum gave him a pitying look. 'I'm sorry, Connor, but it's the truth. Why else do you think Anna broke up with you and went to London? It must have been because she found out for herself. Perhaps Kate told her.'

Connor felt as if he'd been frozen to the spot. The truth was a rising tide, steadily flooding past his defences, no matter how hard he fought to hold it back. Now everything started to make sense.

Anna had known. That was the reason she had suddenly broken up with him. It was why she had been unable to give him an explanation. It was what had made her run away to London.

He longed to talk to her again, to tell her that if she couldn't be his girlfriend, then he wanted her as his sister.

If only he had known, he would have begged her to stay. Yet even when she returned, she still hadn't been able to tell him the truth. Now she was gone forever and he felt as if he had lost her all over again. Hot tears trickled from his eyes, running down his cheeks, splashing to the floor. 'Why couldn't she tell me, Mum? Why did she go?'

Sarah sat tight-lipped, saying nothing.

And then another truth dawned on him. 'You told her, didn't you? You told Anna she was my half-sister!'

Sarah's face was as hard as stone. 'She needed to know. Things couldn't go on the way they were. You and her, it was indecent. I had to tell her, before things got worse.'

'You forced her to leave!' Connor stood up suddenly, pushing himself away from the table. 'This is all your fault!'

His mother eyed him nervously. 'What are you going to do?'

He brandished Anna's phone. 'I'm taking this to the police, like you should have done in the first place. I'll say it just turned up under a cushion or something.'

'No, don't do that,' pleaded Sarah. 'Throw it away. Don't risk incriminating yourself!'

'I have nothing to fear. I didn't kill Anna.'

Then a horrifying thought seized him. What if his mother had killed Anna to be rid of her once and for all?

Suddenly Sarah lunged at him and tried to grab the phone out of his hand. He pushed her away, holding the phone out of reach. Then he fled from the pub, taking it with him.

'Come back!' shouted his mum. 'We need to talk!'

But Connor ignored her. Talking to his mum was the last thing on his mind.

CHAPTER 33

Time was running out for Raven to continue holding Sid Sutcliffe in custody. In a matter of hours he would have to charge him, apply for an extension, or release him. He was keen to restart the interview process, but Becca still hadn't turned up for work. It wasn't like her to be late. He hoped she wasn't avoiding him, although he wouldn't blame her if she was. He scanned the office to see who else was available.

'Jess, can you sit in on an interview with Sid Sutcliffe?'

Jess jumped to her feet, her keenness brimming over. 'Happy to.'

'Becca not in today?' asked Raven, as they walked to the interview suite. He tried to keep his voice casual but was sure he sounded anxious.

'Not yet,' said Jess. 'Maybe she's sorting out her new flat.'

'Her new flat?' This was news to Raven. 'She's moving?'

'Didn't she tell you? I just assumed you knew. She's found a place in Castle Terrace.'

'Castle Terrace? That's...'

'Just up the hill from you,' Jess supplied cheerfully.

Raven tried to hide his surprise. Becca moving to a new flat was one thing, although strictly speaking it was none of his business. But moving to a street that overlooked his own house? His mind was filled with all kinds of thoughts.

After his appalling behaviour yesterday, she might be doubting the wisdom of moving so close to him. Maybe she'd had second thoughts and was now urgently trying to wriggle out of a tenancy agreement. He didn't want her to do that. At the very least he needed to see her and apologise for his unacceptable behaviour in Brandon Holt's office. She liked chocolates, didn't she? Maybe he should buy her a box, although this hardly seemed an adequate reward for saving him from destroying his career.

A uniformed officer was standing watch over Sid. He gave a curt nod and left the interview room as soon as Raven and Jess entered. Jess took a seat at the table and Raven spent a moment surveying his prisoner. He frowned at what he saw. Was that bruising around Sid's neck? Was one side of the man's face redder than the other? Surely he couldn't have come to any harm in the cells overnight.

Sid himself gave no sign of wanting to raise a complaint, so Raven took a seat next to Jess and prepared to begin the interview. The previous day, Sid had been unwilling to name any of his criminal associates, apart from Davy, but a night in the cells seemed to have had a profound effect on the old man. Before Raven could start the recording machine and run through the preliminaries, Sid reached out a bony hand to stop him. He leaned across the table and gave a hoarse whisper.

'I think we can help each other out.'

'How?'

'Information in return for immunity from prosecution. And I'll need protection – for me and my family.'

Raven hesitated. He couldn't make a promise he couldn't deliver on. He was in enough trouble already with Gillian without incurring the wrath of the CPS too. 'That's not how this works, Sid. If you've got something to say, then start talking.'

Sid thought for a moment, then nodded. 'All right. You asked me yesterday how Roger Hepworth died.'

Raven could hardly believe his ears. Was Sid about to spill the beans and admit to pushing Roger overboard after all? 'I have to get this on tape, Sid. What you tell me can't be used as evidence otherwise.'

Sid dropped his voice even lower. 'No, listen. You can't record this. I'll only say owt if it's off the record.'

Raven shifted in his seat, catching Jess's eye. This was wrong. He couldn't allow himself to be played by a suspect. Anything Sid said off the record could never be used in court. On the other hand, it was clear he would say nothing if Raven persisted in sticking to the rules. *Hell.* 'Go on, then,' he urged Sid. 'I'm listening.'

Sid blinked once, then began to speak. 'I always denied killing Roger, and that's the truth of it. But it weren't an accident. It were like this, see. Roger and I weren't just mates, we were business partners.'

'Are you talking about the smuggling business?'

'Aye. We used to take the boat out together to pick up the goods. Anyroad, there were other folk involved. Nasty folk, the kind you don't want to cross. Roger wanted out. But you can't just walk away from a business like that. He knew too much. So one of the bastards made sure he wouldn't ever go running to the cops.'

'You're saying he was murdered? Who did it?' Raven stared at Sid, willing him to talk, yet fearing the consequences. What good would it do to have a confession that was inadmissible in court? Yet if shaking the man would have loosened his tongue, Raven would have picked him up and shaken him like a salt cellar.

The wait felt agonising, yet eventually Sid said, 'Superintendent Brandon Holt. Except in those days he were just plain old Sergeant Holt. He were still as much of a bastard though.'

At Raven's side, Jess gasped in astonishment. Yet Raven felt no surprise whatsoever at the news. It was Holt who had killed his mother, Holt who had investigated Roger Hepworth's death. And Chief Constable William Seagrim who had presided over the whole rotten show. Nothing would surprise him about that pair.

'Everyone blamed me for Roger's death,' continued Sid. 'And I couldn't breathe a word about what really happened. I just had to lie and say it were an accident.'

'Why are you telling me this now?' asked Raven. 'What's changed?'

It wasn't too hard to guess. If Holt really was running the smuggling operation, it wouldn't have been difficult for him to pay Sid a visit overnight and make some threats. Those marks on the old man's face weren't Raven's imagination after all. Holt must have banked on Sid being too terrified to speak, and yet Sid had weighed his options and decided that coming clean to Raven was the lesser of two evils. Ironically, if Holt had kept his distance, Sid would probably have maintained his silence.

'Who else is involved in this business of yours?' asked Raven.

'A loan shark by the name of Donovan Cross and his henchman Jackson Webb. Cross provides the cash, but Webb is the one who delivers it to Robin Hood's Bay. Holt stays in the background and creams off the profit. But it wasn't always that way. He used to be the frontrunner, back when Seagrim was boss.'

Raven allowed his thoughts to return to his mother. Was that how it had happened? Holt returning from Robin Hood's Bay with some gear stowed in the back of his car? Driving too fast, not paying attention to a pedestrian about to step into the road. If he was carrying illegal drugs in the car, no wonder he'd been afraid to stop at the scene of a road traffic accident.

Raven made a note of the names Sid had given him. The name Donovan Cross rang a bell. He'd have to check with Tony where he'd heard it before.

'This is all very interesting,' he told Sid, 'but if you want me to do anything about it, I'll need proof. What evidence have you got?'

Sid shook his head. 'Nowt.'

There was a knock at the door and Jess went to answer it. 'Sir? It's Becca.'

Raven looked up. Now wasn't really the time for Becca to be making her entrance. He owed her an apology but he needed to get back to Sid and try to coax him into putting his story on tape. But he could tell from her face that she had something important to say.

'It's Connor Hepworth,' she said. 'He has news you'll want to hear right away.'

*

Connor Hepworth was clearly very upset, and it had taken courage for him to come forward to the police. After listening to what the lad had to say, Raven returned with Becca to the incident room. The information that Connor had given them now took precedence over his interview with Sid.

Raven gathered his small team for an impromptu meeting, letting his gaze fall on Becca, Jess and Tony. He would need to go to Gillian and request more resources if he was going to follow up the lead that Sid had given him, but right now his priority was to act on what he knew.

'Okay, listen up everyone. Anna's phone has surfaced at last. It seems she left it behind in the Waterfront when she went there on Saturday, most likely late in the evening. It was found by Sarah Hepworth on Sunday morning but has only just been handed in. I've passed it to the forensics team, so we'll have to wait and see if they recover any relevant information. In the meantime, the other big news is that Anna was Connor's half-sister. Sarah just told him that Anna was Joe's daughter, not Davy's.'

'That certainly changes the dynamics,' said Becca. 'It explains why Anna broke up with Connor and moved to London. She clearly wanted to make a fresh start away from her family.'

'It also explains why Joe kept in close touch with her,' said Jess, 'and why he was seen giving her a hug on Saturday night. He wasn't romantically involved with her, he was her father.'

'Yes,' confirmed Raven. 'We'll need to interview him again, but for the moment I think it's fair to assume that he knew Anna was his daughter. An obvious question is whether Davy knew. If he did, it adds fuel to the theory that he killed her. We know for a fact that he has a violent temper and that he abuses Kate. Both Kate and Sid have confirmed that after Davy found out that Anna had stolen the money, he went out searching for her.'

'When I found his cigarette butt on the Cleveland Way,' Jess chipped in, 'I never bought the idea that he'd just gone for a walk in the middle of the night.'

'Precisely,' said Raven. 'Connor's statement validates Davy as our prime suspect.'

'I'm worried about Kate,' said Becca. 'If Davy killed Anna, then Kate's safety is at risk if he returns.'

'Agreed,' said Raven. 'One of us should go over to the house immediately.'

'Sir!' Tony interrupted, looking up from his screen. 'I've just picked up a signal for Davy's phone. It's been switched on and he's back in Robin Hood's Bay.'

Raven didn't have to ask Becca if she was happy to go with him. She was already heading towards the door.

CHAPTER 34

It had been going on for years. A slap here, a punch there. Sometimes worse. Mostly, Kate kept out of his way and tried not to antagonise him, especially when he came rolling home after a night out. There was no one she could turn to for help. Sid had warned her not to go to the police. 'We don't want coppers poking their snouts into our business,' he'd told her. He preferred to pretend that nothing was happening. After all, it was Sid who had introduced her to Davy in the first place, after she and Joe had split up.

There was a hymn she used to sing at school – *Eternal Father, Strong to Save*. It was intended for seafarers – *O hear us when we cry to Thee, for those in peril on the sea*. You couldn't grow up in Robin Hood's Bay without understanding the perils of the sea. That part of the coast had a long history of shipwrecks and drownings. Kate could still recall the words of the hymn – *the restless wave, the foaming deep*. Often she wished *the foaming deep* would swallow Davy and his damn boat and she would never have to set eyes on him again.

The only person she'd been able to confide in about her

troubles was the vicar, Reverend Mark Taylor. He had found her one day sitting in the church, alone and afraid. He had listened without judgement, the only man, besides Joe, who had ever taken her seriously. He'd shown real compassion, genuine understanding. She had started visiting him more often, helping out with cleaning and other jobs. He was lonely too, carrying the problems of his parishioners on his shoulders. One thing had led to another and, well... She knew he regretted their brief affair – probably saw it as a sin, given his line of business – but she would never call it that. It had been a comfort in a life fraught with pain and sorrow.

But Anna's death had changed everything. She couldn't go on any longer. It was time to leave Robin Hood's Bay for good. There was nothing for her here. She hated everything about the place – her hand-to-mouth existence, the criminal activities that put the family in constant danger yet never seemed to pay more than a pittance. In a fit of fury she had burned the boat that had brought nothing but misery. She knew there would be no insurance payout, but without the boat, she hoped Davy would find proper work. But instead he had run away.

That's what she was going to do now. She pulled an old suitcase from the top of the wardrobe and blew the dust off it. She should have gone with Anna when she left home a year ago. Anna had the right idea. She had always been the smartest in the family. She had probably inherited her brains from Joe. Her only mistake had been to come back when she needed money. Kate wouldn't make that same mistake.

She unzipped the suitcase and started stuffing it with clothes. She wouldn't be able to take much with her, but she didn't have a lot that was worth keeping. She would head up the coast to Whitby first, see if there were any jobs in the hotels. Or she might try Scarborough. She could clean, or work as a waitress. Anything. She filled the suitcase until it was bulging. And that was when she heard the key in the front door and the voice she dreaded most.

'Kate! Where are yer, woman?'

The door banged shut and she dragged the suitcase onto the floor, pushing it under the bed and cursing herself for not having gone already. She heard his footsteps on the stairs, slow and heavy, reminding her of all the times she'd lain in bed trembling with fear as she awaited his return from the pub. The landing floorboards creaked and she felt her knees grow weak.

But she wasn't going to stay a victim any longer. Those days were finished.

She steeled herself and took a deep breath before stepping out to meet him on the landing. He stood at the top of the stairs, unwashed, unshaven, and stinking of stale cigarettes and body odour. How she loathed him.

'Where've you been?' she demanded. 'The cops have been round 'ere looking for you.' If he knew the police were after him he might just turn around and leave. She hoped so.

'What did you tell 'em?'

'I didn't say owt.' It wasn't exactly the truth, but Davy didn't deserve the truth. 'I didn't know where you were.'

'I were 'anging with a mate, getting me 'ead together.'

'You should 'ave stayed there.' The words were out of her mouth before she could stop them.

'What did you say?' Davy took a step nearer and glowered at her through bloodshot eyes. 'I live 'ere, don't I? I've a right to come back to my own 'ouse.'

Kate gripped the newel post for support. 'It's not your house. It belongs to my father.'

'But I'm yer 'usband. What's yours is mine.'

He raised a hand but instead of flinching, she stood her ground.

'You're the world's worst husband and father. You weren't even Anna's real father. That were Joe Hepworth and he's been laughing at you behind your back for twenty years.' There, she'd said it now. He would probably beat her black and blue.

But instead of punching her, Davy threw back his head

and roared with laughter. 'How stupid do you think I am, woman? Do you think I didn't know that? Do you think I didn't notice the similarity between Anna and Joe?'

Suddenly the laughter stopped dead and he stared at her, his eyes full of hate. 'You dirty slut.' He threw out an arm and shoved her against the wall. 'You tricked me into marrying you. If I'd known you were carrying another man's child, I would never have touched you, you whore!'

'I wish you hadn't!'

He hit her then. A hard slap to the side of the face. Her head banged back against the wall. He put a hand to her throat. 'Everything's your fault. You brought that bastard daughter of yours into this house and she stole my money.'

'You shouldn't have left it lying around.'

'Oh yeah?' Davy let go of her and dropped his voice to a hoarse whisper. 'Do you know what? I went after Anna, all the way across the cliffs in the middle of the night, and when I got to Boggle Hole, do you know what I found?' His face was inches from hers, his breath rank and stale. His quiet voice was sinister and calculating and it frightened her more than when he was bellowing. 'Anna were lying at the bottom of the steps, already dead, her head cracked open on a rock. Someone had got to her before me. And I think you know who.'

Kate's whole body trembled with fear. Fear of violence, fear of the truth.

Somehow, Davy had worked it all out. 'I didn't mean to kill her,' she protested. 'It were an accident. I just gave her a shove down the steps. I never meant to kill my own daughter.'

He looked at her, reassessing her, a kind of fear creeping into his eyes. And in that moment she knew what she had to do. She had already crossed a line. She had taken a life, one most precious to her. Davy's life meant nothing. He was vermin. He deserved to die.

With a cry she flung herself forwards, putting her hands to his chest. He was bigger and stronger than her, but that made no difference. A lifetime of frustration had been building to this moment.

He tottered backwards, losing his footing. 'What the–'

But his protests meant nothing to her. She drove forwards, putting all her weight against him. His back leg slipped and he stumbled towards the top step of the rickety old staircase.

'You're a bastard, Davy Capstick!' she bellowed, readying herself for one final push. When it came to it, it was easy and she wondered why it had taken her so long to find the courage. She drove herself forward one more time with all her might and watched as his eyes grew wide and he tumbled headlong down the stairs with a shriek.

*

For once, Becca raised no objections when Raven put his foot to the floor. They arrived in Robin Hood's Bay in record time.

He barely slowed down as he took the hill, and the car screeched to a halt at the bottom. The burned-out shell of the boat was still there, propped up on blocks, the grey sea silent behind it. Becca leapt out of the car and ran ahead of him up the path. Cursing his leg, he followed as quickly as he could.

When he reached the house, Becca was rapping loudly on the door. There was shouting and screaming coming from within. Becca peered through the living room window. And then they heard it. A screech of terror followed by a series of loud thumps.

Then silence.

Raven threw his weight against the front door. The timber frame was weak and gave way with barely a struggle. He pushed the door wide open and entered the house.

He surveyed the scene before him, afraid of finding Kate, beaten or worse. But instead it was Davy Capstick whose limp body filled the hallway, his arms and legs in an untidy tangle at the foot of the stairs. Blood was seeping from his ear, staining the bare boards dark red. His eyes stared vacantly into space.

Raven knelt and felt for a pulse, but there was nothing.

Kate was standing at the top of the stairs, hugging herself with her thin arms.

Raven walked halfway up. 'Are you okay?' he asked. 'Did he try to hurt you?'

'He's been hurting me for years.' Kate heaved a sob. 'I'm not sorry I pushed him. He were asking for it. Anna too. She told me she'd tell Davy about me and the vicar. She said she'd go to the police and tell them about the smuggling.'

Raven climbed the rest of the way up the stairs. At close quarters Kate was a dreadful sight, her hair lank, her eyes dark from crying. Crimson marks on her face and neck revealed where Davy had struck her. 'What are you saying, Kate?'

Her hands were steady, but her legs were trembling and she clutched the banister for support. 'Anna said we'd all go to prison unless I gave her money. I told her no, but she wouldn't listen. She knew where to find the cash. When I realised it were gone, I had to go after her. I had no choice.' She looked imploringly at Raven.

'So you tried to get it back?' It was all starting to make sense now. Why hadn't he seen it before? 'You followed Anna to Boggle Hole.'

A single nod. 'I knew Davy would go mad when he found out what she'd done. So I went after her, just to talk to her, try to reason with her and make her see sense. She admitted taking the money, but she said she didn't have it on her. I called her a liar. She called me... it doesn't matter what. But I was so angry and scared and it was dark and I couldn't see properly. I'm not sure how it happened. I tried to grab her and she took a step back, and then she fell...' Kate buried her face in her hands. 'I didn't mean to kill her. I was her mother. I loved her.'

CHAPTER 35

Liam walked up the road to Donovan Cross's house as calmly as he could manage, but his heart was pumping like he'd done ten miles on the treadmill. He passed a plumber's van and a car advertising pick-up and drop-off laundry and ironing. This wasn't the sort of neighbourhood where people did their own washing.

Becca had promised him that it would all be okay but Liam wasn't so sure. It had taken a lot of persuading before he had agreed to her plan. But in the end, what choice did he have? He had run out of options a long way back.

He paused on the pavement outside the house. His car – it was still *his* car as far as he was concerned – was parked on the driveway exactly where he had left it. Donovan probably hadn't even driven it. He'd taken it because he could.

Becca said he should never have handed over the keys, but she didn't know how terrified he'd been. Nobody had held a blade to *her* throat. At least he'd managed to keep the truth from Ellie. She still thought the car was at the garage and her money was safe. With any luck she need never be any the wiser.

He took a deep breath, then walked up to the front door and rang the bell. A moment later, the door opened. It was Donovan himself this time. No Mrs Cross to distract him today, thank heavens.

The bald bastard gave Liam a smirk. 'Back so soon? Come on in.' He held the door wide.

Liam glanced back at the street – at safety. The laundry car was moving off and Liam longed to be leaving too. But instead he stepped inside the house.

Donovan took him through to the kitchen again. This morning the huge room was filled with pleasant aromas – freshly brewed coffee and baking bread. Was Donovan an avid baker when he wasn't busy threatening to cut people's throats? Nothing would have surprised Liam anymore.

He almost turned and fled when he took in the sight of Donovan's henchman, Jackson Webb, sitting at the breakfast bar, a tiny espresso cup cradled in his huge hands. Jackson grinned at him with crooked teeth and drew a stubby finger across his own throat – a cruel reminder of that day in the barber's that Liam would never forget.

He swallowed hard.

'Coffee?' enquired Donovan pleasantly. 'Croissants? They're still warm from the oven. Tasty, aren't they, Jackson? Even though I say so myself.'

It was as much as Liam could do to shake his head.

'No? Then perhaps you've brought the rest of my money,' said Donovan.

This was where it got risky. The part of the plan that had taken the most persuasion for Liam to agree to.

'No,' he said, speaking as boldly as he possibly could under the circumstances. 'I haven't brought you a penny. I can't pay and I won't pay. Have you got any paperwork that proves I owe you money?'

Donovan looked more amused than angry. 'Did you hear that, Jackson? The man's asking for paperwork. If he'd wanted paperwork he should have gone to his bank for a loan. Oh, that's right, he did and they refused to lend him any more. And so he came to me instead.'

A trickle of sweat ran down Liam's back. 'You and your exorbitant interest rates. You stole my car! Well, you're not getting any more out of me.'

Donovan appeared to be getting bored with the way the conversation was going. He turned to Jackson. 'What do we do with customers who won't pay up, Jackson?'

The henchman carefully set his coffee cup down on a saucer and pulled a knife from the wooden block on the breakfast bar. Six inches of stainless steel glinted under the ceiling lights.

'Are you threatening me with that knife?' asked Liam.

Jackson slid lazily from his bar stool like a big cat.

'Your call, Liam,' said Donovan. 'Pay in cash or pay in blood. And remember what I said about your girlfriend.'

Liam watched in horror as Jackson took a step towards him, knife in hand. Summoning all his courage he said, 'What did you say about Ellie?'

Donovan chuckled. 'That she's far too pretty to end up with a nasty scar across her face. Cut him, Jackson. I've been too soft with him.'

Liam backed away towards the door. 'Put that knife down!'

Jackson came closer.

'I said, put the knife–'

But his words were lost as the front door crashed open.

'Armed police! Drop your weapon!'

Half a dozen police officers dressed in black tactical uniforms and armed with handguns stormed into the kitchen. Liam dodged out of their way. Within seconds both Jackson and Donovan were on the floor with their hands cuffed behind their backs. Radios crackled as the officers reported back to control outside. Liam had never seen anything so efficient. These guys really knew what they were doing.

When Becca walked in a few moments later, Liam threw his arms around her and gave her the biggest hug ever.

'It worked,' he said, pulling the wire out from under his shirt.

When Becca had told him he would have to confront Donovan wearing a microphone and that the police would monitor from a van in the street, he'd thought she was pulling his leg. 'No way,' he'd said. 'Not like they do on the telly.' But she'd convinced him it was the only way. They needed evidence of Donovan Cross's criminal dealings. And with nothing else to go on, only covert surveillance would do it.

'I told you it would work,' said Becca, smiling at him. 'Next time, have more faith in your sister.'

'Next time?' Liam blurted. 'There's absolutely no way you're dragging me into this sort of shit ever again!'

CHAPTER 36

'Have they said anything yet?' asked Gillian.

'Nothing,' said Raven. 'Both Donovan Cross and Jackson Webb are refusing to cooperate. Their solicitor has advised them to "no comment" everything. It would be easier to crack a macadamia nut than persuade either of those two to blab.'

It was Sunday afternoon and Raven was sitting in Gillian Ellis's office. The twenty-four-hour limit for holding the loan shark and his henchman had expired that morning and Raven had requested an extension to thirty-six hours which Gillian had obligingly authorised. She had even given up her weekend to come into the station and complete the necessary paperwork.

Yet in contrast to Kate Capstick, who had willingly confessed the whole sorry affair of the night she killed her daughter and the day she pushed Davy down the stairs, neither man was talking.

Raven still had nothing more to use than the recorded intelligence that Liam had obtained. And that was flimsy, to say the least.

He really wanted to bring charges against them not only

for illegal money lending and threatening behaviour but also for their role in the drug smuggling operation, as that was the most promising way to nail Superintendent Brandon Holt.

But for that he needed a lot more.

'I visited the barber's where Liam alleges the assault with the razor took place,' he told Gillian, 'but the shop has closed down. The shopkeeper next door said the barber has gone back to Turkey.'

'It's unlikely we'll be able to obtain a statement from him,' said Gillian. 'What about Sid Sutcliffe? What does he have to say for himself?'

'Sid has been surprisingly cooperative. He's given us full details of the entire smuggling operation. According to Sid, William Seagrim was originally the boss, but Brandon Holt took over when Seagrim retired. Donovan Cross supplied the ready funds and Jackson Webb delivered the cash and picked up the goods. Sid and Davy's job was to sail out and meet the boats coming over from continental Europe. It's been going on for years and would have continued if Anna hadn't stolen the bag of money. We also have Sid's allegation that Brandon Holt murdered Roger Hepworth.'

Gillian shook her head. 'It's nowhere near enough. All we have against Holt is Sid's word against his. We'll need more than that if we're going to move against a highly-respected police superintendent, never mind one who's just won an award for his role in reducing drug-related offences.' She gave him a sympathetic smile. 'I know this means a lot to you, Tom. But I don't see how we can take it any further.'

He thanked her politely and left her office. He couldn't argue with Gillian's logic. She had already gone out of her way to help him gather evidence. The extension for holding Donovan and Jackson, the application to the Chief Constable for Liam's wiretap, the very fact that she was entertaining the notion of bringing charges against a police superintendent. She had gone as far as she could, and yet his goal was still as distant as when he began his unofficial investigation into his mother's death.

He was about to tell Becca the bad news when his phone buzzed with a text message. He stopped in his tracks, read it twice, then immediately changed direction and headed outside to his car.

★

The door to the house opened before Raven even had a chance to ring the bell.

'Come inside. He's expecting you.' Nurse Bradshaw's manner was as brisk and efficient as ever, but Raven thought he detected a sadness behind her eyes. It must be a difficult job, caring for the sick and dying.

'How is he?'

She responded with a shake of her head. 'It won't be long now.' She opened the door to the sick room and stepped aside so that Raven could enter.

It was like entering a spider's lair. But a spider hovering at death's door.

The smell of sickness invaded Raven's nostrils as soon as he stepped inside. The figure in the bed had shrunk even more since Raven's last visit. His cheeks were hollowed out, his skin waxy. His eyes were closed and Raven had to look closely for any sign that the old man was still breathing. A barely perceptible rise and fall of the bedsheet told him that Seagrim was still in the land of the living. Just.

Raven gently touched the old man's fingers with his own and spoke his name. Crusty eyelids fluttered open.

'It's DCI Tom Raven,' said Raven. 'You wanted to see me?'

Seagrim turned his watery eyes on Raven. His lips moved and Raven leaned forward to catch the words. 'Thank you for coming.'

'There's something you wanted to tell me?'

Seagrim lifted a shaky hand and pointed to a dressing

table in the corner of the room. 'Over there. Fetch it.'

Raven walked across the room. A black folder lay on top of the dressing table. 'What is it?'

'You might call it my insurance policy. I don't need it anymore. It's for you now.'

Raven picked the file up and flicked through its contents, his heart racing. It was a meticulously compiled dossier of evidence detailing the drug smuggling operation, the murder of Roger Hepworth, and – Raven could hardly believe his eyes – the missing car logbook from 1991. He turned to the relevant date and saw it in black and white. Brandon Holt had been driving the car that hit and killed his mother. He had exactly what he needed to ensure that Holt faced justice.

Raven sat down on the chair beside the bed. 'Why are you doing this for me? After all this time?'

'Do you want the long answer or the short?'

'I don't want to tire you out.'

'Hardly matters.' Seagrim coughed, but he had no strength and the sound was a mere splutter. 'It all started to go wrong with Anna's death. The money disappeared, the shipment was missed, the boat was burnt. Police were crawling over Robin Hood's Bay looking for Anna's killer. I knew that sooner or later you were going to discover the smuggling ring.' He stopped to catch his breath. 'I told Brandon to deal with it but he was too weak. Then you arrested Sid and I knew he would sing like a canary. Brandon should never have killed Roger Hepworth. Roger was Sid's best friend. It turned him against us forever. Now I hear you've arrested Donovan Cross and Jackson Webb, too. The game is up. The people at the top of the chain are angry. And they are ruthless. They'll step in and mop things up. It's Brandon's fault for letting everything get out of hand.'

It was quite a confession from Seagrim. Raven was glad he'd had the foresight to switch on the voice recorder on his phone before entering the house, although whether it would be admissible in court was another matter. A defence would argue it was merely the ramblings of a dying man dosed to the hilt with diamorphine.

The dossier was another matter entirely, and would surely guarantee that Holt, Cross and his henchman all went down for a long time.

'And what's the short answer?'

Seagrim turned his rheumy eyes in Raven's direction, the bones in his neck creaking. 'I haven't got long for this world. There's no point taking my secrets to the grave.' He grasped Raven's hand. 'Do you believe in God, DCI Raven?'

Raven pursed his lips and held the dying man's gaze, not knowing what to say. By confessing his sins, was Seagrim seeking Raven's forgiveness?

'It doesn't matter what I believe.' Raven stood up, pressing the file to his chest. He had got what he needed. If Seagrim craved forgiveness he would have to look to a higher power to grant it. Without another word, he left the room.

CHAPTER 37

Liam was over the moon to have his car back. The police had returned the keys to him that morning after verifying that he was, in fact, the legal owner. He slid into the Corvette's leather seat and caressed its steering wheel like an old friend, almost like a lover. When he started the ignition, the engine roared into life. He pressed the accelerator, and the Chevy responded with a deep throaty howl. He could have cried for joy.

As he headed back along the Foreshore and rounded the headland, he decided he would take Ellie on that road trip after all. Now that Donovan was off his back and his debt was as good as cancelled, since it had never legally existed in the first place, he would find the money and they would get away for a few days. Scotland. The Lake District. Cornwall. Ellie's tastes weren't very budget-friendly, but at this time of year they would surely find reasonably priced hotels if they looked hard enough. Liam had contacts in the business he could lean on for a sweet deal.

Ellie was right; he needed a holiday. The past months had been so stressful he'd lost sight of what was most important in life – relationships. He vowed to be a better boyfriend, brother and son moving forward.

He parked outside the apartment and sprinted up the stairs, excited to whisk Ellie away on a dream trip. When he opened the door, he was surprised to find bags and suitcases already packed. She must have anticipated his plans, although he hadn't expected to be setting off immediately and even Ellie wouldn't need quite so much stuff for a quick jaunt around the Highlands.

'I'm back!' he called.

She emerged from the bedroom with another suitcase and dumped it next to the already substantial mound of luggage. She dusted off her hands and placed them on her hips.

Liam sensed that all was not well.

'I got the car back from the garage,' he said, dangling the keys in front of her. 'I thought we could go on a little road trip around…'

He trailed off when he saw the expression on her face.

'I'm not going anywhere with you, Liam Shawcross!'

'But…'

'You lied to me,' said Ellie. 'You swindled money from me and Dad under false pretences to pay off your debts and then you said your car was at the garage when in actual fact you had given it to a loan shark for money you couldn't repay.'

Oh shit. Had Becca been talking to her flatmate? It hadn't occurred to him that she would spill the beans to Ellie.

'I can explain,' he muttered. 'It's all sorted now and your money's safe.'

'Save your breath,' said Ellie, holding up a hand. 'Really, Liam, you call yourself a businessman but you don't know the first thing about running a business.'

That stung, and Liam swallowed hard.

'I have the brewery to think about,' continued Ellie. 'I can't let your failed schemes put that at risk. I have my employees to consider. And so does Dad with the bistro.

Besides, how can I ever trust you again?'

'So that's it?' said Liam. 'Are we over?'

'Done and dusted.'

'And you're throwing me out?' His eyes slipped towards the luggage. 'Right now?'

'I am.'

He felt the shock like a punch to the gut. He thought he'd lost everything when he'd given his car to Donovan Cross. But now he really had lost everything that mattered.

'I haven't got anywhere to live,' he moaned, hating the begging tone that had crept into his voice.

Ellie regarded him coldly, as if he were dirt. 'Don't your parents run a bed and breakfast? I'm sure they'll be happy to put you up.'

★

Raven looked on with satisfaction as the team made the arrest. It was out of his hands now. The arrest of a police superintendent on suspicion of murder wasn't taken lightly, and the decision had been made at the highest level of authorisation. The Chief Constable of North Yorkshire, no less.

A chief superintendent from Northallerton had come to carry out the deed. Brandon Holt made no comment as he was read his rights. He would no doubt refuse to answer any questions that were put to him when interviewed. Holt knew better than anyone how this game was played.

That made no difference. The case against him was cast iron. He would go down for a very long time.

The disgraced police officer locked eyes briefly with Raven as he was led away, but there was scarcely any hint of recognition there. Holt had obviously decided not to give Raven the benefit of that acknowledgement. But both men knew that Raven had been instrumental in bringing his mother's killer to justice. And Raven would have the satisfaction of watching the court case unfold and knowing the part he had played.

After leaving the police station, he got into the M6 and set off in the direction of the North Bay. He had another important appointment to keep.

★

Raven had insisted on helping Becca move house, and she hadn't liked to say no. She would have preferred to do it on her own, but after all that had passed between them, she didn't feel she could turn him down.

She wasn't even sure how he had found out about her move. Jess was the only other police officer she'd confided in. Then again, Raven was a detective. Who knew what secret avenues of intelligence were open to him?

A big part of her was sorry to be leaving the apartment, especially now that Liam had gone.

Ellie seemed to have guessed the reason for her leaving. 'It must have been hard having your brother under your feet.'

Becca gave Ellie a rueful smile. Her friend was perceptive as ever. 'We'll still see each other,' she promised. And she meant it. She didn't want Ellie to become just another Facebook friend who she never saw in real life.

'Of course we will,' said Ellie, bright and cheerful as always. But Becca sensed the sadness in her friend's smile and drew her into a tight embrace. Ellie had done the right thing in ditching Liam, but she still felt sorry for both of them. They had been good for each other in some ways, although Liam was still too immature to maintain a long-term relationship. Perhaps he would learn his lesson, being sent back to the guest house for a spell.

Becca didn't regret telling Ellie about the mess he'd got himself into. He had deceived her, obtaining money under false pretences. Ellie could do a lot better.

'Here comes your knight in shining armour,' said Ellie, looking out of the window as Raven's BMW pulled up outside. 'It's very gallant of him to help you move your stuff.' She gave Becca a quizzical look.

'What?' said Becca, a little more sharply than she'd intended.

'I was just wondering why he's going to so much trouble.'

'I think he feels he owes me.'

'Oh?'

'It's complicated.'

Becca was saved from having to explain further by the ringing of the doorbell. She buzzed Raven into the building and waited for him to climb the stairs. It occurred to her that her boss wasn't the most able person to help her move house, what with his dodgy leg and the obvious unsuitability of his car for carrying luggage and navigating Scarborough's oldest and narrowest streets.

But it was too late to worry about that. He was already at the top of the stairs, trying not to look out of puff.

He entered the apartment and stood awkwardly in the kitchen-diner. He seemed too tall for the confines of the apartment, too dark in his black suit and winter coat for the bright open plan space. Becca didn't know what to say but Ellie quickly came to her rescue.

'Detective Chief Inspector Raven.' She held out her hand. 'How nice to meet you again, in happier circumstances.'

The pair had got to know each other during a case involving Ellie's cousins, including Sam, Becca's boyfriend at the time. Becca had no contact with Sam now but occasionally heard from Ellie that he was getting on well in Australia.

'Right,' said Ellie, looking expectantly from Raven to Becca. 'Shall I help you load the car?'

When the rather small boot of the BMW was filled to capacity and the rest of her gear was piled up on the cramped rear seats, Becca gave Ellie one last hug, then slid into the passenger seat. She'd picked up the keys to the flat earlier in the day from the estate agent. Her mum had made one last-minute effort to persuade her to move back into the B&B, but that was the last place Becca wanted to go now that Liam was back there. Besides, she was determined to go it alone at last. At the ripe old age of twenty-eight, it was about time she became a fully-fledged adult.

'All set?' said Raven.

She nodded and they drove off, Ellie waving them goodbye.

They headed along North Marine Road, past the B&B where Liam's car was now ostentatiously parked, then turned into Castle Road for the steep climb up the hill to St Mary's Church, Raven grimacing whenever an oncoming car appeared in the road and he had to pull over.

'I really could have managed this on my own,' said Becca. 'My car can easily nip along these narrow streets.

'I wanted to help,' said Raven through gritted teeth.

She decided not to mention it again.

They began the descent down the other side of the headland, Raven manoeuvring the M6 around the quaintly named street of Paradise and into Castle Terrace.

'It's just here,' said Becca, indicating the house that had been converted into flats.

Raven insisted on carrying the heaviest suitcases. That just left Becca with some medium-sized cases, a rucksack and some carrier bags. They managed it in two trips.

She hadn't told him that her flat was on the top floor of the building. By the time they had hauled everything up the stairs, he looked exhausted.

'Where do you want these?' he asked once they were inside the flat. It was smaller than Becca remembered it, or maybe it was just that Raven seemed to fill so much space.

'Just dump them there,' said Becca, indicating the centre of the living room floor. 'I can sort them out later. Thanks for your help.'

He deposited the suitcases then wandered over to the window that was built into the sloping roof. 'Does this thing open?' He lifted it up and stepped outside onto the makeshift balcony, leaning out across the metal railings. The late September sun cast a long shadow on the floor behind him. 'Lovely view.'

'It is,' agreed Becca, coming to join him.

'You'll be able to keep an eye on me from up here,' he joked. 'That's my house down there.' He pointed to a rooftop at the bottom of the hill. Beyond it, the boats in the harbour bobbed gently in the sunlight.

'I'm sure I won't need to do that,' said Becca.

'You might.'

She sensed he wanted to say more so she kept quiet.

'If you hadn't intervened that day when I... lost control, it would have been the end of the road for me. I owe you my career.' He turned his face to hers. 'Thank you. For everything.'

The balcony wasn't big enough for two people to stand side-by-side without brushing against each other, and Becca felt his leg against hers. But that no longer seemed wrong. They had crossed a line at some point and were now more intimate than just work colleagues. Yet what were the parameters of their new relationship, exactly?

She suddenly felt too overwhelmed by emotion to speak. She had spent so much time in Raven's company recently, working on their secret assignment. She had saved him from himself and felt closer to him than ever before, but in getting so close she had glimpsed the darkness within his heart.

That darkness frightened her. Another time, she might not be able to stop him so easily. Raven was dangerous to know.

'I–'

'Anyway–'

Raven smiled. 'You go first.'

She shook her head. 'I don't really know what I was going to say.'

He nodded gravely before turning away from the window. 'Well, I hope you'll be very happy living here. And if you'll excuse me now, there's something I have to do.'

★

The walk was familiar to Raven but new to Hannah. Up the steep and narrow cobbles of Castlegate, casting a sideways glance over his shoulder in the direction of Becca's new loft apartment on Castle Terrace. Over the hill and down the other side, the grey stone walls of the castle standing firm against the breeze that buffeted the headland. Hannah threaded her arm through Raven's, and Quincey scurried ahead, straining at his leash, sticking his eager twitching nose into every filthy nook and cranny he could find.

They carried on through town until the houses thinned out, and they reached the chapel at the end of Dean Road. Here they crossed from the land of the living into the city of the dead.

'There's something I have to tell you,' said Raven. This was going to be painful. He was dreading Hannah's judgement, but he couldn't put it off any longer. He had already told her about Brandon Holt's arrest. But Hannah deserved the real truth, not just a version in which her father was the hero.

'What is it?'

They walked arm in arm between mossy gravestones worn smooth by the passing of the years. Trees spread their golden autumn canopies overhead. There was no better place for Raven to unburden himself than here. He took a deep breath. 'The night your grandmother died... it was my fault.'

Hannah stopped and turned to face him. 'What do you mean, it was your fault? How could it be? That man, Brandon Holt, was driving the car.' She searched his face, looking for answers. Her gaze felt heavy, reminding him uncomfortably of his ex-wife, Lisa.

'It was my fault,' he repeated. 'I should have been at home studying for my GCSEs. Instead I was out on the town with my friends, getting up to no good.' Hannah said nothing so he pressed on, letting the words tumble out, the words he'd kept locked inside himself for so long. It was time to set them free at last. 'Mum came looking for me – she wanted me to do well at school so that I wouldn't end up like Dad in a dead-end job with no prospects. She was walking along the Foreshore, searching the amusement arcades when the car hit her. If it wasn't for me she would have been safe at home.'

'Oh, Dad!' Hannah gripped him by the upper arms. 'You can be such a fool!'

'I know, I'm sorry.' He hung his head in shame. She was going to hate him now. He deserved it.

'That's not what I meant, Dad.'

'It isn't?'

She shook her head. 'I meant that you're a fool for thinking the accident was your fault.'

'But–'

'No, listen,' she said firmly. 'The only person to blame is Brandon Holt and he's now going to be brought to justice because of what you did. You need to stop carrying all this guilt around, Dad. Otherwise, it will be the death of you.'

Raven nodded dumbly. Hannah was right. He felt as if a huge burden had just fallen off his shoulders. The feeling of lightness was unfamiliar and strange. Hannah didn't blame him for her grandmother's death. He would have to get used to the idea of not blaming himself. He didn't know if he would manage it, but he would give it a try. For Hannah's sake.

Quincey tugged at his lead and they carried on to their destination, a small grey headstone much like all the others.

Hannah knelt and cleared away the old flowers Raven had brought on his previous visit. In their place she arranged fresh chrysanthemums, placing each flower with careful reverence, positioning each stem so the leaves and petals formed a pleasing pattern.

'You have a talent for that,' said Raven. 'Just like your

grandmother.'

They stood together, arm in arm, admiring the flowers and silently reading the words engraved on the stone.

Jean Raven, born 1946, died 1991. Beloved mother and wife.

Raven threw an arm around Hannah's shoulders and held her close. The weather was turning colder, but he felt a warmth in his heart that had been absent for a long time.

★

The phone rang late in the evening and Raven picked it up idly, glancing at the screen to see who was calling. Not work, he hoped. He had only just wrapped up one major investigation. Gillian surely wouldn't assign him to another so soon.

But the name on the screen wasn't that of a police officer.

Liz Larkin.

Raven frowned. Why was a journalist from the BBC calling him? He had bumped into Liz on a number of cases, and it was fair to say that their encounters had not gone smoothly. Liz was the kind of journalist who was always hungry for information, and when Raven had been unable – or unwilling – to provide it, she had proven herself to be quite vindictive. Raven fought back unpleasant memories of Liz and her team ambushing him during the course of various high-profile investigations over the course of the past twelve months. One of his TV appearances had even gone viral on social media, much to Hannah's amusement and Raven's annoyance.

On the other hand, she had helped him out once or twice.

His finger hesitated over the red button but in the end he swiped on the green and hoped he wouldn't live to regret it. 'Raven?' he answered gruffly.

Her well-articulated voice came over the speaker. 'I have something for you, Detective Chief Inspector.'

It wasn't quite the opening line he'd expected. 'Is this a trick? Usually, you call when you want something from me.'

'No tricks involved, I assure you. Do you want to hear what I've got?'

Raven shook his head at the woman's cheek. How could he turn down such a brazen lure? 'Go on.'

There was a long pause before she spoke again. 'Not over the phone. Come and meet me in person and I'll give you the name of a murderer.'

A DYING ECHO

**An unsolved mystery. An echo of the past.
A dark-fated future.**

When DCI Tom Raven's longstanding adversary, TV journalist Liz Larkin, invites him to a rock concert, Raven reluctantly accepts. Liz claims she has groundbreaking information about the fate of the band's former lead singer who disappeared decades previously on the eve of their debut US tour, leaving behind a trail of mysterious clues, a cult fan following, and a web of conspiracy theories. But the evening ends in tragedy when the new lead singer collapses on stage.

As Raven plunges into the case, he's drawn into the tangled lives of the band members, their manager, and record label executive, all of whom hold pieces of the puzzle. But Raven's judgement is clouded by his complicated relationship with Liz.

Can Raven untangle the mystery before more tragedy strikes the band he idolised in his youth? Or is the band fated by its gloom-ridden songs and dark legacy

Set on the North Yorkshire coast, the Tom Raven series is perfect for fans of LJ Ross, JD Kirk, Simon McCleave, and British crime fiction.

THANK YOU FOR READING

We hope you enjoyed this book. If you did, then we would be very grateful if you would please take a moment to leave a review online. Thank you.

DCI TOM RAVEN CRIME THRILLERS

Tom Raven® is a registered trademark of Landmark Internet Ltd.
The Landscape of Death
Beneath Cold Earth
The Dying of the Year
Deep into that Darkness
Days Like Shadows Pass
Vigil for the Dead
Stained with Blood
The Foaming Deep
A Dying Echo

BRIDGET HART

Bridget Hart® is a registered trademark of Landmark Internet Ltd.
Aspire to Die
Killing by Numbers
Do No Evil
In Love and Murder
A Darkly Shining Star
Preface to Murder
Toll for the Dead

PSYCHOLOGICAL THRILLERS

The Red Room

ABOUT THE AUTHOR

M S Morris is the pseudonym for the writing partnership of Margarita and Steve Morris. They are married and live in Oxfordshire. They have two grown-up children.

Find out more at msmorrisbooks.com where you can join our mailing list, or follow us on Facebook at facebook.com/msmorrisbooks.

Printed in Great Britain
by Amazon